Oh Sweet

CHARITY

SEVEN VIRTUES RANCH ROMANCE BOOK 3

BECKY DOUGHTY

Oh Sweet Charity: Seven Virtues Ranch Romance Book 3
Copyright © 2018 by Becky Doughty

Published by BraveHearts Press
All rights reserved.

The story, all names, characters, and incidents portrayed in this production are fictitious. No identification with actual persons (living or deceased), places, buildings, and products is intended or should be inferred.

Book Cover by BraveHearts Press Designs

Author Information: BeckyDoughty.com

ISBN: 978-1953347374

CHARITY

"Where there is charity and wisdom,
there is neither fear or ignorance."

Francis of Assisi

ONE

IT WAS ALWAYS THE same, the dream. And every time it came, Charity awoke with a start, breathless from the exertion expended in her sleep. Theo standing just off to her right, not speaking, not moving, just standing, waiting. Waiting for her.

And smiling in that heartbreakingly tender way he did when he looked at her.

In her dream, she was always trying to get to him, her legs moving in slow motion as she maneuvered the rough terrain between them. If she kept her gaze fixed on Theo, the way seemed easy and short, but the moment she glanced down to see where she might put her next step, boulders and mud pits, sand dunes and brambles would form before her eyes.

She hated those dreams.

But she always lay there in the dark after each one, waiting for her pulse to slow, for the trembling in her limbs to still, holding onto the fleeting images for as long as she could. Because in those dreams, she saw her husband more clearly than she did any other time.

And he saw her.

Right after Theo died, he appeared everywhere. She'd wake up to find him sleeping beside her, the alluring curve of his spine sweeping up to that vulnerable hollow at the base of his skull, his broad shoulders smooth and muscular in the morning light. In that place between sleeping and waking, she'd reach out to trace the border of a scapula with her fingertips, or to slide her hand, ever so gently, around his waist so she could draw from his furnace-like body heat.

She'd head down the hall in their apartment, and he'd be just ahead of her, slipping into the bedroom or the little office.

She'd be cooking his favorite meal, and from the corner of her eye, she'd catch a glimpse of him standing in the doorway, his face lifted like he was sniffing the air.

But her hands always met with the aching emptiness of his side of the bed, she'd inevitably find the rooms of their home unoccupied, and when she turned from the stove top to smile at her man, he wasn't there.

Charity had moved back home to Seven Virtues Ranch less than a year later, half afraid that if she stayed in their hollow, haunted apartment, she might one day wake up and decide she couldn't live without him anymore.

It'd taken her a few months to readjust to living with her sisters, her niece, and her father, but she'd eventually found her place in the household. Ironically, it was in the kitchen, a space so densely populated by Goodacres that there wasn't room for Theo's ghost.

But alone in her room at night, when she closed the rest of the world out and burrowed deep into the covers of the bed she and Theo had shared, he came to her, smiling, his eyes shining with love for her, a beacon that even death couldn't snuff out.

She swung her legs over the side of the bed and sat up. "I miss you so much, Theo," she whispered, closing her eyes in the dark of the predawn morning, desperate to capture the memory of him. Guilt seeped into her bloodstream; no matter how hard she tried to hang on, she was slowly losing the ability to conjure up a clear image of his face. Of the way his mouth moved when he talked, how his eyes crinkled at the corners when he laughed. The upright posture, his shoulders straight, his chin lifted, as though never out of uniform. His confident swagger, because yes, Theo did have a delicious swagger.

The last time she'd said goodbye to him, he'd pumped up the swagger as he walked away, just to get a smile out of her. That was right after he'd kissed her so sweetly and told her he'd be back before she knew it.

"Might as well get my day going," she mused aloud, glancing over at the clock on her nightstand. The sun would be up in less than an hour, but she had a full schedule before noon, and getting a jump on things wasn't a bad idea. It was a big day over at Whispering Hills, the expansive ranch next door to Seven Virtues. Skid and Ernie Maddox from Maddox and Sons Construction, along with their crew of more than a dozen men, were putting the finishing touches on a massive pole barn and indoor arena for a new Quarter Horse breeding program. The program, in fact, wasn't new; Cord Overman, the new owner of Whispering Hills Ranch—and husband to Charity's oldest sister, Faith—had purchased much of the best stock from a well-established breeder outside Louisville who was closing his doors. The horse breeders, Dennis and Nancy Bastion, were ready to retire, but had no children to take over the business. They also happened to be long-time friends of the Overman family, and when the Bastions learned that Cord was interested in their operation, they'd been only too happy to work with him. They planned to deliver the horses themselves the following week.

Accompanying them was one of their most sought-after trainers, Terrell Jackson, but Terrell would be staying on at Whispering Hills. He'd accepted a position to take over running the breeding and training program at Whispering Hills, and he'd been out to the site multiple times throughout construction, giving his stamp of approval all along.

Today, they were celebrating a job well done. The stables were ready, tack rooms stocked, the surrounding pastures cleared and newly fenced, corrals and paddocks cordoned off, round pens and wash stations, even a brand new two-bedroom foreman cabin that Terrell would soon call home. The whole crew would gather at noon for Charity's famous smoked ribs, bacon mac and cheese casserole, oven fries, and dilly bean potato salad, along with a few other assorted side dishes. She'd been cooking meals for Cord and his work crews and ranch hands for over a year now, and these were some of their favorites.

Yesterday, Charity had coated the racks of ribs in her own special dry rub and had sealed them in plastic wrap to rest overnight, letting the salts, herbs, and spices go to work tenderizing the meat. She needed to get back over to Whispering Hills first thing so she could pack the ribs into the two huge smokers by six o'clock that morning. They needed as many hours as she could give them before noon; the lower heat and long grill time made the meat practically fall off the bone. Her mouth watered just thinking about the scent of the mesquite and apple wood chips she always used, and between the rub, her secret mop sauce, and the homemade barbecue sauce she slathered on generously at the end, she knew she'd be fending off hungry men all morning.

She made her bed, kissed her fingertips and pressed them to Theo's pillow, then hurried to dress in the quiet of the still sleeping house. Daddy would be up any time now, and as much as she loved sitting with him in the early hours, sharing a cup of coffee and some quiet conversation, today, she wanted to slip away. Dreams of Theo always left her feeling introspective and withdrawn.

Carrying her boots, she tiptoed down the hall to the kitchen. On the counter where she wouldn't forget it was the gallon jar of dilly beans that she'd canned last summer. They'd had a bumper crop of beans, and this was her contribution to the meal today. Her dilly bean potato salad was practically legendary with the guys.

She shoved two huge muffins from the breadbox into a brown paper lunch bag; she'd make a fresh pot of coffee next door. Knowing Binks, he was probably already up and prowling around for the day, and if he saw her truck, he'd stop in to say good morning. He always took pleasure in whatever homemade breakfast treat she shared with him.

She snatched her keys from the hook by the back door, then ducked out, making sure not to let the screen slam behind her. On the top step of the porch, she shoved her feet into her boots, climbed into her pickup, then headed down the gravel drive toward Carpenter Road.

Whispering Hills was less than a mile up the road, so it wasn't long before she was wending her way up the pristine blacktop driveway flanked by pastoral fields to the beautiful ranch house at the top of the knoll.

Cord and Faith and their daughter, Jasmine, didn't live in the big house, but in a darling two-story home Cord had built for them. It nestled right up against the property line between Whispering Hills and Seven Virtues and had been his wedding gift to Faith and Jasmine. Their future plans for the big house were still a little ambiguous, but they'd made its renovation a top priority job as Cord wanted to make sure there was a place to stay for visiting family, friends, and guests—like the Bastions—who came and went. He'd turned the large, somewhat dated farmhouse into a gorgeous ranch house that managed to retain the old school feel, but with all updated amenities.

Especially the kitchen. It was practically state of the art, with stainless steel appliances, granite counter tops, beautiful hardwood cabinets, a massive butcher block island, and a pantry large enough to operate a small grocery store out of. He'd hired Charity early on to cook for his work crews, so he'd made certain she had everything she could possibly need or want at her fingertips, and all the room she needed to cook for the masses.

For Charity, the last year had been like the sweetest dream working in that gorgeous kitchen, mostly alone and uninhibited by the presence of anyone else around. She loved the homey feel of Seven Virtues, but she felt so professional and legitimate in the Whispering Hills kitchen. She was queen of her domain there.

Binks, the old foreman, sometimes poked his gray, fuzzy head in the door. More often than not, he just stopped in to greet her, or to catch a whiff of whatever she was whipping up that day, but he always asked if she needed help with anything. She rarely did, although she wasn't above coming up with small tasks that he could do for her. Binks had married young, had lost his wife early on, and had never remarried, and Charity liked having him around; she felt a kindred spirit with him.

Other times, if he'd catch her singing some old Elvis or Patsy Cline song, he'd join in. "You've got great taste in music, Mr. Binks," she'd tell him. He'd nod and return the compliment before heading back outside to tend to whatever business he had on hand.

Charity pulled around the house and parked near the back porch with its door that led into the kitchen. The black sky was just beginning to soften to a murky violet, darkness reluctantly giving way to the light, as she climbed out of her truck. With the jar of beans in one arm, her bag of muffins tucked gingerly into the crook of the other so she wouldn't smash them, she fumbled with her keys to find the right one.

She nearly dropped the beans when a voice reached her from out of the shadows on the back porch. "You look like you could use another hand."

TWO

It was never the same, the nightmare that haunted him. Oh, it always *ended* the same, but the circumstances changed again and again. Every horror story he'd ever heard came to life in his dreams. The buried IED detonating underfoot, the insurgents hiding in the ruins, ready to ambush the convoy as they drove through what was supposed to be a deserted village, the suicide bomber charging into camp, screaming the name of his god in zealous triumph—or terror—before tripping the wire that would end his life...along with all his intended victims.

Victims Frank couldn't save. Victims he couldn't reach in time. Victims who called for him, begging for his help. Victims who belonged to him, men and women under his care and leadership.

"Help me, Sarge."

"Mama. I wanna go home."

"Oh, God. I'm hurt real bad, Top." It was the ones who'd earned the right to call him Top that really ate him up.

Their voices echoed in his mind long after the dream faded. Especially Stanley's. "I'll be okay, Top. Go help someone else."

They both knew Stanley wasn't going to be okay.

Stanley was just a kid from New Jersey. No one special, not according to his paperwork, his rank, or even his stature. But in some ways, Stanley had been the lifeblood of their unit. His voice rose above the others during drills, he sang like an angel during their small Sunday church service, and his laughter could be heard throughout camp at all hours. That laugh. It was irritatingly contagious. Something in that cockeyed grin, the missing eye tooth, and the way he talked about home made the other guys hold on to hope. The kid had been in his unit for almost a year before Frank learned that Stanley had no home to go back to. His fiancée sent him off to war with a Dear John letter, and the only family the guy had was an elderly grandfather who'd raised him, but who'd been left behind in a nursing home. Stanley's paycheck covered his grandfather's expenses over and above what his meager Social Security and retirement didn't.

By the time Frank had recovered enough to hunt him down, Stanley's grandfather was dead. Knowing the old man had spent his last days utterly alone tore Frank's guts out every time he thought about it. And when Stanley showed up in his dreams, Frank woke up in tears.

It was the only time he cried. And he hated it every time.

Tonight, Stanley had been there, running alongside him, just out of reach. When the first bullet ripped through the underbrush, Frank had lunged for Stanley, but the kid had laughed and kept running, straight into the fray. Had gone down in slow motion, his body twitching and jerking as he was hit time and time again, his laughter turning to mournful song, before those final, whispered words. "I'll be okay, Top. Go help someone else."

There was no way Frank could go back to sleep. Beyond weary, he began his midnight pacing around the small set of rooms that made up his apartment, his crutches squeaking and clicking irritatingly with each jarring step. But tonight, nothing soothed him. Not the Scripture he repeated like a mantra in his head about keeping his eyes on the goal, about running the race, about staying the course. Not the hitched cadence as he hobbled around and around the room. Not the pain that spiraled up his tibia like a serpentine branding iron, or the ache in his left ankle where they'd fixed the joint with titanium pins. Not the ice-cold water splashed on his heated features, not Harry Connick, Jr. crooning on the stereo.

Not the pain pills calling out to him from behind the bathroom mirror. He wanted to be done with them. He *needed* to be done with them.

"I gotta go," he muttered, the words coming out a low growl of frustration. His skin crawled with his mounting anxiety, his forehead and upper lip beaded with perspiration, and sweat trickled in an irritating rivulet down the middle of his back. "I gotta get out of here."

He didn't care where he went, not really. But by the time he'd put fifty miles under his wheels, he knew exactly where the road was taking him.

Home.

Whispering Hills didn't belong to him anymore, but he had no doubt that Cord Overman would welcome him back, even showing up unannounced the way he was. He hadn't told anyone he was stateside. Not even his own mother. He'd had no intention of staying stateside so long, but his recovery had been hindered by one infection after another, by flesh that had been damaged beyond repair. They'd released him from the hospital last month to continue therapy as an outpatient, but his physician warned him that as long as he opted to keep his leg, he'd be living with debilitating pain the rest of his life.

Frank raged against the choices he'd been given; keep the leg, endure months, maybe years of therapy and surgeries, and, of course, the never-ending pain—and still, there would be no guarantee he'd be able to go back—or let them take the leg, as well as the pain that went with it. An amputation would definitely speed up his recovery time, and with advancements in prosthetics these days, there was a good chance he could remain on active duty...at some level. The thought of sitting behind a desk while his men were out there running missions without him just about crushed his soul.

He'd seen too many men and women leave the Armed Forces with fewer limbs, though, and he didn't want to be one of them. Not because he thought any less of them, but because he was reasonably sure losing his leg meant losing his career.

And yet, there was no way he could pass any of the physical tests they'd require of him with his leg intact, at least not in the foreseeable future.

Neither option sounded favorable to Frank, period.

Maybe he was going about this wrong. Perhaps enduring therapy on the parallel bars at the rehab center while waiting for the next surgery wasn't the way for him to regain his strength and endurance, his balance and health.

Home. He knew what Cord had going on back at the ranch. He knew there were a dozen or more projects that Frank could jump in on at

Whispering Hills. His crazy horse, Hidalgo, was still in the stables, and there were miles of ranch land Frank could lose himself on if that's what he needed. Surely, he could figure out how to get on a horse and just ride, if nothing else.

He drove all night, arriving just before dawn. He motored slowly up the long, paved driveway, taking in what changes he could make out in the long beam of his headlights, marveling at how different things looked, and yet how much it still felt like coming home. He eased the car as quietly as he could manage into what appeared to be a small parking lot at the top of the drive, turned off the engine, and peered out the front window at the house he'd grown up in. Everything was dark, except for a low-wattage porch light at the front door, and a soft glow inside the entry. He already knew there wasn't anyone living in the house. It was a shame; Cord had done wonders with the place. It looked like a classy old broad with a really good facelift and some new duds. Frank wondered what the inside looked like. He was especially curious about what had become of his old room. He suddenly wanted to crawl into his childhood bed and bury his head beneath the covers.

He shook the thought away as he sat in the driver's seat of the Challenger that he'd bought on impulse three weeks ago. A muscle car to pump him up, for sure, but he'd chosen that particular model because it came with a beastly automatic transmission. He wasn't in any condition to work a clutch.

Frank's leg ached from sitting in one position for so long, and for a moment, he was grateful for the pain. He was beginning to have second thoughts about his impulsive decision to fly the coop—he didn't do impulsive—but without the Percodan he'd left behind, there was no way he could endure another two and a half hours back the way he'd come without taking a break first. He pushed open the door but had to shove a hand under his thigh and manually lift his leg out from under the dashboard. Why had he tossed his crutches in the trunk with his duffel bag? He wore only the strap-on gel brace he slept in, and although he'd packed the other one with all the bells and whistles, it was in the trunk, too. Without the security of The Beast, as he'd not-so-affectionately named his brace, he wasn't supposed to put any weight on his left leg. When he'd set out a couple hours earlier, he'd had no trouble hopping around the car, but now, he wasn't so sure that was a good idea.

He stood slowly, lowering his left leg to rest on the ground. Maybe, just maybe... but when the pain lanced all the way into his low back, making his breath hiss out between his teeth, he knew he'd overdone it.

No pills, no crutches, no plan.

Glad for the dark, he leaned heavily against the car as he made his way on one foot to the trunk. Perching on the back bumper, he switched out the braces, but when he stood again, it was all he could do to bite back the groan that formed a tight ball in his chest. "Walk it off, man. Walk it off," he muttered under his breath. But walking it off wouldn't help; he knew that. He needed to lie down. He needed to elevate and ice his ankle.

He needed his pills.

I need my mama. The thought came unbidden and he snorted self-deprecatingly. His mother had been gone for more than a decade.

He jerked the crutches out of the trunk and hobbled across the driveway toward the house, eyeing the steps that led up to the front door. He shook his head; he only wanted to do steps once if he could help it. He circled around back; if the kitchen door was locked, surely Binks would be awake soon. Frank could wait for him on the back porch.

To his relief, he found a new set of patio furniture that included matching, remarkably comfortable chaise lounges. Easing his leg up onto the seat, he lay back and focused on his meditative breathing, willing the fire in his bones to subside.

The sound of wheels on gravel warned him of company, and he opened his eyes and turned his head to watch as a small truck rounded the side of the house and parked in the gravel strip nearby. A woman practically fell out of the driver's side, her arms loaded. She seemed oblivious to his presence.

Frank sighed. He didn't want to startle her, but he knew there would be nothing graceful or subtle about his attempt to get up out of the lounge chair. His pain was easing off a little, but ever the gentleman, he wasn't going to sit by and watch the lady struggle with her load. He took a deep breath, clenched his jaws together against the surge of pain as he maneuvered his leg off the cushion. "You look like you could use another hand."

He lumbered to his feet, making the chair scoot noisily backward, knocking one of his crutches to the ground with a loud clunk. He swore under his breath when she let out a blood-curdling scream that was sure to wake every armed man and woman in a ten-mile radius.

THREE

THE MOMENT THE SCREAM let loose, she wanted to suck it back in. She sounded like a high school girl at a Band Perry concert. The man on the porch didn't look like he was poised for assault, and besides, she had her pepper spray.

"Not that it's going to be of any help," she mused to herself. Her spray was in her purse on the floorboard of the passenger side of her truck, and by the time she got the door opened and started digging around in her floppy hobo bag, the guy could have her tossed over his shoulder and—

"Hey." He waved both hands in the air in a show of truce. "I won't hurt you, ma'am. I used to live here. Frank Flanner. Frankie to folks around here." He slowly made his way along the porch railing toward her.

Frankie Flanner? Judge Flanner's son? Charity squared her shoulders and peered up at him. The porch light was fixed to the wall behind him, back-lighting him so she couldn't quite make out his features, but there was definitely something familiar about him. She hadn't seen Frankie—did he go by Frank now?—in ages, so it wasn't a surprise she didn't immediately recognize him. "Not to mention you rose up out of the dark night like some phantom freak," she grumbled, then grimaced when she realized she'd said it out loud.

"Like a what?" He'd reached the top of the porch steps and stopped.

Charity didn't miss the fact that he held tightly to the handrail, nor did she miss the brace that ran from ankle to mid-thigh on his left leg. "Sorry," she said, hoisting the beans up a little higher. Her palms had gone slick with adrenaline sweat, and the last thing she wanted to do was drop her lovely dilly beans. "Just talking to myself." Should she get back in her truck and return later? Or did she dare brave walking up those steps past him and going in? He seemed harmless enough, especially with the way he was babying that leg...but then again, wasn't that how Ted Bundy got his victims? Hobbling around on a pair of crutches, playing on the tender mercies of unsuspecting young women... alone in the dark... no one around to hear— "Whoa. Get a grip, girl."

"You always talk to yourself?" he asked.

She could hear the hint of mockery in his tone, and she frowned. Could she ask him to please leave and come back when normal people were awake? Then again, if he really were Frank, who was she to tell him he couldn't be there? "I wasn't expecting anyone to loom up out of the dark like that."

"No kidding." He chuckled, a sound so pleasant, it grated against her nerves. "That was some scream."

He was laughing at her. What a jerk. "You know what? Never mind." She'd didn't need this. Not this morning. She'd escaped her own busy household for the peace and solitude of the Whispering Hills kitchen. She'd just come back after the guy was gone, and the crew would have to wait for their ribs if need be—she'd blame any delay on Frank Flanner, impostor or not. "I'm not sorry. I don't care who you are; that wasn't a cool thing to do." She reached for the handle of her truck door, nearly dropping the bag of muffins.

"Wait," he called out. "I'm the one who should be apologizing. I really didn't mean to startle you. I wasn't expecting anyone to show up here at this hour, either." He started down the steps, but when she turned around and glared at him, he stopped, almost as though suddenly self-conscious with her watching him. That wasn't like Frank Flanner at all. The guy she remembered had been a self-assured, cocky cowboy who wouldn't hesitate to take on the fiercest bull, no less some dilly-bean-and-muffin-toting widow.

"What exactly are you doing here?" Charity asked. The question came out surly and rude, but her heart was still pounding against her ribcage in fight or flight mode, and he was still grinning at her.

"What exactly are *you* doing here?" he shot back, crossing his arms over his chest and leaning his hip against a support beam.

"I asked you first," she said, regretting her childish response the moment it was out. "I mean, how do I know you're Frankie Flanner?" she amended.

"How do I know you're not some strange, crazy lady breaking into my childhood home?" Oh, he was enjoying this far too much. He shifted a little, and the light shone more directly on his face. Yeah, it was Frankie, all right. And still cocky after all. Maybe not a cowboy anymore, but in spite of the leg, he looked pretty self-assured. The moment of vulnerability seemed to have passed; perhaps she'd just imagined it.

"I work here. That's what I'm doing here." Charity squeezed the jar of beans against her side, fighting the urge to hurl them at his head. She might not be a very big package at five-foot-three, but she had an arm on her that could make a grown man weep. Especially if whatever she threw his way actually hit him.

"How did you get here?" she asked. "Did someone drop you off?" She waved the bag of muffins at his brace. "I doubt you walked." When he shifted his weight self-consciously, she inwardly groaned. She hadn't meant to be unkind.

"I parked around front," he said, his grin still there, but no longer quite so playful. "And I *walked* around the house." His emphasis on the word only made her feel worse. "I was waiting for Binks; I figured he'd be the first one up. He usually is."

"Sorry," she mumbled. "That was rude of me." Binks would probably be thrilled to see the guy.

"It was," he returned. "What did you say your name was?"

He really was a jerk, she decided. Apologizing for her outspokenness wasn't usually difficult for her—she had a bad habit of blurting out whatever thought passed through her mind, and it had gotten her into trouble more than once. But then, people were usually a little more receptive to her apologies, too. Granted, she wasn't usually so unkind... "I didn't say."

He nodded slowly, then waved a hand toward the kitchen door. "Well, then, be my guest, Mystery Lady. Apparently, my house is your house."

She squared her shoulders again and started forward, then paused at the sound of hurrying footsteps on the gravel drive.

"What's going on out here?" It was Binks, hurrying from the direction of his cabin. "I heard you scream, Miss Charity. You all right?"

"I'm fine, Binks. You have a visitor." She thrust her chin toward Frank again. "He scared the living daylights out of me, creeping around in the dark—"

"I wasn't creeping around in the dark," Frank said with another laugh. "Hey, Binks." He pushed away from the post to stand upright, still not putting much weight on the braced leg. "Good to see you, man."

"Frankie?" The old man moved past Charity and up the steps. "What are you doing here, boy?" Binks stuck out a hand, but Frank pulled him into a man hug instead. "Why didn't you tell us you were coming?" Binks asked when he stepped back.

Frank made an odd face. "I didn't know myself until I was halfway here," he said by way of explanation. "I didn't want to wake anyone, so I came around back here to wait for you. No creeping around, I promise. I don't do much of that these days, not with this thing." He patted the side of his brace in an affectionate manner. "In fact, I was resting peacefully before I was interrupted by that tiny, little thing with a great big voice."

"Miss Charity?" Binks asked with a chuckle of his own. He turned back to look at her, noticed her hands were full, and came back down the steps to take the jar from her. "Let me help you, young lady."

"Wait. Charity?" Frank cocked his head and sized her up. "Charity Goodacre from next door?"

"No," she snapped. "Charity Banner."

"From next door, though, am I right? I recognize you." He nodded as she followed Binks up the steps. "You're married?" he asked as she passed just close enough that she could smell the cologne he used.

"Yes, and yes," she said. Then she decided not to breathe because the smell of him nearly knocked her off her feet. It wasn't cologne after all, but the clean, old-fashioned aroma of Barbasol shaving cream. Theo swore by it, and catching a whiff of it on Frank Flanner made her senses reel uncomfortably. She quickly located the key to the door, pushed it open, and headed inside ahead of Binks. Frank appeared in the doorway a few moments later, a pair of crutches tucked under his arms. Seeing them, she felt even worse for her unkind comment.

She flipped on the overhead lighting and glanced behind her at Frank when she heard his sharp intake of breath.

"Whoa," he said, surprise and pleasure coloring his tone.

Charity watched him from under lowered lashes, not to be coy, but because she couldn't help staring, and she didn't want to be super obvious. In the artificial light of the kitchen, she saw the telltale signs of fatigue on his face, half-moon shadows under his eyes, the way the corners of his mouth dragged down, the day or two's worth of growth covering his jaw. In spite of it all, something about Frank Flanner had her feeling a little stirred up; her pulse fluttered erratically just under her jaw. He wasn't exactly handsome, but he had the chiseled features and squared-off look that made a uniform look good. Granted, he wasn't wearing one at the moment, but she could totally picture him in one, and the fact that she could completely unnerved her. Even with his messed-up leg, he carried himself the way Theo had, shoulders squared, chin up, and his eyes—she couldn't tell from across the room if they were green or maybe hazel—took in every little detail of his surroundings. Including her. She blinked rapidly and glanced away when he quirked a questioning brow at her.

"My cousin has been busy," he finally stated.

"He sure has," Binks agreed. He slid the jar of beans onto the big butcher block table in the middle of the room. "This whole place got renovated, but he handled things with care, son, so don't you worry."

Frank nodded. He pointed at an ornate wall clock mounted above the pantry door. "Mom's Bulova clock. It looks good up there."

"Sure does," Binks said, peering up at the timepiece. "Cord kept the things that belonged."

Charity bit back a smile when she noticed what the old man was wearing—a pair of jeans, a threadbare tank top under a denim jacket, and a pair of cowboy boots, the cuffs of his pants bunched haphazardly at the top of them as though he'd pulled everything on in haste. She set the bag of muffins next to the coffee maker, then crossed the short distance to put an arm around the foreman's waist. "Thank you for coming to my rescue, Binks."

Binks gave her a quick, self-conscious hug, and shook his head. "Nothing to rescue you from, Miss Charity. Frankie here wouldn't let anything happen to you."

"Thanks for the vote of confidence," Frank said from where he stood just inside the kitchen door. The grin was back. "But I think she was referring to you rescuing her from me."

"You know what?" Charity said with a frown. He may be hot stuff in or out of a uniform, and sure, he was sorta family by marriage, being her brother-in-law's cousin, but that didn't mean she had to like him. She moved around Binks to the massive refrigerator. "I have a lot of work to do this morning, so why don't you boys get on out of here and leave me to it."

"You work here," Frank said. It wasn't a question, but an opening to a conversation. The guy couldn't take a hint.

"I do," was all she'd give him. She pulled the first stack of ribs out of the fridge and turned to place them on the butcher block table.

The two men just stood in their respective spots, watching her.

"What?" she asked, placing a hand on her hip. "Is there something you need from me?" She narrowed her eyes at Frank who still wore that stupid grin, then turned her attention fully on Binks.

"You planning on making any coffee this morning?" the old man asked, his brow furrowed as he looked back and forth between Charity and Frank.

"Coffee sounds good to me," Frank interjected in a winsome tone as he moved further into the room. He leaned his crutches against the counter and turned to plant both hands on the table so that he was facing her.

Charity pressed her lips together and frowned at him. "You know how to use that machine?" she asked, waving in the general direction of the coffee maker.

"I do. Would you like me to brew a pot?" He straightened, as though preparing to do just that, his pie-eating grin softening his angled features, making him look much more like the boy next door she remembered.

"No, I do not," she shot back. The idea of Frank lingering in her space any longer than was absolutely necessary was more than she wanted to deal with right now. "Why don't you go... I don't know. Check on your room, or something, while I make coffee. Does Cord know you're here? Or Faith?" Surely, Faith would have mentioned it if she knew he was coming.

"Nope. Like I said earlier, I didn't even know I was on my way here until about an hour or so out. Figured I'd surprise everyone."

"Well, you can check that off your list." She rolled her eyes and turned back to start pulling the rest of the racks of ribs out of the fridge. "I'll have coffee ready in fifteen minutes. You can come back then." She'd be ready to take the load of ribs out to the smokers by that time, and hopefully, he'd take his coffee somewhere else and be gone when she got back to start on her side dishes.

"Actually, I think I'll pass on coffee for now," Frank said, a hint of regret in his voice. "I've been up all night, and I think an hour or two of sleep might do me some good. Mind if I take a rain check?"

"Take whatever you want. It's your house." She hated the way she sounded. Besides, technically, it wasn't his house anymore, not since he'd sold the place to Cord. What was it about him that set her off so badly? Sure, the guy was easy to look at, and he wasn't exactly the most sensitive man in the world, but she spent every working day around a crew of guys just like him. Skid and Ernie Maddox were both good-looking local boys who had the world by the tail, but neither one of them affected her the way Frank was now. It couldn't be just because he'd startled her and hadn't really bothered to apologize, could it?

Her stupid pride, maybe? Although, that didn't seem to make a whole lot of sense, either. She'd been embarrassed by her ridiculous reaction, but it was the kind of thing that usually set her laughing at herself.

That was something else she was known for—her contagious laugh. Well, she'd been known for it before Theo died. She didn't laugh very often these days.

From the corner of her eye, she saw Frank nod. "Will do. Thank you. And Binks?" Leaning heavily on the table, he moved toward Binks, and thrust out his hand toward the old man. "It's good to be home. I'll look for you in a few hours, okay? If you see Cord before I do, let him know I'm here."

"I will, son. It sure is good to see your face around here again. You planning on staying for a bit?"

"You know, I wasn't planning on coming here at all, so..." Frank shrugged one shoulder, a wry expression on his face. "Not exactly sure how to answer that."

"Well, even so," Binks said, reaching up to pat Frank on the shoulder. "You being here is all right by me."

Charity leaned into the open door of the fridge to pull out a flat of eggs that needed hard-boiling. "No one bothered to ask if it was all right by me," she muttered under her breath. Did this mean he'd be staying in his old room upstairs? That she'd have to start sharing her sanctuary with Frankie Flanner?

FOUR

"THERE YOU GO AGAIN, talking to yourself," Frank said as she straightened, letting the fridge door close behind her. She jumped, nearly dropping the tray of eggs, and he reached for them, his reflexes as sharp as ever. One unfortunate egg flipped out and fell to the floor with a wet crack. "Oops. Sorry."

"Seriously?" she gasped, grabbing the tray back and glaring up at him. She snatched up a handful of paper towels from a holder on the counter and made quick work of the mess. "Why do you keep sneaking up on me like that? What is wrong with you?"

Frank tried not to laugh, but Charity's expression of petulant rage made it impossible to hold it in. He hadn't meant to scare her again—surely, she'd heard him approaching, his ungainly stride not subtle at all. "What's wrong with me? Let me see. Where do you want me to start? I have a bum leg, I'm getting old and have no one to call my own, and my childhood home belongs to someone else now. Someone who apparently has a penchant for hot-headed chefs."

Charity made a sound that might have been a squawk if she was a chicken. A little mad hen, that's what she reminded him of, huffing and clucking and ruffling her feathers.

A very cute little mad hen with all that blonde hair and those flashing blue eyes. Eyes that were zeroed in on him.

Binks guffawed, then pushed open the back door. "I'm heading home to get dressed properly. You two try not to kill each other before I get back. And Frankie?"

"Yes, sir?" Frank turned to salute the foreman.

"A word of advice. Try not to rile up the cook. Especially not on rib day."

"Too late for that, Binks," Charity called after him. She brushed past Frank, purposely nudging him out of the way as she did so, making him stumble slightly. For such a little thing, she sure knew how to throw her weight around.

Frank could still hear Binks' chuckle even after the screen door slapped shut. "Come on, Charity. How about we start over? Let's be friends."

"Why?" she asked from where she stood at the sink, filling a large stock pot with water. "We never were before, and believe me, you haven't really endeared yourself to me since I got here."

"What do you mean, we never were before?" Frank said, his tone now cajoling. He leaned back against the counter, bracing his hands on either side of him, and took the weight off his throbbing leg. Bed still sounded really good right now, but sparring with Charity Goodacre—Charity Banner—was helping to take his mind off his pain quite nicely. "I was friends with everyone in the hollow."

"No, you weren't," she contradicted him. "You were a hotshot teenager when you lived here, and coming home to visit your folks for a day or two every couple of years doesn't make you exactly friendly to the rest of the folks in the hollow. Just because everyone knows who you are—I mean, you are practically royalty around here, you know—doesn't mean everyone is your friend." She didn't even bother looking at him while she spoke, so he took advantage of the opportunity to take a gander at her. She wore a western style navy blue plaid shirt tucked into jeans that followed her curves like they'd been specially tailored for her, a pair of simple cowhide boots, and the biggest hoop earrings he'd ever seen on a woman. Her blonde curls spilled down her back, but they were clipped up and away from her face with what looked like glass butterfly wings. His eyes traced her profile with her slightly upturned nose, arched brows, and that jaw thrust forward obstinately. Was it all a show, or was she really as tough as she made herself out to be?

He lifted one hand in surrender. "Did I somehow wrong you in the past? I mean, is this aversion to me all because I was creeping around and rising up out of the dark like some... What was it you called me?" He winked at her when she tossed a dark look at him over her shoulder. "A phantom freak? Was that it?"

"Why are you still here?" she asked, making him laugh out loud.

"Because I'm curious about whatever this is between us, Ms. Charity." He was goading her, he knew, but he couldn't decide whether he should be offended by her blatant animosity or flattered by it.

She spun on her heel and threw her hands in the air in frustration. A drop of water hit him on the cheek, and he reached up to wipe it away, his eyes locked with hers. "What are you talking about?" She asked, her voice tight. "There is nothing between us, Frank Flanner. You are an egotistical, rude man who scared the snot out of me and then mocked me. You haven't quit mocking me since. You're like a school yard bully, it seems. Is this the way you treat your men, soldier boy?"

"That's First Sergeant Soldier Boy to you," he said dryly, his gut clenching at the thought of the troop he'd left behind. What was left of them, anyway. "I'm a decorated war hero, I'll have you know." He made a sweeping motion with his hand, lifting his leg for her to see.

"Wow. Big whoop-de-do. Did you get a boo-boo?" She practically snarled at him, her eyes flashing angrily. "At least you're still here to complain about it." She shook her head and gave him one last scathing look. "You're in my territory now, Frankie. Which means unless you're a decorated *cake*, you need to leave."

"Wow," he echoed her, but not in the same sarcastic tone she used. Mad hen, indeed. What had he done to set her off so badly? And why on earth was he contemplating sticking around to find out?

Before he could come up with a good response, she let out a heavy sigh and dropped her head to her chest. "Thank you," she murmured.

Frank reached up to run a hand over his hair. He was a couple weeks overdue for his bi-monthly buzz cut, and the longer hair felt as foreign to him as standing in this kitchen across from Charity and her all-over-the-map emotions. "You lost me," he said.

"Thank you for your service." She fluttered a hand at his leg, then lifted her gaze to his just long enough for him to see the stark pain in her eyes. "Thank you for your sacrifice." The statement seemed to almost strangle her, but without another word, she turned back to the tray of eggs and began loading them into the stock pot, leaving Frank at a total loss for words.

When Charity lifted the heavy load out of the sink to carry it to the stove top, Frank started forward, wanting to help, but his knee buckled at the sudden weight, and he grabbed at the counter to steady himself. How he hated the limitations this leg put on him. He couldn't even be the gentleman his father had raised him to be.

Charity turned glistening eyes on him—ah geez, had he made her cry?—then she said in a much kinder voice, "You should go lie down. Rest that leg. None of the rooms on the second floor are being used if you can manage the stairs."

He hesitated, not liking the way this encounter was ending, but his all-nighter was catching up to him, and he was suddenly beyond fatigued. "Will you still be here in a couple of hours?" he asked.

She nodded, switching on the burner under the pot, then turned to face him. She spoke flatly. "I'll be in and out of the kitchen most of the morning, but I won't have time to play hostess, if that's what you're asking. I'm cooking for a big barbecue out on the deck behind the barn later today. You're welcome to join us if you'd like. There will be plenty of food." She'd gone from startled, to wary, to angry, to... was she sad now?

"Thank you," he said, his voice a little gravelly. He wasn't sure if it was from lack of sleep or because he was so bothered by her roller-coaster emotions. "I'd like that." He eyed the stacks of ribs on the butcher block. "You need any help before I go?"

She shook her head, glancing tellingly at his leg. "No thank you. I've got this."

Frank nodded. She was right. Charity didn't need the help he could offer her. His leg hurt too much to even attempt walking without his crutches right now, and even then, he'd be lucky to be able to carry half of what she could without tripping over his own foot or having his knee buckle and end up dropping something important. "Right. Sure. Okay, well, I'll see you later today then. Looking forward to the ribs." He squared his shoulders and reached for his crutches, then started toward the arched opening with the swinging doors that led from the kitchen to the rest of the house.

As they swung closed behind him, he heard her say, "Welcome home, Frankie."

He lifted a hand in acknowledgment but said nothing. For years, home was on the front lines. Home was sleeping back-to-back with a comrade, one eye open, ears tuned to any suspicious sound. Home was where men and women looked up to him, followed his commands at the risk of life and limb... a risk that had become a reality for him, and now he wasn't sure where home was.

The bed in his old room had no sheets on it, but the navy and gray comforter was soft, and he'd showered before he climbed into his car several hours ago. He slipped out of his sneakers, removed the leg brace with a groan of relief, and lay back, his head on the bare pillow. He wrapped the blanket around him like a sleeping bag, then he closed his eyes as morning light began seeping its way through the wooden blinds on his window. Surely, now that the dark was gone, he'd sleep like a baby.

His last thought was of the pretty woman bustling around in the kitchen downstairs. What was her story?

FIVE

CHARITY HAD TO GET him out of her head. She slipped her phone from her back pocket and dug out the pair of earbuds she kept in a drawer she'd claimed as her own. It held her personal items like nail clippers and a file or two, a toothbrush, lip balm, a packet of tissue, a travel-size sewing kit, tampons, a tube of her favorite lipstick, and a change purse with a few dollars in it. It was essentially her purse, and everyone knew not to dig around in it.

She shoved the speakers in her ears and found the audiobook she'd started last night, a Nora Roberts novel about a woman who, as a girl, helped one of her serial-killer-father's victims escape. Now as an adult, she was being stalked by a copycat killer. It was intriguing enough to hold the thought—and smell—of Frank Flanner at bay, and Charity worked with dogged concentration on the task of putting together the huge meal she had planned.

By ten o'clock, she was ready for a break. The ribs were starting to color nicely, the smoky, sweet aroma wafting across the pastures, distracting hardworking—and drooling, according to Binks—crew members. The potato salad was marrying flavors in the refrigerator, the chicken pieces were cut and marinating in a seasoned brine—she'd dip them in eggs and breading at the last minute before deep frying them in a pot of hot oil—and several gallons of tea were out brewing in the sunshine. Nothing like sweet sun tea at an early summer barbecue.

She had at least half an hour before she needed to baste the ribs again, so she headed into the living room of the big house to her favorite reading chair where she could put her feet up and lose herself in the novel she was listening to. It was getting really creepy; no wonder she'd freaked out when Frank had appeared out of the darkness early that morning. Sometimes she wondered why she loved thrillers and murder mysteries as much as she did. She'd only started reading them after Theo's death, and Faith thought it had something to do with Charity being able to tap into her emotions in a way that felt safe and distanced from her reality. Her sister was probably right—it was a lot easier to embrace the fear of fictional characters than it was to tap into the bottomless well of her own grief.

She lowered herself into the chair, drew a large soft footstool close, toed off her boots, and sank back into the cushions behind her. On the occasional table beside her was a cold glass of lemonade and a platter of tomato slices and mozzarella sprinkled with shredded basil, salt and pepper, and drizzled in olive oil. She closed her eyes and tried to imagine the wooded scene the narrator was describing.

A loud crash jolted her upright and she snatched the speakers from her ears. Had something blown up in the kitchen? Had she left something in the oven?

A thunk, followed by a terrible cry of alarm, or pain—*not* coming from the kitchen, but from somewhere on the floor above her. Charity leaped to her feet. "Frankie." Without questioning the wisdom of her actions, she hurried up the stairs, taking them two at a time in her haste. She'd only been on the second floor a few times, mostly just to check on the progress, but she was familiar enough with it to know which room had been Frank's.

All the doors were open except for the one at his end of the hall. She knocked, but there was no response. No sound at all, in fact. "Frank?" she called out. "It's Charity."

Still no answer. Taking a deep breath, she slowly turned the handle and pushed the door open just enough to peer inside. "Frank? You okay?"

Still getting no response, she let the door swing open a little wider and did a quick scan of the place. It was a good-sized room, complete with a large closet along one wall, a built-in nook desk, and a window that overlooked the long front drive coming up from Carpenter Road, but it was evidently empty. How had he gotten out of the house without her knowing? She supposed he could have slipped out while she was outside at the smokers, but surely, he would have stopped in the kitchen for something to eat, a cup of coffee, or even just to poke fun at her again. Besides, she'd heard him up here. Or at least, she assumed it was him. Someone—or something—had made that loud crash, and she hadn't imagined that terrible cry, either.

"Frankie?" she said, her voice a little quieter this time. His shoes sat side-by-side on the floor at the foot of the bed, his leg brace propped up beside them, his crutches leaning against the wall nearby. The bed was bare; had he slept without linens? She was a little freaked out now, the shroud of the audiobook hovering around her, putting her senses on high alert. "Where are you?" She made her way across the room to the closet doors, then reached for one to slide it open. A sound, muffled, harsh, made her freeze, her hand lifted. "Frank?" she whispered.

What was she doing? What if he was one of those guys who suffered from PTSD? What if in his agitated state, he attacked her, not knowing she wasn't the enemy? A rush of adrenaline surged through her, making her skin tingle and her hair stand on end. She spun around, hurrying past the bed to get out of the room. "Stupid, stupid, stupid," she chided herself. "What are you think—" Her mutter ended in a shriek of terror as a hand shot out like a tripwire from under the bed, sending her sprawling to the floor. She rolled onto her side, fists up defensively, but suddenly, Frank was on top of her, flattening her beneath him.

"Shut up," he growled against her ear, his voice fierce and desperate. "Don't move."

"Frank," Charity gasped, his shoulder pushing painfully into her cheek, forcing her head against the floorboards. "You're—you're crushing me."

"Stop fighting me," he grunted, wedging his good knee between her legs.

"Frank!" she cried out, a new kind of terror rising up in her. She tried to push him off, her efforts futile as she lay powerless against his superior strength. Her eyes burned with unshed tears, but she was too scared to cry. "Get off me! Frank!"

He pressed his hips against hers, one large hand slamming down over her mouth, partially covering her nose, too, making it almost impossible to breathe. "Shut up, man," he ordered, his voice a harsh command. "You'll get us both killed."

Charity went completely still beneath him, her tears spilling over. Her chest heaved in a silent sob, but she didn't move otherwise.

Every muscle in Frank's body coiled tightly over her. A tiny tremor coursed through him like a current of electricity, a hum that traveled through them both. He barely breathed, sprawled over her like a boulder, protecting her from some unseen assault.

Protecting her. Covering her.

Slowly, his hand began to relax over her mouth, then he lifted it away completely and rose up on his elbows to peer around the room. His eyes, glassy and red-rimmed—they were hazel, almost amber—saw things she didn't, his jaw was clenched so tightly she was sure his teeth would break. A few moments later, the tension in his big body began to ease, too, relieving some of the pressure off her abdomen so she could breathe easier. She still said nothing, just watched his face, waiting for him to realize where he was, for reality to register.

He looked down at her beneath him. "You're going to be all right, you hear me? We'll get you out—" He broke off mid-sentence, his eyes going wide with shock. He froze, his body going rigid once again.

"Frankie?" Charity whispered, holding his gaze with her own. "You're home. This is Whispering Hills Ranch." She tried a half smile, but it was probably more of a grimace. "It's me, Charity Ban—Charity Goodacre. From next door. Remember?"

Slowly, almost trance-like, Frank eased off her, rolling onto his back and bringing an arm up to cover his face. "I'm sorry," he ground out, the muscles of his jaw bunching visibly. "I'm so sorry. Did I—did I hurt you?"

"No," she whispered, darting a sideways glance at him, then looking back at the ceiling. She straightened her right leg out; it had been bent uncomfortably beneath his.

"I hurt you." It wasn't a question this time. "You're crying."

"It's okay." What could she say? Her tears kept flowing, even though she willed them to stop. He'd surprised her—blindsided her—but as she did a quick mental assessment, she found that nothing hurt. It was a little hard to breathe still, but Charity was pretty sure that had more to do with a pressing need to unleash a torrent of emotions than because she was somehow injured.

Finally, he lowered his arm and turned his head just enough to look at her. "What are you doing up here?"

SIX

HE COULD HAVE KILLED her. Had the dream been different, had it not been Stanley lying beneath him, fighting to breathe, begging for help....

He couldn't go there. Couldn't think that way.

"Why are you in my room?" Frank asked again, mortified that she'd seen him like this, sick to his stomach that she lay on his floor, tears streaming from her eyes. What had he done to her?

"I—I heard you. There was a loud crash. I thought—I thought maybe—" Her voice cracked, and she lifted her hands to cover her face. "I'm sorry for intruding."

"No, no," he said, rolling onto his side to face her. "Don't apologize. I'm not angry, Charity. Please don't cry. I already feel like a monster." He touched the back of her hand but withdrew quickly when she flinched. His leg throbbed painfully; how had he ended up on the floor with her beneath him?

"I don't know why I'm crying," she whimpered behind her hands. "I just can't seem to stop."

"I hurt you," he said, certain he had. He'd been spread eagle on top of her, for Pete's sake, and he was pretty sure he hadn't been gentle about getting there.

"I'm not hurt," she repeated, shaking her head.

"Well, I must have scared you pretty badly. I'm so sorry," he said again, knowing there were no words to make this situation right.

"Don't apologize. You were trying to—trying to protect me," she finished in a trembling voice.

"Trying to protect you," he scoffed, returning to his back and scrubbing at his face with both hands. "From what? The sun motes streaming in the window? The dust bunnies under the bed?" He glanced over, the sarcastic comment triggering a memory. Sure enough, there was the comforter he'd wrapped himself in, balled up and shoved into the tight space. He must have launched himself out of bed and crawled beneath it to hide. "Was I under there?" he asked quietly, but he didn't need her affirmative answer to his question. It had been a long time since he'd pulled that maneuver, but he shouldn't have been surprised. Change often triggered his more active dreams.

She nodded, then swiped at her cheeks with her fingers in a futile attempt to brush away the tears that kept flowing.

Frank frowned when she winced, and he leaned closer, studying her face carefully. A red smudge colored her cheekbone, and he didn't think it was just from crying. He reached over and brushed the pad of his thumb across the high ridge, and then grunted softly when she pulled away. She brought her hand up to cover the spot, her wedding ring flashing accusingly at him.

"Your husband is going to kill me," he muttered, easing up to a sitting position. "That's going to leave a mark."

Charity let out a broken sob and rolled away from him to sit up, too, but with her back to him, her face in her hands again.

"I'll talk to him, Charity. Man to man. He'll understand." He hoped. Frank wasn't sure he'd understand if the roles were reversed, if Charity came home to him with a bruise like that on her face.

Charity shook her head, but she was crying so hard, all she could get out was, "You—you ca—can't."

"Of course, I can," Frank insisted, reaching over to put a hand on her shoulder. She seemed almost afraid. Of what? "I won't tell him this happened in my room, if that's what you're worried about."

She shook her head again, emphatically this time. "I need a tissue," she managed to squeak out.

Frank closed his eyes and grimaced. Without his brace on, and without his crutches, hobbling down the hall to the bathroom would be nothing short of an adventure, but by the time he put the brace on, she could be there and back from getting the tissue herself. If she came back at all.

"Here. Use this," he said, stripping off his t-shirt, balling it up and leaning forward to hold it in front of her. She opened her hands a tiny bit to look at his offering, then shook her head again.

"I can't. I need to blow my nose."

Frank chuckled softly. "Believe me, this shirt has seen far worse. Take it." After another moment of hesitation, she did, covering her face with it.

He turned away to give her some privacy. Reaching under the bed, he grasped a corner of the comforter and pulled it out, then scooted over to grab his brace, giving himself a few moments to gather his own courage. If she ever lowered the t-shirt and looked at him, she'd see exactly how much of a monster he was. He kept his face averted as he put the brace on, cinching the Velcro straps in place, buckling the brackets around his ankle and knee, glad she wouldn't see the mangled remains of his leg, too. The scars on his torso were shocking enough.

The silence between them dragged out so long that he finally turned to glance over his shoulder at her. She still had her face buried in his shirt, but her breathing seemed steadier. "I'm really sorry about this, Charity," he repeated.

"You smell like him." She spoke so softly that he wasn't sure he heard her right.

"Like whom?" he asked, pivoting on his backside so he could rest his shoulders against the bed. He stretched his leg out in front of him, the support of the brace helping to relieve some of the ache.

Charity lowered his shirt, wearing an expression of such misery he had to look away. "Like my husband. You shave with Barbasol, don't you?"

Frank frowned, a little taken aback by the personal question, and returned his gaze to her just in time to see her face go carefully blank as she took in the puckered skin, the ugly ridges and discolored splotches that had once been smooth, muscular flesh. He forced himself to breathe normally, fighting the urge to snatch back his shirt from her—tears, makeup, snot and all—and cover himself up with it. "I do. My dad taught me to shave with it, and I've never used anything else."

"That's what Theo said, too. He loved that stuff." She lifted his shirt and sniffed it. "I can smell it, even with my stuffed-up nose." Fresh tears welled in her eyes. "I'll wash this and bring it back tomorrow. Will that work? Or are you leaving sooner than that?"

"Theo is... your husband?" Frank had no idea when he was leaving, and at the moment, he didn't care about the shirt, either. Not only had she not even acknowledged his horrific scars, but the whole husband thing was taking a new twist. "And you can keep the shirt."

"But do you have something else to wear? You didn't bring a bag with you." She gestured around the room. "At least, you didn't have one when you came in this morning."

"I was planning on going shirtless while I was here," he said with shrug, opting against subtlety and going for a direct hit instead. Get it out of the way. Acknowledge the elephant in the room. He lifted his arms and flexed, exposing his whole shredded side to her. *Look at me, I dare you,* he wanted to tell her. *Look at what's left of me.*

Charity snorted, then covered her mouth with a hand. For a moment, he thought she had burst into a fresh batch of tears, but her shoulders shook too rapidly to be sobs. No, she was laughing, a sound that bubbled up from somewhere low in her belly and burst out of her mouth like a fountain. He was reminded of Julia Roberts—that huge smile and unchecked laugh she let loose in every movie she starred in. Ms. Roberts had taught women the world over that laughter—the full-throttled, genuine kind—could be a huge turn on. And Charity's laugh was surprisingly contagious. Kind of like Stanley's. Frank chuckled softly, enjoying the sound of it, even if he wasn't sure exactly what she was laughing about.

"I'm sorry," she finally said between hiccups. "My goodness. I haven't laughed like that in a long time." She turned teasing eyes on him. "I wasn't laughing at you, I promise."

"Well, that's reassuring," he said, absentmindedly running a hand down the mangled mess of his side. "I was trying to impress you with all this manliness, not send you into fits of laughter."

"Oh, you impress me, all right, Frankie Flanner." She waved a hand at his scars. "All of that impresses me." She gestured at his leg, then reached out to touch his brace, her hand momentarily resting on the hinged bracket at his ankle. "This impresses me."

It felt to Frank like a blessing.

She'd grown suddenly serious. "I can see how hard you're trying, you know. I'm not blind. I can't imagine what you went through, but I know it's not really over, is it? The fact that you're here, worrying about me and my stupid tears, taking the very shirt off your back for me?" She met his gaze. "You impress me, Soldier Boy."

"That's First Sergeant Soldier Boy to you," he said with a grin, a rush of heat flooding through him at her words.

She lifted a hand to salute him. "Yes sir, First Sergeant Soldier Boy." A moment later, she slid on her backside to sit next to him, leaning back against the bed like he was. "What happened?" she asked quietly. "Do you mind me asking?"

Did he? She was one of very few civilians who'd seen his scars; but after what had just happened, didn't he owe her at least some kind of explanation? He took a deep, cleansing breath, then let it out slowly. "I don't mind. I can't tell you much, partly because I'm not allowed to divulge a lot of the details, but also because I don't remember much of it." Which was why his dreams put scenario after scenario together for him to live through—as badly as he wanted to know, as hard as he tried to remember, he couldn't recall what actually happened that terrible day. Glimpses and pieces came back to him over time—the cries he heard, the sound of rattling gunfire, his own labored breathing, Stanley urging him to go help someone else.... "It was an ambush. We'd been working with this guy for weeks; he'd been helping us maneuver through some pretty rough terrain." He spoke slowly, carefully, choosing his words to keep it vague, yet to the point. "But one day, he didn't show up. Against my better judgment, we waited for him. We were like sitting ducks." He swallowed hard and crossed his arms over his chest. "I lost some good men that day."

"Oh, Frank," Charity whispered, her eyes glistening with compassion. "I'm so sorry."

"Yeah, me, too," he said with a nod, no longer wanting to talk about it.

"What now?" she asked, brushing her fingertips along the rigid steel bar that ran down the side of his thigh. "What's going on with this?"

He frowned and stared at his leg, picturing the twisted mess beneath his Ferrosi pants. He'd taken to wearing hiking and climbing gear because the fabric was thin, breathable, and didn't rub roughly against his scars that were still hypersensitive. Because they were so lightweight, they worked well under the brace, too—he had no desire to wear shorts, that was for sure. He shrugged one shoulder. "I've had several surgeries so far. They want me to take a short break, then I'll probably go back under the knife in about five or six months. I think it may be a while before they're through cutting away at me."

"That sounds awful," Charity murmured, not hiding her horror or trying to act unaffected. It was rather refreshing to be able to read her reactions so clearly.

"It hasn't been a joy ride," Frank admitted. Then, lest he sound like he was pouting or complaining, he cleared his throat and shot her a quick smile. "So, I have a question for you. If you don't mind me asking, of course."

She angled a look up at him, then shook her head. "I don't mind. Ask away. I can always plead the Fifth, right?"

"Sure," he nodded. One side of his mouth quirked up. "So, what *were* you laughing at? Me hiding under the bed like a scared little boy?"

"No!" she said, elbowing him in the side. "I wouldn't laugh at something like that. What do you take me for?"

"Then what was so funny? I thought you were going to pass out from laughing so hard."

She brought his shirt up to cover her face again, her words muffled behind it. "I'm too embarrassed to tell you, now that we got all serious."

Frank chuckled. "You're kidding, right? I just fell out of bed, crawled underneath it to hide from the nonexistent boogie man, laid you out on the floor, and made you cry. Then I had to take off my shirt so you could gawk at my mutilated body—"

"Impressive, mutilated body to you, First Sergeant Soldier Boy," she interrupted, lowering the shirt again and giving him the stink eye.

"Right. So, you could gawk at my impressive, mutilated body, and you think you're embarrassed?" He shook his head. "Nope. Not good enough. Spill."

She lifted both hands in surrender. "Fine. *Fine.* But I have a disclaimer. I don't read this stuff, okay?"

"Read what stuff?" he asked, arching a curious brow at her. She was blushing. Her cheeks were turning a very pretty shade of pink right before his eyes.

"You know those sexy cowboy romance novels?" she asked.

Frank smirked and nodded. He could picture her curled up in a chair, her nose buried in a spicy romance novel. "Sure," he teased. "But I don't read that stuff, either, okay?"

"Stop it," she said, poking him in the shoulder. "And I'm serious. I read mysteries and thrillers."

He shot her a disbelieving look but remained silent. Charity rolled her eyes before continuing.

"Well, when you said that thing about going shirtless around here, I got this picture of you as one of those cowboys on the cover of one of those books, all bare-chested and slathered with baby oil, maybe in a denim or leather vest—" She snorted, then continued. "Your hat tipped low in front so that your eyes are half hidden, your thumb hooked over the big silver buckle of your belt." She was chortling now, her voice laced with delighted humor. She was enjoying this all too much, and at his expense. And he didn't even mind. "Your two-day growth airbrushed to perfection. Your horse resting his head on your shoulder, your dog leaning against your leg. Oh!" She waved a hand in front of her as she giggled again. "Your big old Silverado parked behind you."

"Well, I've got the shirtless part handled. All I need is a leather vest, a hat, a big silver belt buckle, a horse, a dog, and a truck," Frank quipped sarcastically, but he was grinning like an idiot. It was kind of nice to imagine Charity picturing him that way.

"Don't forget the oil," she retorted, covering her mouth to keep back another bout of laughter. Then she stiffened and scrambled to her feet.

"Oh no! I forgot about the ribs. I gotta go, Frankie." She held out a hand to him. "Let me help you up."

Now it was his turn to guffaw. "I have about a hundred pounds on you, little lady."

Charity planted her hand on her hip and quipped, "Believe me, I know that. Remember you going all Rambo on me back there?"

He shot her an apologetic smile. "I suppose I've been called worse. But I think I can manage." He pushed up off the floor with his good leg, leaning on the mattress until he was upright, bearing all his weight on his good leg. The throbbing pain in his left leg made him light-headed and a little sick to his stomach. "Do you need any help out there?" He didn't know how much good he'd be, not with the way his leg felt right now, but he'd manage if she said she did.

"No, no," she assured him. "I just need to keep the ribs basted. Believe me, you'll appreciate my efforts," she quipped, tucking his t-shirt against her side and smoothing her fingertips under her eyes. "Do I have black mascara all over?" she asked, lifting her face so he could see.

He gazed down at her, appreciating the gentle curve of her cheeks, the wide lines of her mouth, her pretty lips, her bold chin. Her earrings bobbled against her neck, a few strands of hair tangling in the huge hoops. Her eyes, crystal blue after her crying jag, her funny little nose....

He shook his head. Married. She was married.

And she wanted to know if she had mascara all over her face. He didn't even know for sure what mascara was, but the answer was easy. "You look good. Great. You look very pretty."

She also looked very vulnerable, and Frank had a sudden, wild urge to cup her face in his big hands and lower his mouth to hers.

SEVEN

Charity hurried down the stairs to the kitchen, shoved Frank's t-shirt in her drawer, then scooped up the large mixing bowl of sauce and the long-handled brush on her way out the back door. One of the secrets to her ribs was the consistent application of her tangy mop sauce throughout the smoking process, and she was a good fifteen minutes past time for another slather. "Please don't be dried out and nasty," she said aloud as she rounded the side of the barn toward the new outdoor kitchen Cord had installed last year.

To her relief, everything looked just fine, and the smell of the grilling meat made her stomach rumble in anticipation. She slathered the racks generously, then made her way back inside. She hadn't touched her mid-morning snack, so she'd appease her stomach with the Caprese Salad still waiting for her in the living room.

She was just settling back into the chair, having had to reset the audiobook back several chapters as it had kept playing in her absence, when she heard footsteps on the stairs behind her. She turned to see the still shirtless Frank making his way down on his crutches, a careful smile on his face. She smiled back, then averted her eyes, for some reason, a little shy now that they were out of the crisis mode they'd been in upstairs.

Part of her discomfort stemmed from the complete flipflop of emotions she was feeling toward the man. Just a few hours ago, she'd been so angry at him, she'd contemplated hurling a jar of pickled beans at his head, and now, she was having a difficult time trying *not* to imagine touching all that exposed skin. She hadn't slid her hands over the curve of a man's shoulders or traced the line of hair that ran down the center of his chest in a very long time, and her fingers tingled with the memory of the feel of Theo's flushed skin beneath her touch.

"I'm heading out to my car to grab my bag," Frank said as he drew nearer. His features were tight, and he looked a little pasty to her. He looked like he was in a lot of pain.

"Do you need help?" she asked, sliding forward in her chair and turning to look up at him. *Don't look at his chest. Don't look at his chest.* His shoulders were ridiculously wide, and the scars on his side did nothing to mar the beauty of his form. "Did you hurt your leg when you, um, you know?" She wasn't sure what part of their encounter to refer to.

Frank grimaced slightly. "I think maybe when I launched out of bed—or fell out, more likely—I might have tried to stand on it, or something. I'm supposed to sleep with a brace on for that reason, but I left my sleeping brace in my trunk. I might need to beg some ice off you if you don't mind."

"Sure, sure," she said, rising to her feet. Her phone slipped off her lap and crashed to the floor with a sound that made her groan. It slid face down to stop less than a foot in front of Frank, and they both stared at it for a weighted moment.

Not another cracked screen, she inwardly moaned. She'd replaced one just a few months ago when she'd dropped the phone while climbing out of the truck at church. She hurried forward and bent to pick it up, then straightened again, coming up much too close to the man for comfort. She stepped back awkwardly and shoved the phone and the attached earbuds into her back pocket. She'd check out the damage later. She gestured toward the front door. "Do you want me to get your bag for you? I mean, with your leg and all?" Gah. She was making the situation worse.

"No, I'm fine." His smile grew wider, he was evidently getting a kick out of her discomfort. "Nothing a little ice and elevation won't help. But I do have one other request."

"Absolutely. Fire away." She picked up her untouched cheese and tomato plate and her glass of lemonade, preparing to take them into the kitchen with her.

"I'm starving—"

"Oh! I can make you something. Want a fried egg sandwich? An omelet?" She sounded nervous, even to her own ears, but come on. A half-naked guy was standing in front of her wanting food. *Chill, Charity.*

Frank shook his head quickly. "No, no. I can cook for myself. I just don't want to intrude in your space, and I gather you've got a lot going on in there." He tipped his head toward the kitchen. "But I would like to raid the pantry and whip something up really quick, then I'll be out of your way."

It was Charity's turn to wave his protestations away, although she did so gingerly since she was holding her full glass. "Don't be ridiculous. You're right about it being my space. My domain. You want food? The only way you'll get anything out of my kitchen is if I cook it for you."

Frank grinned. "Are you sure? I know you have your hands full."

"I'm sure. You go get your stuff, then come on in the kitchen. I'll put together one of my famous omelets and a couple pieces of bacon. I think I have some French bread left over from yesterday—we had spaghetti for lunch. Would you like some of that toasted? Or if you like sweet stuff for breakfast, it makes great French toast." She shook her head. "No, wait. That's a lot of eggs for one meal. You know, with the egg batter and all. Oh, I know. How about I whip up a batch of biscuits instead—" She broke off when she noticed his expression. "Sorry. Get me going on food, and I blab incessantly." Man, she sounded like a ditz.

But his chest.

"Sounds like you love what you do," he stated. "Let's keep it simple, though, for your sake, okay? Eggs and toast would be great."

"Sure, sure. Kiss, right?" Charity nodded agreeably, then bit her bottom lip as she felt the flush creeping up her neck. Why in all of God's green earth did she say *that*?

Frank cocked his head, one eyebrow lifting in question. "What was that?"

If her hands were free, she'd have covered her burning cheeks. "Never mind." She ducked her head to hide her embarrassment, and then turned toward the kitchen. "I'll make you an omelet and some toast, then."

"I don't know. I think I might prefer the kiss." She didn't have to look at him to know he was teasing her. "Since you're offering."

"I'm not—I wasn't—" She shot an exasperated look over her shoulder at him. "It stands for 'Keep It Simple, Stupid.' K-I-S-S," she spelled out. "Surely, you've heard that before."

"Ah, yes. Of course. An unfortunate utilization of a very fine word, don't you think?" He shrugged, his broad shoulders moving fluidly, and Charity fled to the kitchen. He was far too comfortable in his skin, and she was far too distracted by all of it to continue their conversation.

"Please don't show up for breakfast half naked," she muttered as she pushed through the swinging doors into the sanctuary of her domain.

"Wouldn't dream of it."

Charity nearly dropped the Caprese Salad, and her lemonade sloshed precariously. "Cheese and crackers, Faith! You scared me to death!" she gasped, resisting the urge to throw something at her sister. "Why is everyone set on giving me a heart attack today?"

"Who were you talking to?" Faith asked, ignoring the question and crossing the large kitchen to duck past Charity. She pushed open the doors that were still swinging and peered out into the large open living room, then turned back to eye her sister. "Was that Frankie? Binks said he was sleeping off a long night, and he'd be out to see Cord when he got up."

Charity set her dish down on the counter and went to the fridge to pull out items to prepare Frank's breakfast. "Yes, it was Frankie, but I think he goes by Frank now. And he just got up, so I told him I'd make him some breakfast." She wasn't quite ready to share how the morning had really played out. She was still trying to make sense of it all herself.

Faith crossed her arms and smirked at Charity. Her hair was thick and shiny, a result, Faith claimed, of the prenatal vitamins she was taking. On Mother's Day last month, the Overmans had shared the good news that they were pregnant again. Jasmine, their preteen daughter, was ecstatic at the prospect of *finally* getting a baby brother or sister.

"You look really pretty today, Faithy." Charity waved a hand at her sister. "You've got that legendary pregnancy glow."

"Thank you," her sister said, her smile growing. She picked up Charity's fork and ate several slices of the tomato and cheese platter. "Yum. This is so good, girlie. And I feel fantastic. No morning sickness for me, I'm happy to say. I'm telling you, Charity, this is nothing like it was with Jasmine. Remember all the puking I did?"

Charity huffed good-naturedly. "How could I forget? I had to clean up after you because the thought of cleaning up after yourself made you throw up."

Faith came over and put an arm around Charity's shoulders. "You deserve an extra halo for that, little sister. But don't change the subject. Tell me about the half-naked Frankie Flanner coming to breakfast."

"Shh." Charity put a finger to her lips, her eyes wide.

"Is he really half naked?" Faith whispered, wiggling her eyebrows up and down in a rather lascivious way. "He's pretty nice to look at, as I recall."

"Faith Overman, you are a married woman."

"I'm not looking for me, girlie. I'm fat and happy with my own cowboy—soon to be a whole lot fatter, indeed." She pointed at the remaining Caprese Salad. "You going to eat this, or can I?"

"Have at it, Preggers. And just so you know, you don't need to be looking for me, if that's what you're implying." Charity moved away from Faith, not liking the direction the conversation had suddenly taken.

"And why not?" Faith kept her voice low, thank goodness, but the question hung like the resonant clang of a bell in the air between them. "Someone's gotta do it." She set the empty plate in the sink and reached for an apple in a wicker basket on the counter. "Mmm, Pink Lady. My favorite apple," she said, polishing it against her jeans before taking a huge bite.

In a rare show of self-control, Charity bit back the retort that wanted to jump out. Just because Faith had her happily-ever-after didn't mean she needed to try to hunt it down for everyone else. Especially not for her. Charity had already found—and lost—her happily-ever-after in Theo Banner, and she didn't want anything or anyone else. "You eating ribs with the crew today?" she asked.

"Oh, no, you don't. The fact that you're trying to change the subject tells me there's more to this little breakfast arrangement than you're letting on." Faith waved her apple at the frying pan where Charity was laying out strips of bacon. "In fact," she said, narrowing her eyes to look more closely at Charity. "You look all flushed. Almost like you've been crying." Then she reached over and tipped Charity's chin up. "You *have* been crying. What's going on?"

Charity pulled away from her sister's grasp and turned her attention on the bacon sizzling in the skillet. "Nothing, Faithy. I promise." When Faith just raised an admonishing brow at her, she rolled her eyes, and said, "I dreamed about Theo last night, okay?"

Faith nodded slowly and stepped away, chomping loudly on the apple as she studied her sister. "And that's really all?" she finally asked. "Frankie—Frank—didn't upset you?"

How did she know? "No, of course not. I mean, he practically scared the life out of me when I first got here this morning—I wasn't expecting some strange guy to be sitting on the back porch in the dark, you know?" It was the truth. Not all of it, but Faith didn't need to hear all of it right now. "Didn't Binks tell you about it? He thought it was pretty funny. They both did." She rolled her eyes and added, "I wasn't very happy to see either one of them at five this morning. I came early for some alone time."

"What happened to your cheek?" Faith asked, nudging Charity's face toward the light so she could see it better.

She'd forgotten about Frank's shoulder shoved against her cheek, pressing her head to the floor. "I couldn't say," Charity told her, reaching up to touch her cheekbone. She frowned at the tenderness beneath her fingers. "Is it ugly?"

Faith scoffed. "Of course not. Nothing on you could possibly be ugly." She put her arms around Charity and gave her a quick squeeze. "And I'm not the only one who thinks that, little sister. I heard Skid Maddox asked about you yesterday."

Charity pulled back and gaped up at her tall sister. "Skid? No way." She shook her head emphatically, then grabbed a fork and flipped the strips of bacon. Skid and his brother Elmer were in charge of the majority of the construction and renovations going on all over Whispering Hills, and Charity interacted with both of them just about every day, since she was responsible for feeding their crews their midday meal. Skid was one of those ridiculously handsome guys who wore a tool belt over jeans and flannel shirt over a white tank top in real life. He always had some pretty lady on his arm—rarely the same pretty lady from one day to the next, according to his reputation. Charity had never gotten much more than a flirtatious vibe from the guy, not in all the time they'd worked together, so Faith's assertions sounded almost silly.

"Yes way. Mr. Skidmore Maddox has been talking about you. He actually asked Cord if you were seeing anyone."

"Okay. Stop." Charity held up both hands. "I don't want to hear any more about Mr. Skidmore Maddox." She grinned at Faith. "Who names their kid Skidmore, anyway?"

"Who names their kids after the Seven Virtues?" Faith shot back, tossing her apple core into the compost bin Charity had opened to drop her eggshells into. "I mean, we have the weirdest names in Plumwood Hollow, all things considered."

Charity nodded. "You and Hope got off easy, that's for sure."

"Poor Abby," Faith murmured, but she said it with a smile. For whatever reason, Abby—short for Abstinence—had embraced her moniker, wearing it like a badge of honor. "But seriously. You should consider Skid. He's a good guy. Makes a good living. And he's nice to look at, too." She nudged Charity playfully with her hip.

"I won't argue with you there. Both those Maddox boys are. But I think 'good guy' might be pushing it a little, especially where Skid is concerned. Bad boy is probably more like it."

"Yeah, he is a little salty, isn't he?" Faith shrugged, picked up a piece of the bacon Charity had just pulled from the pan, and popped it in her mouth. "Like this bacon. Mm-mmm! But hey, maybe you need a salty bad boy in your life, you think?"

"Like I need a hole in my head," Charity shot back, shooing her sister away with the tongs she was using.

"I'm sure if you give him a little sugar, sweet Charity," Faith sing-songed, "he'd let you call him something other than Skid, you know."

Charity giggled. "How about Studmore? Or maybe Mad Maddox? He does kind of have that whole Tom Hardy thing going for him."

Faith chortled along with her. "I'll send him in here half naked for breakfast; I'm sure you'll come up with something."

Charity grabbed her sister by the shoulders and turned her around so that she faced the back door. "Enough. Out. I'm trying to work." But she was laughing too hard to give any credence to her command.

"No, wait!" Faith countered, pushing back. "I promised Cord I'd check on Frank, and if he's wandering around here half-naked and scaring you to death, then I need to personally size up the situation," she hooted. "It's my duty as your big—"

The double doors swung open, and Frank—fully clothed—pushed his way into the room. "Ladies," he said, his expression deceptively neutral, eyeing their matching guilty looks.

EIGHT

What had he just overheard? Wasn't Charity married? Why on earth were they talking about her entertaining Skid Maddox when she was already married? And Skid, of all people.

Frank had a few memories of the Maddox brothers that didn't sit well with him, not in light of the conversation he was unintentionally eavesdropping on. Especially Skid. The guy had been trouble back in high school—he was a couple years younger than Frank, but they'd both been on the football team, and unless the guy had changed drastically, Frank wouldn't want Skid anywhere near a woman like Charity Goodacre. Or Banner. Whatever her name was these days.

Sure, people changed. He glanced down at the clunky brace on his leg; look how much he'd changed. But according to the conversation coming through the kitchen doors, Skid sounded like the same player he'd been back in high school.

But what kind of woman did that make Charity, that she would consider messing around with someone like Skid? What kind of man did that make Charity's husband?

When he heard his own name, followed by the words 'half naked and scaring you to death,' he decided he wasn't going to stand around and let them make a mockery of him. The fact that Charity had already told anyone—was that Faith in there with her?—about their encounter upstairs in the bedroom, and that they were giggling about it behind his back, had his blood running hot beneath his skin. He'd given her far more credit than that, and honestly, he was more disappointed than angry. But that didn't mean he was going to let her insensitivity go unchecked.

"You were asking about me?" He directed his question at the woman standing behind Charity. Yep, Faith Goodacre. Faith Overman now. His cousin by marriage.

"Hey, Frankie. Long time, no see." She skirted her sister and held out her arms for a hug. "What a nice surprise," she added, before wrapping him in a strong embrace. "Why didn't you let us know you were coming?" she asked when she stepped back. "I would have had your room all set up and ready for you."

"I didn't know until I was halfway here," Frank said, starting to feel like a broken record. "I apologize if I'm putting you out." He found it odd that no one seemed to make a big deal over his messed-up leg. Sure, Charity had taken a shot at him earlier—*Big whoop-de-do. Did you get a boo-boo?*—but he'd kinda had that one coming. And yes, they'd talked about the circumstances behind it after he'd jumped her upstairs in his sleep-deprived, out-of-his-mind state. But otherwise, no one acted like it made any difference in who he was. Binks hadn't even mentioned it, and now Faith acted like she couldn't see the bulky brace or the crutches he leaned on.

He couldn't decide if that was good or bad. Why weren't people more shocked or worried? Or something. His injuries changed everything for him. They were a constant reminder of what had happened. Of whom he no longer was.

"You aren't putting us out," Faith assured him, reaching up to squeeze his shoulder. "Charity is just finishing up with your breakfast; if you've never had one of her omelets, then you're in for a real treat. No one does fluffy, cheesy eggs like my little sister."

Frank nodded slowly, eyeing Charity over Faith's shoulder. She was carefully folding an omelet that looked like it might grace the cover of a magazine. The aromas in the kitchen were tantalizing, and the blush on Charity's cheeks was rather distracting, too. Yeah, well, she should be embarrassed, having been caught maliciously gossiping about him. "Looking forward to it," he said, keeping his tone casual. "Maybe I should take it to go, though," he said, not really wanting to spend any more time with the woman right now. "If that's not too much trouble, of course."

Turning back to Faith, he explained, "I need to check in with your husband before I let any more time go by. I've taken advantage of him enough already."

"Don't be silly," Faith countered, shaking her head. "You sit and enjoy your food. I'll let Cord know you're awake, and he can come by here to see you. Besides, Charity just put on coffee. No one can make coffee like she does, either, and when I tell my husband she's got a fresh pot in here, he won't need you as an excuse to pop in." She pointed at an open shelf of stacked coffee cups above the coffee maker, and then at one of the stools tucked under the table in the middle of the room. "Pour yourself a cup and have a seat. I'll go get my man."

Short of being downright rude, there was little else he could do but agree to wait for Cord to join him. He glanced over at Charity, but she appeared inordinately fascinated by the food she was preparing for him. Did she have anything to say about him being in her kitchen while she worked? He'd heard what she'd said when her head was buried in the refrigerator: *No one bothered to ask if it was all right by me,*

As soon as Faith slipped outside, Frank leaned his crutches against the counter, and gingerly made his way around the kitchen, following the aroma of the robust roasted beans. "Your sister doesn't seem to be too worried about leaving you alone with a half-naked scary guy," he began, refusing to feel sorry for her.

Charity closed her eyes and grimaced. "You heard that?" she asked, still keeping her face averted from him.

"You two weren't whispering," he shot back. "She wasn't afraid I'd attack you again?"

Her eyes popped open and she turned to shoot him a narrowed look. "If you're asking if I told her about our...uh, *encounter* upstairs, then the answer is no. Which also means, no, she's not worried about you attacking me again."

Way to go, man. "Well, thank you," he said, scrambling to cover for his faux pas. "I appreciate you allowing me to maintain a modicum of dignity." He snorted softly. "Although, I think I just proved myself unworthy of your consideration." He watched his hostess as he poured himself a cup of the dark brew, bothered by how hard she was trying to avoid looking at him. Without asking, he poured a second cup for her, and instead of sitting down, he slid the cup along the counter in front of him as he hobbled around to where she was plating up his breakfast. "For you, Mrs. Banner," he said, holding the mug out to her. "I'll trade you."

She hesitated, still not quite meeting his eyes, then nodded. "Thank you." She took the proffered cup and set his plate on the table in front of a stool. "Enjoy your breakfast."

"Will you join me?" he asked, then wanted to bite his tongue. He didn't really want her to join him, truth be told. He was having a hard time reading her, and that didn't sit well with him. He was, by nature, rather skilled at reading people—and his job required it—but the woman across from him was a conundrum. One minute she was angry and snippy, the next, grateful and generous with her praise. Tearful and vulnerable, then gossiping and crass a few moments later. Bold enough to charge into a violent man's room unarmed because she thought he needed help, then shy and reserved to the point of awkwardness the next. He couldn't keep up... and yet, something about her made him want to try.

"I shouldn't," she said, shaking her head hard enough to make her coffee slosh over her fingers. "Yikes! Hot!" she murmured under her breath. She finally angled a tentative smile up at him. "I'm not usually such a klutz, you know. Dropping keys, eggs, knocking heads with folks. You just make me nervous." Sudden color suffused her cheeks, and she dropped her gaze again. Evidently, she'd said more than she meant to.

"I make you nervous?" he asked, angling his head to the side so he could better see her face. In a good way or a bad way, he wondered. "You don't have to be afraid of me, Charity. What happened up there in the room. That's not normal. I'm coming off pain pills and not sleeping well, and although that sounds like an excuse, it's the truth."

"No, no," she said, shaking her head, then braved an apologetic look at him. "That was totally my fault for barging in on you like that."

"You were trying to help."

"A lot of good that did." She waved his words away. "No, it's not that."

"Then...." He dragged the word out, then paused, waiting for her to explain. When she said nothing, he grinned. "If it's the half-naked cowboy thing, I'll adjust my plans to include a shirt."

"At the very least," she giggled, "a denim or leather vest, okay?" She smiled, then thrust her chin at the plate of food. "Sit down and eat. That's getting cold and I won't stand by and let you eat one of my omelets cold. Won't do it justice."

"Please. I know you said you don't have time to play hostess, but will you join me?" he invited again, realizing that he did, indeed, want her company after all. When she nodded and lowered herself onto one of the stools, he moved around the table and sat opposite her. He wanted to be able to look at her while they talked.

"Did you sleep okay, other than the nightmare?" she ventured to ask. "I have cream and sugar if you want it," she added.

"I drink my coffee black," he assured her. "And yes, I did sleep well," he said, testing his coffee. Faith was right. Ambrosia. "I think I got a solid four hours, which is a big chunk for me. Especially since I'm weaning myself off the hardcore pain meds. I hate what they do to me."

Charity nodded. "I've heard horror stories about that stuff," she murmured, but said nothing more.

Frank took a bite of the omelet and closed his eyes in appreciation as flavor exploded in his mouth. Cheese—Havarti, maybe?—and tart tomatoes, slivers of red peppers and caramelized onion, dill, and basil, and some other flavor he couldn't quite put a finger on. It was remarkable how intense a lowly omelet could taste. "Wow," he murmured after he'd swallowed the bite. "Faith wasn't kidding, Charity. This is amazing." He picked up a slice of bacon and held it aloft. "Even your bacon is cooked to perfection."

Charity blushed and looked down into her coffee cup. "Thank you. I'm glad you like it. That was my husband's favorite breakfast. He used to ask for it—"

"Frankie!" Cord burst into the kitchen, his booming voice echoing around the quiet room. He tossed his hat on the counter and rounded the table. "Cousin. Good to see you, man."

Frank had risen from his stool by the time Cord reached him and wrapped him in a brutal bear hug, but Charity's words had his pulse racing.

Was? Used to? Past tense.

Where was Charity's husband?

NINE

CHARITY ROSE TO GET Cord a cup of coffee, sliding it across the table to him. "You two catch up," she said by way of greeting. "I'm going to go check on my ribs." Then she ducked out, waving away their protests. The men had a lot to talk about, even without Frank's ambiguous reasons for showing up at Whispering Hills unannounced, and she'd only be in the way.

Besides, she needed to get the deck set up for the barbecue. It'd be buffet-style, but she still had to move the tables and chairs out to the deck. She wanted everyone outside today, not in the big mess hall where she usually served them. The sun was shining brightly, but a cool breeze made the day absolutely gorgeous, and there was no better way to enjoy chowing down on ribs than outdoors in the summer sunshine.

In spite of the fact that the meal was for ranch hands and construction workers, Charity made a concerted effort to give the setting some class. Red checkered tablecloths, bud vases with red and yellow columbines from her mother's garden—they were Faith's favorite flowers, and Charity was beginning to see the bushes popping up in random spots around Whispering Hills—trays for condiments, salt and pepper shakers, and extra napkins. Mason jar glasses lined up in rows on a table beside beverage dispensers for sweet tea and water. She set out caddies with real utensils—no one broke more plastic forks than a work crew—and a stack of heavy-duty paper plates on either side of the buffet table where chafing dishes waited to be filled with food. When she was satisfied that all was ready, she headed back inside, hoping Cord and Frank had cleared out. She'd been gone almost an hour, and the Maddox crews would be making their way in shortly. She had a lot to do last minute, and other than Faith who knew the drill backward and forward, no one else could really 'help' her without just getting underfoot.

Charity was glad for the urgency of the pending meal. She was terribly unsettled by how much Frank made her think of Theo. It didn't help that she'd had her husband fresh on her mind after waking up from the dream of him that morning, but it was almost as if she'd conjured Frank up instead of Theo. It felt wrong, seeing her beloved in this new man.

To her dismay, Frank had burst into the kitchen in the middle of hers and Faith's conversation wearing a shirt that Charity could have sworn came out of Theo's closet; it was a Louisville Slugger t-shirt in a faded gray wash with a red stripe on each sleeve. She'd given Theo his while they were still dating, and he'd worn it so often, it was practically threadbare in places. Frank's was in much better condition, but it was still the same shirt, there was no doubt. The two men looked nothing like each other when their features were compared side by side, but it was something besides appearances that had Charity's heart aching. The similar military postures, the teasing quality in their voices, the side looks they angled at her, even the way they both cocked their heads when they were trying to get a gauge on her mood.

Frank wasn't as big as Theo had been—her husband had the smooth musculature of youth, and the bulk that came from a long line of Viking blood, while Frank was sinewier, more defined and leaner. But she hadn't had the weight of a man on top of her since Theo, and her mind kept going back to the intimacy of the encounter, in spite of the shocking circumstances, Frank's knee between her own, his hips pressing against hers. It was wrong, she knew, but it had triggered an ache in her that had nothing to do with force and fear. Between all that and the Barbasol, every one of her senses felt under attack.

To Charity's relief, the kitchen was empty, Frank's dishes were washed and put away. The mug she'd been drinking from sat beside the coffee pot, a saucer turned upside down over the top of it. As highly as she thought of her sister's wonderful husband, Charity had a feeling the considerate gesture was that of a certain First Sergeant, not Cordell Overman.

She pulled out a large, plastic bin and began filling it with anything she thought they might need for the meal—tongs, carving knives, serving spoons, toothpicks, and more, then she carried the load out to the deck. She met Binks on the way back and asked him to round up a dolly to cart a few coolers of ice over, then Faith showed up right on time to help. Between the three of them, they made short work of transporting food, beverages, sauces, and more to the deck, and by the time the guys showed up, hungry and already complimentary, everything was ready.

Charity manned the grill station, Faith commandeered the buffet, and when it appeared everyone was present and accounted for—including Frank, Charity noted—Cord stood on a bench and offered up a prayer of thanksgiving for God's provision and protection over him and his household and the men and women who gave of their time and energy to turn Whispering Hills into what it was today. After the low rumble of amens, suddenly, the whole place came to life as men and women slid chairs and benches back and they lined up for food, talking and laughing and congratulating each other on all they'd accomplished. And every single person who stepped up to Charity's station for ribs expressed their deep appreciation for her delicious food. Even Frank had hobbled through the line using one crutch, sliding his plate along the buffet table in front of him while he piled it high with the food she'd prepared. He, too, complemented her on how good everything looked before taking his full plate over to sit at a long table across from Binks and Cord.

Skid Maddox, with his charming grin and undeniable appeal, actually circled around to her side of the grill, draped a big, beefy arm around her, and called out, "We couldn't have asked for a prettier chef, right guys? The fact that she can cook is icing on the cake." Charity's cheeks blazed with embarrassment as a chorus of agreement rose up, and she nudged him away with her hip.

"Stop it, you big goon." She pointed her tongs at the other side of the grill. "Back in line—you're in my personal space."

Skid leaned close and murmured, "I kinda like being in your personal space, sweet Charity." But he didn't linger; he just winked at her, gave her shoulders an affectionate squeeze, and headed off to find a seat at one of the tables.

Charity didn't dare look over at Frank. Surely, he'd seen that exchange, and she was pretty sure he'd overheard at least part of the conversation she and Faith were having that morning before he stepped into the kitchen. How could he not have? In fact, he'd probably burst in when he did because he caught the mention of his own name. Charity cringed every time she thought about him standing on the other side of the door, listening to what Faith had said about him being half naked and scaring her.

Besides, every time she glanced his way, she found him watching her. He wasn't rudely staring, just being attentive to her, and when their eyes met, he smiled in acknowledgment and carried on with whatever conversation he was engaged in. But clearly, he had something on his mind; his expression was thoughtful, almost apologetic. Was he worried about her being hypersensitive over her kitchen? If so, he could chill on that. He just happened to arrive on an extremely busy day for her. Most of the time, she didn't even show up until mid-morning; she rarely put in more than five or six hours at Whispering Hills between preparation, serving, and clean up. She'd have to clear the air between them. She didn't want him feeling unwelcome in his own home. It didn't matter that Cord now held the deed to the place; Whispering Hills Ranch would always welcome Frankie Flanner, as long as the Overmans had any say in it.

When everyone else had been served, Charity and Faith dished up plates for themselves, then headed to the big table where Cord, Binks, Frank, and the Maddox brothers sat with several other crew members. As they approached, a few men shifted in their seats to make room for them. Charity pretended she didn't hear Skid call out to her to sit beside him, and instead, she settled in next to Faith who'd wedged a space for them between Binks and her husband. Unfortunately, that put her directly across the table from Frank, who gazed openly back and forth between her and Skid, as though sizing up the situation.

It was the first time she'd felt so completely uncomfortable with the crew for whom she'd been cooking for over a year.

And she blamed it on Frank.

And Theo.

And Skid.

Oh, and Faith, too, for pointing out Skid's obvious admiration for her. She'd been so blissfully oblivious to it before today; how on earth had she missed it? And the frustrating thing about it was that if Frank hadn't been in the mix—sitting across from her with a knowing twinkle in his eyes—she was certain she would have made light of the whole thing in a way that would let Skid know she wasn't interested in a relationship with him while still making him feel good. With Frank's eyes on her, she could hardly remember her own name, much less have the wherewithal to come up with something savvy to say to Skid.

Someone nudged her foot under the table, and she froze, her mouth full, her eyes on the chunk of potato she'd just loaded onto her fork. A moment later, it came again, gentle, but intentional. From the corner of her eye, she studied first Binks, then Faith on either side of her, then she finally braved looking up and across the table.

Frank was staring right at her. "Hey," he said when their eyes met.

"Hey," she said after she'd swallowed the bite of meat that she'd almost forgotten to chew first.

"This really is amazing." He moved his hand in a circular motion over his plate. "Everything. All of it. The ribs are the best I've ever had."

"Amen to that, buddy," Skid called out from several seats away, and Charity wanted to slide under the table and disappear.

Frank kept his gaze locked with hers, all but ignoring the man at the other end of the table. There was something serious in the way he looked at her, something protective about the way he studied her. "You all right?" he asked quietly, keeping his tone casual. Under the table, he nudged her leg again. "That bothering you?"

For a moment Charity thought he meant him playing footsie with her, but then she saw the slight tip of his head in Skid's direction. She shook her head slowly, almost as imperceptibly as his nod. "I'm fine. It's fine," she murmured, trying to keep her own response vague. "Nothing unusual about it."

Frank lifted his jar of sweet tea in her direction, then took a sip. "Even your tea is perfect," he said, keeping his voice low as if their conversation was suddenly very important and personal. "You know, my mom used to make sweet tea with peaches and raspberries floating in it. Have you ever tried that?"

She nodded, leaning forward and speaking barely above a murmur, herself. "I love peach tea, but I haven't tried it with raspberries. I'll have to give it a whirl while you're here so you can tell me if I get it right."

"Maybe I'll show you how to make her chicken gumbo, too," Frank added in a tone that suggested he was about to divulge some great secret to her.

Binks, apparently catching on, leaned forward and all but whispered, "Your mama's gumbo was the best, boy. You know how to make it?"

Frank grinned and nodded. "Of course, no one makes it like Mama, but mine comes close."

"I bet Charity here could master it in a heartbeat," Faith interjected softly, a knowing grin on her face as she, too, leaned in.

Cord, on the other hand, wore an expression of such befuddlement, that when he said, "Why are you guys whispering about gumbo?"

Charity burst out laughing, surprising even herself. Then she covered her mouth with both hands, trying to get her fit of giggles under control.

Everyone around her went silent as they listened to the rare sound, then Faith joined in, and Binks added his halting chuckle to the mix. Soon enough, people went back to their own conversations and meals, and Charity shot an apologetic look at Cord. "I'm so sorry," she said. "I'm not really laughing at you."

Faith put her arm around her husband and laid her head on his shoulder. "I'm laughing at you, Mr. Overman, but only because you're so cute."

"At some point, you'll have to explain what's going on," Cord said, a bemused smile on his face as he shook his head in resignation. "I'm assuming it has nothing to do with gumbo."

"You catch on quick," Frank said from across the table, his tone laced with teasing sarcasm.

Under the table, Charity nudged Franks good foot. But when he looked at her, an eyebrow raised in question, she suddenly had second thoughts about what she'd intended to say. It wouldn't come out right, she knew that for certain, and in the mixed company, she didn't want to have to try to explain. She dropped her gaze to her plate, crossed her ankles, and drew them back under her seat.

It had felt good to release that unchecked laugh. Again. Twice in one day, she'd let loose a belly laugh with Frank Flanner, and she'd wanted to thank him.

TEN

Frank sat across from Cord while his cousin continued talking about all the changes and upgrades he was implementing at the ranch. They'd moved to a small table out of the sun, and he listened carefully, impressed beyond measure at what he was hearing. He continued to study Charity as she moved among what little of the crew still milled about the deck. The crowd had thinned as people went back to work, but Skid had commandeered a handful of guys to set the deck furniture back in place, dissemble the extra tables and chairs, carry trays and serving equipment back to the kitchen, and to haul off the trash. With their help, Charity and Faith made quick work of putting everything back in order, then the two ladies headed back to the kitchen, themselves, to start on dishes. Skid, Frank noted, accompanied them, carrying on a companionable conversation with both women.

Frank's reservations about the man hadn't lessened in the hour they'd spent sharing a table. He'd seen Charity's discomfort when Skid drew everyone's attention to her, and he hadn't missed how deftly she'd avoided taking the empty seat on the bench beside the man. He'd been saving it for her, Frank was certain, and had been forced to slide down to make room for the women squeezing in at the other end of the table. Oh, he'd been good-natured about the whole thing, seemingly unfazed by the subtle rebuff, but Frank hadn't been promoted to First Sergeant after only ten years in the Army because he was ignorant to the way people's minds worked. He may not be able to read Charity so easily, but men, he knew. Men, he understood. And men sizing up the competition and marking their territory and honing their weapons, especially. Skid Maddox seemed to be setting his sights on Charity Goodacre Banner, and from what Frank could tell, the man was pretty sure the victory was already his.

Not that Skid was a bad guy, Frank grudgingly admitted, at least not from what he'd heard from his cousin and the old ranch foreman. He obviously had solid leadership skills; according to Cord, most of the work crew had been with Maddox Construction for years, under Skid and Ernie on bigger jobs like this one. They were loyal and hardworking, and the Maddoxes took good care of their employees in turn, intent on maintaining the reputation their father had created for the family business.

But that didn't change the fact that the Maddox brothers—Skid, in particular—was a modern-day Adonis, who had a good handle on the art of wooing and winning the ladies. He was complementary, attentive, and quick to offer assistance, but he also seemed to know when to back off. Frank couldn't tell if that made Skid more of a threat, or less of one.

A threat to what? And why was it his place to be on the lookout for threats in this place? A temporary traveler, a short-term visitor, that was him. Who was he to decide whether Skidmore Maddox's intentions toward Charity were honorable or not?

But then again, after what Cord had divulged about his sister-in-law's husband, something in Frank *did* feel responsible for looking out for Charity's best interest. Frank had actually survived the same kind of attack that had taken Theo Banner's life, leaving Charity a widow. Her words stampeded through his mind for the thousandth time since Cord told him what had happened. *At least you're still here to complain about it.* Indeed, he was, and indeed, that's exactly what he'd been doing for the past few months. Complaining about his injuries. Oh, not out loud. He hadn't dumped a sob story on anyone, not that he was aware of, but in his head, he railed against the fates that had left him mutilated and incapacitated for service. He shook his fists in rage over the fact that he'd survived and so many of his men hadn't. He ranted internally that the medical care he received wasn't good enough, the doctors not skilled enough, the therapists not knowledgeable enough, when in his heart, he knew none of the above was true. He'd received excellent care at Fort Campbell, the very best they had to offer.

"Frankie?" Cord's voice broke through his ruminating thoughts. "Frank? You hearing anything I'm saying?"

"Sorry, man." He shook his head abruptly. "Drifted there for a minute."

"Good food, full stomach. Warm sunshine," Cord said, waving off his apology. "Do it to you every time."

"Yeah, I don't think I've been this relaxed in a very long time." It was true. In fact, sitting there on the deck overlooking the lake at the bottom of the pasture was as close to a vacation as Frank had taken since long before his father died almost three years ago. Once he'd made the decision to turn the ranch over to Cord's capable hands, he'd poured himself with renewed vigor into his military career, and taking time off for himself seemed frivolous. "It's good to be back, Cord. Thanks for letting me crash here for a few days." He didn't know how long he'd stay, but he'd been instructed to treat Whispering Hills as his own for as long as he needed it.

Frank had some phone calls to make that afternoon, and he wasn't exactly looking forward to them. Leaving the way he did had the potential to create problems, but he had some strings he could pull, and he intended to pull them. He'd only been at the ranch for eight hours, and he already knew this was what he needed right now. He'd been away too long.

"Hey, come out to our place for dinner this evening, okay?" Cord leaned forward, a contemplative expression on his face. "Get some rest this afternoon if you can—you look like you could use some—but plan on eating with us." He leaned back in his chair and called out to Faith, who was making her way back toward them. "Honey, what time do you plan on us eating tonight? I've invited Frank to join us."

"You just finished eating, Cordell Overman, and you're already thinking about food again? What's the deal? I'm the one who's pregnant here," Faith shot back, a teasing glint in her eyes. "And I was about to ask you the same thing. What are you planning on cooking for us, husband of mine?"

"If I'm cooking, it's spaghetti with sauce out of a jar."

Faith rolled her eyes and circled the table to perch on Cord's lap. She looped an arm around his neck and kissed the top of his head. "If you really want to deal with my heartburn all night, then by all means, Cowboy. Pop open the marinara sauce."

Frank straightened, his eyes going wide as he gawked at Faith. "You're pregnant?" He turned to Cord. "You're pregnant, man, and you didn't even tell me?" He stuck out a hand and shook Cord's vigorously. "Congratulations, man."

Faith leaned back a little and frowned down at her husband. "Did you forget already? Just because I haven't grown out of my jeans yet—"

Cord reached up and cupped the back of his wife's head, his fingers winding through her hair as he brought her mouth down to meet his for an indecently affectionate kiss. "Not even for one moment, Mrs. Overman," he growled against her mouth.

"Okay," Frank said with a chuckle. "You two have at it. I'm going back to the big house to clean up and see if Charity needs rescuing from Skid." He rose and pushed in his chair, then positioned his crutches under his arms. It would be good to take a load off for a couple hours.

Faith—who'd lifted her head to look at him, but whose eyes told him she was hoping his disruption wouldn't take long—let out a breathy giggle, and said, "Poor Skid. He doesn't stand a chance with her, but he's not one to back down so easy. Oh! I almost forgot. I was supposed to ask if you wanted her to pack up leftovers for you for dinner tonight."

Frank averted his eyes when he saw the fingers of Cord's other hand slide around to cup Faith's backside. "I'll go talk to her," he said. "I'll see you two—and Jasmine, of course—for dinner tonight. Since neither of you seem to want to cook, do you want me to ask Charity to put together a leftover meal for all of us? Say, around six?"

Faith chuckled, then rested her cheek on top of Cord's head. "That sounds lovely," she said. "I ate too many ribs to manage more than a small piece of her fried chicken, so load up on that for us, will you?" She hugged Cord's neck—he didn't seem to mind that the side of his face was pressed tightly against her bosom—and said, "You don't have to cook tonight after all, delicious man of mine."

And that was Frank's cue to bail. Were they always that affectionate, he wondered? If so, he wasn't so sure he wanted to join them in the privacy of their home. "Maybe I'll ask Charity if she wants to tag along for dinner tonight." The moment the words were out of his mouth, he knew he'd put his foot in things just by the way Faith cocked her head and narrowed her eyes at him. "You know. Since it'll be her food we're eating," he quickly amended, getting to his feet.

Faith nodded slowly. "Yeah," she said. "That's actually a good idea, Frank. Since she already turned down Skid's invitation to Schooner's tonight, I know for a fact that she's free." She grinned saucily and pointed at him. "Don't take no for an answer now, you hear? She needs to get out more, and since she won't go out on the town, at least getting her over to our place will have her away from Seven Virtues. And with you there, she won't show up in her pajamas."

An image of Charity in a white tank top and soft sleep pants flashed through his mind so vividly that he had to clear his throat to get his thoughts in check. He made a show of saluting Faith, hoping she was too distracted by the slow, circular pattern Cord's hand was making on her low back to read Frank's thoughts about her little sister. "Yes, Ma'am," he said, then turned and headed toward the house, moving carefully along the gravel drive, wary of where he set his crutches with each step. A glance back over his shoulder revealed that Faith and Cord were not at all offended by his hasty retreat.

On the steps leading up to the back porch, Frank paused long enough to gather his thoughts before heading inside. First off, if Skid was still in the kitchen with Charity, Frank wanted to have his wits about him so that he didn't do or say anything stupid. Charity had already turned down the guy, which made Frank feel a little better. At least she wasn't blinded by his pretty face. But Frank would wait until Skid was gone before putting her on the spot about dinner with her sister's little family and him.

But there was also the matter of Theo Banner that needed to be addressed. Charity had led him to believe that Theo was still alive, saying she was married, not correcting Frank when he'd assured her that he would explain the mark on her face to her husband. Maybe she hadn't outright lied about it, but she certainly hadn't set him straight on multiple occasions throughout the morning.

Then again, maybe she'd been afraid to tell him. From her perspective, he probably did come across as a little creepy. Showing up in the predawn dark unannounced, physically assaulting her in his upstairs bedroom in an otherwise empty house. Maybe she'd been playing it safe by acting like she had a husband who was alive and well, someone he'd have to answer to. In fact, the more he thought back over the events of the morning, the more he realized how carefully she'd handled the situation. Sure, she probably shouldn't have barged in on a military man in the throes of a nightmare—his therapist insisted he suffered from PTSD, but Frank kept assuring the guy that his vivid dreams were his way of working through the things he couldn't remember. Besides, if he agreed to the diagnosis of PTSD, he'd be required to endure that much more therapy before they let him go back. *If* they let him go back.

Aside from her not-so-great decision to race upstairs and check on him, she'd rather clearheadedly and effectively steered the majority of their interaction away from her and back to him. She'd stilled beneath him as soon as she realized he was seeing Stanley and not her, not arguing or trying to set him straight. She'd insisted she wasn't hurt or frightened, even though he knew she was, and she'd shifted the conversation away from her husband by asking Frank about his own injuries, and then teasing him about being on the cover of a romance novel.

Even with his horrific scars. It was almost as though she simply didn't see them.

In hindsight, he was glad it had been Cord who'd told him about Theo Banner. His cousin had given him the details of the suicide bomber who'd stumbled out into the middle of the road in front of Theo's convoy, a woman with a bag slung over her shoulder, begging for help for her and her baby. The bag, however, held explosives, not a baby, and Theo wasn't the only one in his unit who didn't make it home alive. Having lived through an experience similar enough to make him break out in a cold sweat as he listened to the details, Frank felt compelled to acknowledge Charity's loss, if for no other reason than to honor the man who'd given his life for his country.

And if he was being honest, having that conversation with Charity about her husband might help Frank process through some of the unresolved grief and guilt he was harboring over his own failure to protect his men.

He took a clarifying breath and squared his shoulders, preparing to head inside, but when he glanced over to where Charity's truck had been parked all morning, he stopped in his tracks. It was gone. He frowned, crossed the porch as quickly as he could manage, and pushed open the door. The kitchen was empty, spotless, and quiet. Clipped to the refrigerator door was a piece of paper with his name on it. Frank made his way around the worktable and snatched the note from under the magnet.

Frank - I've packaged up a ton of leftovers for everyone - you, Binks, and Cord and family - so please feel free to eat as much as you like. It's there for the taking. I won't be in tomorrow until about midmorning to make lunch for the crew. Just wanted to give you a heads up so I don't catch you by surprise. We set some fresh sheets and a couple towels out in a basket at the top of the stairs for you—we figured you wouldn't want us girls rooting around in your room without you there. Sleep well - Charity

ELEVEN

ALL RIGHT. SO, SHE'D run. But between the awkwardness that had followed turning down Skid's very sweet invitation to dinner at Schooners, and her hyper-awareness of Frank Flanner, topped off by her much too early morning and the mad rush of getting such a huge meal served to more than a dozen hungry men by noon, Charity was exhausted. Oh yes. Add in being thrown to the floor and crushed beneath a man fighting invisible demons, and she'd pretty much reached her limit on interacting with members of the opposite sex. She needed to take a nap, or at least put her feet up and relax for an hour or two before heating up the leftovers she'd brought home for her own family for supper.

Besides, she'd recognized the look in Frank's eyes. It had taken her awhile, but she'd finally understood it for what it was. Someone—presumably Cord—had told him about Theo, and now he wanted to talk to her about him. Well, Charity certainly wasn't up for that, either. She'd intentionally led Frank to believe Theo was alive and well when they'd first met, just because she was mad at him, and then, up in Frank's room when she'd had the chance to come clean, the conversation had moved past Theo before she could explain.

She could do with a little down time to clear her head—Frank was taking too much room in there today, and she needed a break.

"Daddy?" Charity called out as she pushed open the back door into the kitchen at Seven Virtues Ranch. She shoved the containers of food in the fridge, then washed her hands. "You here, Dad?"

Jed Goodacre usually took his afternoons inside these days, especially during the summer when the temperature and humidity started rising.

Charity couldn't remember exactly when they'd put central air in the house, but she recalled days from her early childhood when it was muggier indoors than out, and she breathed a sigh of relief at the blast of cool air that welcomed her into the house. Jed called out a greeting from the family room, and Charity made her way through the kitchen to greet him. She found him sitting with his feet up in his recliner, a cup of coffee on the table beside him, and an open book face down on his lap. She bent over and kissed the top of his head.

"You need a haircut, Daddy," she said, flopping into the corner of the old sofa nearby. Her father wore his hair in an old school buzz cut that was short on the sides and a little longer on top so he could slick it back when he wanted to look a little more formal. It was easy for him to care for, but it grew surprisingly fast, and he seemed to always need a trim. Charity had been the one to take over buzzing her father's hair after her mother died. She'd been only nine years old and had been thrilled that he trusted her to do it. She'd been a pro with the clippers by the time she took over keeping Theo's hair closely cropped.

Frank's crew cut was a little grown out, too. She'd noticed him rubbing his palm over the top of it on multiple occasions, the same way Theo used to do when his short hair started growing out enough to lay flat. *I have got to stop thinking about him.*

"Whenever you have time, sweetheart," Jed said with a relaxed smile. "I'm in no hurry, and other than you girls, I've got no one to impress."

"What are you reading?" she asked, waving a hand at the book in his lap. Her weariness was beginning to settle into her bones, and if she didn't get up and head to her own room, she'd pass out right where she sat. On any other day, she'd have been fine to do just that, but today, she wanted to wrap her arms around Theo's pillow and fall asleep with the memory of him in her arms.

"Michener's *Centennial*," Jed said, holding the soft cover up for her to see.

"Daddy, you are so cliché," Charity teased. Her father loved his Westerns. He had every Louis L'Amour book ever published.

Jed grinned. "Nothing wrong with reading about cowboys. It's in my blood. It's in your blood," he added, waving the book at her.

Cowboy romance novels, Charity thought. "Frankie Flanner showed up unannounced this morning." The words were out before she was finished thinking them. She closed her eyes and rested her head on the couch cushion behind her, trying to act as though the statement was nothing more than a bit of gossip she was passing along.

"I heard," Jed said. Something in his tone made her open one eye to look at him. He chuckled and took a sip of his coffee. "Come on, daughter. That was old news by eight o'clock this morning."

Charity sighed and sunk a little lower in her seat. "I forget how alive and well the Plumwood Hollow prayer chain is," she said, her voice dripping with sarcasm.

Jed let out another low laugh, but he didn't reprimand her. Everyone knew the fastest way to get word around town was to mention it to a church secretary, and the fact that Frankie Flanner was practically royalty in the hollow? Well, news of his arrival had phone lines heating up before folks were even out of bed. "How's he doing. Heard he's sporting a brace. Heard a few other things, too, but nothing worth repeating."

"Really?" Charity asked, her curiosity peaked. "Yes, he's got a full leg brace and a pretty bad limp. He uses crutches most of the time. He's also got some significant scarring all up his side." She drew a hand along her ribcage the way she'd seen him do earlier that morning, then she stilled, realizing she'd just so much as told her father she'd seen the man shirtless. She hurried on so Jed wouldn't ask how she knew that detail. "He said his unit got ambushed, and he lost a couple men." This was exactly the kind of conversation she should *not* be having.

"Ah." Jed remained quiet for several minutes, and Charity braced herself for whatever he was preparing to say. Her father was the kind of man who took his time with his words—a habit she wished she could master—and said only what he really wanted to say. He hadn't always been that way. Several years ago, he'd had an accident that had almost cost him his life, and during his long recovery, he'd come to terms with some of his anger and bitterness over his own lifetime of losses, and learned to embrace the gifts he had in his daughters and granddaughter, and in the ranch they called home, and especially in the cherished memories of his beloved Caroline.

But Jed said nothing more, and when Charity finally opened her eyes to look at him again, he'd gone back to reading. As much as she wanted to ask him to share his thoughts on Frank's return to the hollow, she wasn't about to do so, because that would be admitting that she had thoughts about him, too.

"I'm going to go lie down in my room. I woke up way too early this morning, and now I'm pooped. I brought leftover ribs and chicken and all the fixings for dinner, but if you have any greens or salad stuff to add, that would be great." Her father's huge vegetable garden was in full swing, and even though most of the early lettuces were finished, he had a row of hearty Romaine heads that were cut and come again producers. Jed pulled off the outer leaves each day, and the lettuce kept producing.

"Heard you this morning," he said, glancing up at her as she pushed heavily to her feet. "You called out for Theo."

"Yeah." Charity shoved her hands into the front pockets of her jeans. "I miss him today."

"I always miss Caroline the most after I dream of her," Jed said with a slow nod. "You go get some rest. Mr. Michener and I will be just fine on our own." He took a sip of his coffee, then added, "Looking forward to your fried chicken, sweetheart. You know it's my favorite."

She blew him a kiss and headed down the hall. The house was so quiet these days now that Jasmine had moved out. The girl wasn't obnoxiously loud; she was just a busy kid, and now that Faith and her daughter had moved into their own place over the fence at Whispering Hills, the silence seemed to loom up and surprise them every now and then. Prudence worked part time for Trilby's Blossoms and Books and was gone most afternoons, the twins came and went around work, school, the riding lessons they gave, and their own time spent in the arena with their matching horses. Courage and Justice had a trick-riding show called the Twisted Sisters, and although they'd done some of the rodeo circuit in their high school years, they were both in the last year of college now, and most of the performances they did were within a day's round trip. But they'd taken on students to whom they were passing on their knowledge, and it was always fun to go out and watch her sisters showing the next generation the ropes. Abby? Well, who knew where that girl spent her days? She'd just graduated high school, and she was a bit of a loose cannon. She wanted to pursue her music career, but she wasn't quite ready to hit the road for Nashville on her own. In some ways, the youngest Goodacre daughter was as fearless as they came, yet there was another side of her that made her the biggest home body of them all. But she showed her age by not taking too kindly to helpful advice from her big sisters, so the girls left her alone to sort through things. She kept busy playing local clubs on the weekends, and she worked the counter at Ripley's Auto Parts weeknights, so Abby had a little money coming in between her wages and tips. During the day, however, the girl often disappeared for long hours, showing up in time for meals and family functions and work. Their father never said a word, but Charity had seen him silently studying his youngest daughter on more than one occasion, and she, too, had some growing concerns for the girl.

Then again, it was summer, and Abby needed some time to do a little wandering before she had to grow up, right?

In her room, Charity flopped back on her bed and stared up at the ceiling, pulling Theo's pillow close to her chest and hugging it loosely. Even after all these years, she still imagined she caught a whiff of him every now and then. That blend of shaving cream, the body wash he used, the Old Spice deodorant he liked, and that certain something that was uniquely Theo. He was such an old-fashioned guy when it came to his ablutions, and but Charity had never minded, because to her, he always smelled amazing.

An image of Frank rising up on his elbows to look down at her popped into her head. "Leave me alone," she murmured, then closed her eyes, momentarily wondering if she meant Frank or Theo or both. She rolled onto her side and buried her face in the pillow, waiting for the tears that would inevitably come, but they didn't.

The next thing she knew, Prudence was poking her head in the door. "Supper's ready, Charity Pie." Prudence loved to call her that. "You're as sweet as this cherry pie, Charity Pie," she'd announced once when Charity had been showing her how to weave a lattice crust over the top of a homemade pie.

Charity stretched and smiled, feeling well-rested and relaxed after the long, dreamless nap. The tangy aroma of barbecue sauce wafting down the hall from the kitchen. "Thank you for letting me sleep," she said to Prudence. "I must have needed that. Smells good out there."

"Our chef is fantastic," her younger sister gushed. "Everything she makes is divine, even the leftovers. *Especially* the leftovers. But you'd better hurry if you want a chicken leg. Daddy is already claiming his pieces."

TWELVE

When Frank told Faith he'd missed Charity, she'd offered to have everyone come over to the big house to eat so no one had to cart the food anywhere. "I'll have Cord bring Binks with him, too."

The meal was just as delicious as it had been at noon, and the company even sweeter. It had been a long time since he'd sat around the Whispering Hills dining table with friends and family—Binks would always be family—and just enjoyed being a civilian. No formal bearing, no need to monitor his guys, no reason to keep one ear tuned to every sound around them. No, here, he was simply Frankie Flanner, son of Frank "Judge" Flanner, and one-time heir to the family ranch. He'd made the right decision selling it to Cord. It kept the property connected to the family, and there wasn't anyone more capable or more passionate about running the ranch. Cord was bringing the place back to life in a way Frank couldn't fathom doing. His cousin came from money and was not hesitant to sink his resources into making Whispering Hills great again.

But the day had not been without its bittersweet moments. Especially that afternoon. Too restless to sleep—he was beginning to seriously regret leaving his medication behind—Frank wandered as much as his leg would allow. This was home, and yet, so much had changed—for the better, definitely—that it only heightened his feelings of displacement. The main barn close to the big house had been salvaged, but it looked nothing like it had the last time Frank had been home. New stall gates, updated fixtures, replaced flooring, a wholly redesigned tack room loaded with new equipment and gear. Cord had built on an enormous addition at one end off of which the deck extended, overlooking the pasture that swept down to the 5-acre lake. The big room, Cord explained, was currently being used as a mess hall where Charity served the midday meals, a meeting room, and a workspace when weather required projects be brought inside. "It's also been a barn dance hall," he went on. "We try to have one every quarter. Keeps the community up to date on what we're doing, lets them see the progress around here, and it gives us an opportunity to give back to the folks in the hollow on a personal level. I had a bit of a reputation to live down when I first came back here, and Faith agreeing to marry me was only the first step," he explained with a sardonic chuckle. "Folks wanted to see evidence that I'd stick around this time."

His cousin's love story was one for the books, that was for sure. High school sweethearts, a short-lived long-distance relationship, a secret baby, and a second chance at love a decade later. Talk about redemption. Cord and Faith were so ridiculously happy, and seeing them together again gave Frank hope for... well, for the idea of love, at least. He'd poured so much of his life into his military career and had hoped to put in at least twenty years before retiring. At that point, when he had something to offer, he'd find a good woman by being the best man he could be.

Now, here he was, a good four-plus years shy of the mark, and his superiors were encouraging him to take disability retirement.

The worst part about his situation was that no matter how motivated he was, his body refused to comply. His leg continued to hold him back. And the fact that his doctor still hadn't ruled out below-the-knee amputation told Frank that he might need more than motivation and determination to get through this time.

He'd made a few necessary phone calls, and as the evening wound down, he leaned forward in his chair and crossed his arms on the edge of the table. "Listen, man. I've got a proposition for you. Something I'd like you to consider." He looked Cord directly in the eye and waited for his cousin to give him leave to speak.

Faith started to rise, but Cord reached out and took her hand, staying her. Jasmine was in the front room watching a movie, and when Binks raised a questioning brow, Frank shook his head. "No, you stay, too."

"Shoot, Cuz. What's on your mind?" Cord's voice remained steady, encouraging, with no hint of hesitation at all.

Frank wasn't one to beat around the bush, and he'd put this part of the conversation off all evening already. He'd wanted to enjoy the meal first, but there was no reason to delay any longer. "I need to head back to Fort Campbell and check in. I kinda bailed without letting anyone know." He shifted his leg under the table and then went on. "But I'd like to return, this time, with your permission, and see if I can't plug in here for a while. I've plateaued with my rehab progress, and things aren't looking promising for me and this old foot. My doctor is... how shall I put this? Encouraging me...to consider amputation."

Faith's eyes widened, but she said nothing. Cord nodded solemnly, but it was Binks who immediately teared up at the words.

"I'm not ready to make that decision, but from what my medical team tells me, it's not one I can put off for much longer. I need a place to stretch my legs right now, so to speak. I need to assess my options from a different perspective. Things are too close on base. I can't think clearly there; I don't see clearly when I'm staring at folks in white coats. I've requested a leave, and I have no reason to expect it won't be granted." He looked from Cord to Faith, then at Binks. The old man swallowed hard but said nothing. "I'd like to take some time here if you'll have me. I'm not sure what that will look like, exactly, or what they'll give me, but I'm going to request as much time as they'll give me."

Cord and Faith were both nodding before he finished. "This is your home, Frankie," Faith declared, reaching across the table to rest a hand on his crossed forearms, her own eyes glistening now. "You don't need our permission to come and go around here. We'd love to have you."

"Absolutely," Cord agreed. Frank had filled Cord in on how he'd been injured, had apologized for showing up the way he had, and now it was almost as though his cousin wasn't exactly surprised at the proposition. "Like Faith said, this is your home. And you can stay as long as you need, Cuz."

Binks, still overwhelmed emotionally, just nodded his head, his lips pressed together in a tight line, making his scruffy chin pucker oddly.

"I'm not asking for a handout, or a vacation," Frank stated. "I don't want time off. I need to stay busy. I need to keep my mind and my body sharp. In fact, I really need to test a few limits; see what I can do with this leg." He cleared his throat, and added, "See what I'd be able to do without it."

Binks pushed back his chair and rose quickly. "Excuse me," he muttered, his voice so hoarse his words were almost unintelligible.

"Oh, Binks," Faith murmured after the man had pushed through the swinging doors into the kitchen. "He's such a softy."

Cord slid his arm around the back of his wife's chair and drew her close. She rested her head against his cheek. "Go on," Cord said to Frank. "I'll catch him up if he doesn't come back to hear it for himself."

Moved by the old man's response, Frank had to swallow the lump that rose in his throat before he continued. "I'd like to plug into a project here. I don't care what it is, but I think that I might be better on a horse than on my feet." He dipped his head in the general direction of the barn. "I've been over to see Hidalgo, and that old boy recognized me in spite of the change in my gait. He was calling for me soon as I walked in the barn. I'm going to need some warming up — maybe I can hire someone to help me get back in the saddle for the first week or two. I'm hoping he's mellowed a little, but I'd like to see what he and I can do together."

Faith straightened slowly as he spoke. She and her husband exchanged speculative looks, and Cord nodded, a satisfied grin settling on his face.

Faith rested her forearms on the table in front of her and laced her fingers together around her glass of water. "Can you give us a ballpark time frame? At least what you're hoping for?"

Frank hesitated, partly because the answer to that would depend on the decision he made about his leg. "At this point, I'd say five or six months. Maybe even through the new year, if you'll have me. I think that's about all the time I have before I go under the knife again, whether it's to try to salvage the leg or cut it off." He didn't bother tempering his words, and even though Faith winced slightly at his bluntness, she smiled gently in understanding.

Silence settled around the table as they each processed what Frank was saying. Even he, himself replayed his words in his mind. It was the first time he'd spoken so succinctly to anyone other than his doctors. It was rather freeing.

Finally, Cord reached out and rested a hand on his wife's back. "How do you feel about herding cattle, Frank?"

That was a no-brainer. "Absolutely. Give me a chance to get comfortable in the saddle again, and I'm good to go. Like riding a bike, right?" He reached up to scratch his jaw, the rasp of the end of the day growth sounding loud in the quiet room. "It's not much of a full-time job though, is it?"

"Actually," Faith spoke up. "We move our herds every day. On horseback. The cows are much more amenable to us moving in and among them when we're on horses, and we like them to be as low stress as possible. Makes for much better beef. Here at Whispering Hills, we ride out in the evenings to do a visual check on everyone, make sure the dogs are awake and on duty, then first thing in the morning, we move the cows to a new paddock. We have two livestock dogs—wonderful Great Pyrenees and Anatolian Shepherd mixes—who pretty much live with the cows. They follow us back to the big barn to eat after the morning move, but then they head back out to the pasture to be near their charges. They pretty much sleep the day away out there, but they're on duty, and they take their jobs seriously, so if something does approach during the day, they're on it."

"Why every day?" Frank sat back in his chair and studied the couple. "That seems like a lot of work."

"Yep," Faith confirmed. "It is, to a certain degree. But in the long run, it pays off. Once you've had a chance to make some rounds on the property, I think you'll see that things have changed from the ground up, quite literally. We've implemented a technique that goes by several names, but it's essentially high-density rotational grazing. We corral the herd in paddocks just large enough to feed them for a day, then move them to a new one each morning, making a complete circuit of the pastures in about ninety days. By the time they've done a full rotation, the grass in the first paddock is lush and thick again. Because food supply is limited, the cows are more voracious eaters. That means they chomp on the less tasty weeds, as well as the sweet grasses and clover, and trample what they don't eat—like living tillers, you know?—but because they aren't in a paddock long enough to overgraze and strip it, rainwater is retained much better with little to no run-off, roots grow deeper and stronger, and the grass keeps coming back healthy and green almost year round. Weeds are all but eradicated because the soil is good, the grasses are healthy, and the weeds can't compete in that kind of environment. Oh, and we also send the chickens in behind the cattle to scratch and peck and spread the manure around, naturally fertilizing and de-worming without chemicals, all but eliminating the need for us do anything else to the pastures."

"Chickens' digestive systems kill off the majority of the parasites that affect cattle," Cord interjected. "We haven't had to de-worm our herds for the first time this year, and Hope—you remember Faith's sister, Hope, don't you? She's our local vet now. She has been monitoring the herd, and so far, Faith's system is working exactly as she promised it would. She's been using it at Seven Virtues next door for years, and once I took a look at the results she's been getting, I was sold." He tugged gently on one of Faith's curls at her neck. "My wife is a genius, Frankie. I mean, I had no plans to be a chicken farmer, but here we are. What are we up to, honey? Have we hit a hundred birds yet?"

"Just about. We have around forty to fifty layers, and we rotate through at least that many meat birds throughout the year. Needless to say, we never have a shortage of eggs or chicken meat; we cull the meat birds every eight to twelve weeks."

"Wow. Chickens." Frank tried to imagine what that looked like. "Do you herd them, too?" The question sounded silly once it was out, but he was curious about how this all worked.

Faith grinned and nodded. "In a way, yes. We have what we call our chicken caravan. It's a glorified coop I built on a motorcycle trailer to make it mobile. We either manually haul it—it's big enough that two people make the task much easier—or we just hook it up to an ATV and haul it from paddock to paddock. The birds are several paddocks behind the cows—we keep about four days between the two to give the manure time to start breaking down and drawing critters like dung beetles to work their magic—so the ATVs aren't really close enough to the herd to spook them. The chickens stay close to the coops; in the wide-open pastures, sometimes it's the only thing to hide under for safety. The dogs—Remus and Sirius—are fantastic at keeping predators of all kinds away from the birds; they'll launch themselves at a hawk if they think it's a threat. Coyote, possum, raccoon, you name it. And it doesn't matter that the chickens are several paddocks away; the dogs include them in their guard duty. Best investment ever, those two, don't you think?" she asked, turning around to look at Cord.

"Definitely. We'd have no chickens left if it weren't for them."

"Anyway," she continued. "The portable coop is where the chickens roost at night and lay their eggs during the day. So that's part of the job, too—moving the caravan and collecting the eggs." She waved a hand in the general direction of her family's ranch to the east. "Then I do it all again next door at Seven Virtues, except I move my cows in the evening."

Cord picked up the explanation, his hand now moving up and down Faith's back. "Faith has a hundred and ten head on seventy acres next door, and here, we're currently rotating two hundred fifty cow and calf units on three hundred acres. Over the next three years, we're aiming for six hundred head on those same three hundred acres. It's pretty remarkable how little space we need compared to conventional grazing, and our return is exponentially better than it was before we implemented this system. We're producing more calves, more forage almost year-round, and better quality of both on about a tenth of the pasture your dad was running. Even in the winter, we only supplement with our own hay in the worst weather."

"It's hard to wrap my head around it," Frank said. "I'm excited to see it for myself. So where do I fit in?"

Faith sat back again, leaning against her husband, and Cord rested a flat palm on her abdomen.

Frank's eyes widened as the answer dawned on him. "Oh. You can't ride in your condition," he said to Faith.

She smiled softly. "Not for much longer. My midwife tells me I really should stop by six months at the latest." She brought Cord's hand up and planted a kiss in his palm, then leaned forward again and pointed at Frank. "If you're interested in taking over for me, you coming here now couldn't have worked out better if we'd planned it. This will give you about a month to get used to riding and to learn the ropes around here. I'm due the middle of October, so by the time you have to decide about your leg, I'll be well on my way to getting back into the saddle. My midwife says I should wait six weeks after the baby is born, but I have a lot of friends who got back on their horses much sooner than that, and they're just fine. There's no way I'll be able to wait that long if I don't have to, I'm telling you what."

Frank exchanged grimaces with Cord. Riding a horse after delivering a baby didn't sound like something anyone should be looking forward to.

"She comes from sturdy stock, don't you, honey?" Cord teased.

Faith sighed and pressed the back of her hand to her forehead. "Oh, such sweet compliments you give, Cord."

Frank chuckled, appreciating the affection the two shared. They so clearly were two halves of a whole.

"So, what do you think?" Faith asked, her voice casual, but she didn't fool him. Her eyes were alight with hope. "Oh, and my father and sisters can cover for me at Seven Acres. All you'd be responsible for is Whispering Hill's herd."

"We'd pay you, of course—" Cord began, but Frank cut him off.

"No." He shook his head. "Feed me—especially if Charity is cooking—and let me crash in my old room. I don't need money. Right now, I need something to do with myself, and I don't need busy work. I need a real job in spite of my limitations, and this sounds like it might be just the thing for me."

"Sounds like it might be just the thing for me, too," Faith said, her smile widening. "Charity only cooks the noon meal for the crew five days a week, but if you want her to cook other meals for you, talk to her. She's taking on more private clients these days—she's considering starting her own catering business."

Frank shook his head. "No, no. I don't need special treatment. If I can have access to the kitchen, maybe have a drawer in the fridge and a space on a shelf in the pantry, I can feed myself the rest of the time. My mama raised me to know my way around a stove, I can assure you."

They spent the next half an hour hashing out some of the details of the plan, then Jasmine sidled in, rubbing her eyes.

"I fell asleep, my peeps. Did I miss anything?" The girl wasn't quite a teenager, but she had the spirit of one, that was for sure. She was friendly and warm to Frank, taking her cues from her parents, but she had a special connection with Binks that made Frank appreciate her even more. Jasmine went out of her way to get a smile or a chuckle out of the old man, and Frank could tell Binks was smitten.

The Overmans left for home soon after, and Frank headed upstairs to pack up the few items he'd pulled from his duffel. He'd head back to the base first thing in the morning so he could get things rolling on that end. He'd be gone long before Charity came to prepare lunch, but Faith assured him she'd fill her sister in on the change in plans. It was only fair to let Charity know she'd be sharing the kitchen with someone else for several months because if all went well, he'd be back in Plumwood Hollow before the week was over.

THIRTEEN

CHARITY COULDN'T DECIDE IF she was disappointed or relieved by Frank's absence when she arrived at Whispering Hills the next morning. Not that she'd expected him to be sitting at the worktable, empty plate in front of him, waiting for her to serve him. But still, having left a courteous note for him the night before, she'd expected some kind of response; a hastily scrawled 'Thank you' at the bottom of hers would have served.

When she carried the large chafing dishes over to the mess hall in the barn a little before noon, she was glad to find Faith already busy setting out the racks and burners, and Jasmine filling the caddies at the tables with silverware and napkins. The girl had spent yesterday with her best friend—and half-cousin by marriage—and had been sorely disappointed to miss the barbecue. She'd been mollified when her mother had assured her that Charity had saved a huge portion for her. The girl loved barbecue ribs more than anyone Charity knew.

"I'm so sorry I haven't been by yet," Faith said, raising her voice to be heard about the clinking of cutlery and trays. "I meant to stop in an hour ago, but I had a calf down in the pasture next door." Faith was a busy woman these days. She'd opted to keep her Dexters at Seven Virtues after she married Cord, primarily because there was no pressing need to move them right away. In the mornings, she helped Cord move his large herd of Angus to their new pasture for the day, then she'd head next door to do her morning visual check on her own cows. In the afternoons, she left the end-of-the-day check for him to do on his own, then she spent an hour or more moving her cattle and making sure they were settled for the night. Her dog, Jack, always ran out with her both times, but he was a herder and not quite the kind of guard dog they had at Whispering Hills. They'd had very few problems with predators bothering her cows, but in the last year, there'd been an influx of coyotes in their area, and for her birthday last year, Cord had given Faith a guard dog of her own. Jasmine had insisted on naming the dog Sephora because of her hyperactive anal gland, and in spite of her unfortunate malodorous qualities, the animal was sweet-natured, loved people, protected her charges with a vengeance, and got along well with Jack. People always smiled when they saw the huge Anatolian Shepherd at work—she was almost as big as the diminutive Dexters she guarded—but she took her job seriously, even if no one took her seriously. They'd had no trouble with coyotes at Seven Virtues since putting Sephora on the job.

"Everything all right?" Charity asked, frowning at the concern that lingered on her sister's face.

"Yeah, but I'm not sure what's wrong with the little guy. Hope came by, but she couldn't find anything obviously wrong, either, so she's running some lab work now. I'm just waiting for her call."

"Bummer," Charity said, wrapping her in a quick hug. "I'll be praying for good news."

"Thanks. And speaking of good news...." Faith squeezed her in return, then turned to Jasmine. "Sweetie, I'm going to walk back to the kitchen with Aunt Charity, so I can tell her about Frank. You okay here?"

"Got you ladies covered," Jasmine shot back.

"About Frank?" Charity asked, frowning, then Faith linked arms with her and drew her through the barn back toward the house.

"So last night," Faith began. "We came over here to have leftovers with Frank and Binks. Which, by the way, were just as delicious the second time around, made more so because I didn't have to cook. I love you to the moon and back, sister of mine."

"Love you, too, Faithy." She didn't want to seem too interested in whatever news there was about Frank, but obviously, it was important, or Faith wouldn't have made such a concerted effort to fill her in. "What's up with Frank? I haven't seen him all day."

"Right. So, Frank asked us if we would be okay with him taking a temporary leave here. Like, for five or six months, and not a vacation, but to work."

"Oh. Wow. Oh. Here. Like, here at the ranch?" The stilted words slipped out unchecked as she processed what her sister had just said.

"Yes, silly. Here at the ranch. As in, sleeping in his old room upstairs, using the kitchen to cook his own meals—he promised to tread lightly and stay out of your way—and best of all, taking over some of my tasks while he's here. In particular, anything on horseback. As in, moving the cattle here at Whispering Hills every day."

"He can ride?" Charity asked as she stacked two chafing dishes and a huge basket of breadsticks covered with a pretty dishtowel in Faith's outstretched arms.

"He thinks he can. He wants to try. He says he'll be more useful on horseback than on foot." Faith rested her chin on the breadbasket and breathed in deeply. "Oh, my lands, Charity. These smell delicious. Can you please put one in my mouth?"

Charity snickered. "No, I cannot. Wait until we walk back over to the barn, then you can have at 'em."

"But my baby," Faith moaned. "She's shriveling up with hunger. She needs. She needs. She needs." She giggled. "Oops. I'm drooling. Glad you covered them with this towel. Here. Wipe my chin, will you?" She jutted out her chin toward Charity.

"Give me those," Charity said, snatching the basket up. She peeled back the towel and broke the end off one of the breadsticks. "Open up," she said, poking the piece of soft, chewy bread into her sister's mouth. "That should tide you over. Now let's go." She added the breadbasket to the bin she was loading, not trusting the eating machine who'd taken over her sister's body, then backed out the screen door and held it open for Faith. "As soon as you're done chewing, you can tell me how this whole thing came about. Frank didn't say anything to me about it all morning."

Faith nodded and chewed, closed her eyes in appreciation, then quickly opened them to follow Charity down the porch steps. It took a bit, but she finally swallowed the huge bite, then said, "I think he came up with all of this pretty quickly. He called a few people yesterday afternoon, so by the time we sat down to dinner, he had a good idea of a plan, but he's gone back today to try to iron out some of the details. It's an answer to prayer for us, Charity—you know that—and it sounds like we might be an answer to his prayers, too."

"But why here? I mean, isn't he in therapy or getting treatments, or something? Is it okay for him to ride a horse? Won't that jostle things around and hurt like crazy?" They stepped inside the cool interior of the barn, and Faith stopped and turned around to face her. "What?" Charity asked, not liking the odd look on her sister's face.

"I'm not sure if it's my place to tell you this, but he didn't say it was a secret," she hedged.

"Tell me what?" Charity leaned back at the waist to offset the weight of the bin in her hands. "What's going on?"

"What did he tell you about his leg?" Faith asked.

Charity shrugged. "Not much. He told me how he got hurt. He told me he's had several surgeries, that there are going to be more. Poor guy."

Faith nodded. "Come on. If we hurry and get this stuff set up, we'll have a few minutes to chat before the crew starts showing up. Jasmine can cover for us if we need her to." She tipped her head toward the mess hall where they could hear the preteen singing one of Abby's songs.

The girls worked like whirling dervishes, then once again, Jasmine agreed to stand guard—they had to bribe her with two cookies from the dessert tray first—while Faith and Charity slipped around to the side of the barn to talk.

"I'll make this quick," Faith said, glancing at the bulky wristwatch she always wore. "I don't want Cord to worry and come looking for me. He swears I'm going to suddenly get lightheaded and faint, or that I'll trip and fall, and no one will be around to help me up." She held her hands out to her sides. "Do I look like I need help getting up? Maybe in about five months, sure, but right now, I'm perfectly capable of hauling my butt off the ground."

"And then there was Frankie Flanner and his leg," Charity said with a smile, reminding her sister to stay on track. Faith had become a little dingy in the last couple of months. Of course, that was one thing Charity did manage to keep to herself, thank goodness because Faith had also gotten uncharacteristically sensitive about some of the most mundane things. One day her sense of humor was rock solid, the next day, if you laughed when she hiccupped—and she had the silliest hiccups—she cried. Literally teared up.

"Right. Frankie." Faith took a deep breath, growing frighteningly serious. "His doctor thinks he should consider amputating. Below the knee, so it's not as terrible as it could be, but still."

"Ampu—Below the knee? Not as terrible?" Charity gasped, a tingle of fear and trepidation making the hairs at the back of her neck stand on end. "Faith, any amputation is terrible, especially for a man like Frank." A wave of nausea washed through her, not at the thought of Frank losing part of his leg, but at what must be going through his mind right now. Did he have to make this decision all on his own? Did he have good counselors? Good doctors? Was Cord all the family he had left to lean on through this difficult time?

"I know, I know," Faith said, crossing her arms around her middle. "I think it's pretty hard on him right now. Which is why he wants to get away from the base for the next several months. I guess they're pushing for a decision before they do anything else. He's kind of in a holding pattern right now with his progress, and from what I can tell, that's not a good thing. Anyway, he thinks he has a couple of months before he has to give them his decision, but then he'll have to go in right after the new year, whether it's to salvage the leg, or amputate."

"Oh, Faith. He didn't tell me any of that. I mean, I knew things weren't exactly easy, but not—" Her eyes blurred with sympathetic tears. If Faith was correct, then Frank could possibly lose his foot right after Christmas. She swiped at the moisture on her face, then winced as fingertips passed over the bruise on her cheekbone.

Faith didn't miss it and leaned closer to examine the spot. "How did you get that, Charity? It's definitely not your blush, and don't tell me you don't know."

"Frank," Charity whispered, her throat tight with misery for the man. "He threw himself on top of me and shoved his shoulder into my face pretty hard."

Faith reared back. "He what?" Then she grabbed Charity by the shoulders and turned her so that they were facing each other. "Frank did this? Why didn't you say so yesterday?" She was aghast. "Cheese and crackers, Charity! We've given him our blessing to stay here for the next five months or more. We would have booted him off the property had we known he'd pulled this—"

Charity shook her head and waved her hands between them to stop Faith's tirade. "No, no! He didn't mean to. He was dreaming, and I interrupted. He thought I was one of his men and threw himself on top of me to protect me."

Faith's eyes grew even wider. "What? Whoa!" She held up her hands in a halting gesture. "What?" The words were coming out in quiet shrieks. "Oh, my lands. What are you telling me? Did he hurt you? I mean, I can see that he hurt you, but are you okay?" She eyed Charity from the top of her head to the tips of her toes and back. "Do I need to tell Cord or not?"

"Faithy, stop shaking me," Charity blurted out in between her sister's deluge of words. "I'm fine, really. I heard a loud crash, then I heard him moan. Thinking he'd fallen, I raced upstairs and barged into his room." She pulled her shoulders out of her sister's grip. "I surprised him in his sleep, that's all."

"Are you sure?" Faith's expression said she wasn't convinced.

"Yes. And if it makes you feel any better, I'm glad you agreed to let him come back here. I do think it will be good for him to get out of his own head for a while." She sniffed, and then smiled up at her sister. "But I also think it will be good for you, Faithy. You can get off your horse at any time now, you know." Charity hated the thought of Faith riding her horse well into her second trimester, but who was she to argue with a midwife? Charity reached over and put both hands on her sister's still flat abdomen. "Hi, sweet baby. It's your Auntie Charity. I love you," she cooed in a silly voice.

"The little princess says she loves you, too." Faith patted her belly affectionately.

"How do you know she's a little princess?" Charity asked a rush of anticipation at the thought of another baby girl in the family. She'd adored Jasmine from the first time she'd held her tiny infant niece in her arms, and Faith having another girl was fine by Auntie Charity.

Faith shrugged. "I'm just assuming since we come from a long line of far too many females, that she's got to be a girl." She shook her head and narrowed her eyes contemplatively. "I'm so glad we weren't born in a day and age when Daddy had to pay dowries for us. The poor man would have gone bankrupt before he sold off the last of us."

"You're a nut, Faithy." Charity leaned forward and spoke to her sister's belly button. "Your mommy is a nut, little dumpling. But don't worry; your Auntie Charity will take good care of you."

"You know," Faith said, growing suddenly serious again. "It might be good for you, too, Charity."

"What might be good for me?" Charity asked, straightening slowly from talking to Faith's belly. She had a good idea what her sister was referring to, and she didn't really want to hear it.

Faith reached for Charity's hand. "He's been through something similar to Theo. It might do you both some good to talk about it."

She didn't have to ask who Faith was talking about. She tried to pull her hand free, but her sister wouldn't let go. "Just stop. Stop trying to hook me up. First Skid, and now, not even twenty-four hours later, Frank?"

"Hey," Faith said cajolingly. "I'm not trying to hook you up. I'm just saying I think you two might do each other some good because of your shared experiences."

Charity sighed deeply. "I need to go feed your guys," she finally said. "I love you, Faith, but sometimes you don't know when to quit."

"I love you, too, sweet Charity," Faith responded, but with no malice. She spoke gently, almost pleadingly. "But sometimes you don't know when to start."

FOURTEEN

The drive back was uneventful, and after an afternoon of meetings and paperwork, Frank was exhausted, but greatly relieved at how efficiently things had run. Everyone on his care team was supportive of his decision to take some time away, and although the plan was a little unconventional, because of his rank and reputation, there'd been no resistance from anyone. Granted, he didn't come right out and say he planned to get on a horse next week, nor did he let on that he'd be riding that horse every day once he got comfortable on it. But he'd agreed to return every two weeks for maintenance visits with the doctors and therapists to make sure he wasn't losing ground, and they all agreed that as long as he didn't digress, it might do him some good to be around normal life for a change. The duration of the leave at this point was left undetermined based on his medical condition, but they'd been supportive of his plan to decide which course of action he wanted to take regarding his leg before the end of November at the very latest.

He'd take the next few days at Fort Campbell to pack up his apartment off base—regardless of his decision about his leg, it wasn't likely he'd need the place after his leave—then he'd head back to Plumwood Hollow on Saturday. Having a plan in place set his mind at ease in a way it hadn't been in a long time. He was looking forward to being useful again, and the thought of getting back on Hidalgo made his pulse race with anticipation.

On Saturday morning, with his car packed and his apartment key turned in, Frank left Fort Campbell in a completely different frame of mind than he had on Tuesday morning. He had a plan. He had a purpose. It was remarkable what a difference those two things made in his life. He didn't have a decision yet, but he had a strategy for making one.

He also had his pain meds with him; he wasn't foolish enough to think he could take on the challenges ahead of him without them. Not yet, anyway.

But he would have friends and family around to walk through this with him. If there was one thing he'd learned in his years in the Army, it was that no man was an island. Not the lowliest Private, not the highest ranking General, not the cook or the medic, not even the camp dog. The moment a man started pulling away, became isolated or distanced, red flags went up. Working as a team, having each other's backs, picking up or stepping in where the one before you left off, never letting go of your partner, it was, quite literally a matter of life and death. Out there, a man who went solo wore a bullseye on his forehead, and Frank had learned to recognize the signs in his men.

He'd looked in the mirror this week and was shocked to see those red flags flapping around his own soul.

As much as he'd come to appreciate his doctors and therapists, they were a unified team, and he was the rogue player wearing the bullseye. Frank needed men he could call his own, and spending just one day back at Whispering Hills had been enough to remind him that he belonged to more than just the Army. Maybe the ranch wasn't officially his anymore, but the people who lived there were. The folks in the hollow were his folks, and they knew him.

They saw his withdrawal, too; he'd seen the look in Cord's eyes, and he knew his cousin knew. Cord hadn't done any time in the military, but he'd played football for the Bengals—Who dey!—and he knew the importance of teamwork. Cord had taken a few too many hits during his first few seasons, had a few too many bad concussions, and he'd been forced to make the decision that cost him his football career. No, it wasn't the same, not exactly—Cord walked away on two good legs—but he'd still had to make the hard decision to leave. Seeing his cousin making a good life for himself at the ranch, married to the lovely Faith Goodacre Overman after all this time, embracing fatherhood, and changing lives around him, it all gave Frank more hope for himself than anything any medical team member in a white coat had ever offered. Frank wanted to go back to the front lines; that was his heart's desire. The only way he was going to get back there was by leaning into his team, by letting them fill in where he left off. By asking them to have his back for him, to not let go of him while he figured out what he needed to do to stay in the game.

By the time he arrived back in Plumwood Hollow just before noon, he was famished, and although he knew it was Charity's day off, he hoped he'd find some of her packaged-up leftovers in the fridge. The woman could cook. He'd had only one meal prepared by her, and the second time around eating it last Tuesday night hadn't diminished its quality. He was looking forward to sampling more of her wares.

The phrase with its double entendre caught Frank up short. That not-so-fleeting urge to kiss her right before she'd fled his room to check on the grill washed over him, making his blood warm sweetly. The way she'd looked up at him, genuinely trusting him, even though she bore a bruise on her face that was his doing. That Julia Roberts laugh kept echoing in the back of his mind. He'd heard it in his dreams a few times that week. Frank only remembered one of them; he'd been walking the hospital corridors, his leg throbbing with each step, but he was willing to bear the pain because ahead of him, somewhere, he could hear Charity Goodacre Banner laughing, and he knew if he caught up to her, he could lose himself in that smile. And maybe, just maybe she'd look up at him with that trusting light in her eyes, and he'd get to kiss her. He'd awakened from that dream anxious to get back to the ranch.

Oh, he knew that in his condition, at least on the outside, he didn't appear to have much to offer a woman like Charity. He wasn't exactly a prime specimen, hobbling around on his crutches, his leg encased in The Beast, his flesh twisted and warped, his mind in not much better condition at the moment.

But he knew who he was as a man, and whatever the outcome of this injury, wherever he ended up, whether he made it back to the front lines, or took up residence behind a desk, even if he accepted a disability retirement, his identity was still intact. He knew where he came from—his father had instilled in him the value of life and hard work and community. Frank had carried those qualities into every war zone he'd entered, making him the kind of soldier other men automatically looked to and leaned on. And as limited and constrained and frustrated as he felt over his current circumstances, none of those good qualities had changed about him. He might eventually lose his limb, even his career, but that didn't give him license to lose his integrity or his identity. He was a man of God who loved and served his country, who led and cared for the men who followed him. He was Franklin Joseph Flanner, First Sergeant in the US Armed Forces, disabled, retired, or not.

Yes sir, First Sergeant Soldier Boy, he heard Charity quip, and his smile broadened as he turned off Carpenter Road onto the long, winding drive that led up to the Whispering Hills ranch house.

Charity had seen past the outer casing he wore to the man he was beneath; it was there in the way she looked at him. Perhaps he'd read her better than he'd first given himself credit for. Because now, in hindsight, he knew what that flicker was in her eyes.

Awareness. Of him.

Not as a monster, but as a man.

No, on the outside, he wasn't much of a prize. But over the next few months, in this place he'd once called home, Frank intended to prove to himself—and perhaps even to the pretty Widow Banner—that everything he believed about his identity was true. With or without his left foot. With or without his unit. With or without his uniform.

Having Charity Goodacre Banner in his life might be the best medicine he'd ever find.

FIFTEEN

The Goodacres arrived at church at the same time they always did; a full ten minutes early. Charity couldn't remember ever missing the opening worship song that signaled the congregation to stop chatting and start singing. Even when she and Theo had been married, they'd done likewise, joining the family on the Goodacre pew, Theo's sizeable male presence looking far more out of place in the row of females than Jed's. Daddy wasn't a small man, but folks were accustomed to him leading his little entourage up and down the aisle. Theo, big and blond, with shoulders almost twice as wide as Charity's, stood out like a pumpkin in a cucumber patch.

Since his marriage to Faith, Cord Overman now took up a spot in the Goodacre row, usually between his wife and daughter, and Hope, newly married to Levi Valiente, sat across the aisle with the handsome butcher, his daughter, Yvette, and his mother, Naomi, whom everyone simply called Nona. Charity felt the subtle pressure of being the third daughter; folks had begun asking her if she was dating again. It was almost as though they thought it was her turn, simply by order of birth, to land herself another husband. It didn't seem to make a difference that she'd been happily married already, and years ahead of her two older sisters. She knew folks hadn't forgotten Theo, of course not. He wasn't from the hollow, but they'd embraced him as one of their own the moment she brought him home. People couldn't resist falling in love with Theo. His big, booming laugh actually rivaled her own, and his gregarious nature drew folks to him like bees to honey. His kindness and generosity toward everyone was inspiring, and in fact, it was quite likely his readiness to help that had killed him.

That had left her a widow.

That now had her next in line for a husband, at least according to the busybody folks who had no qualms about saying so.

She glanced over at Courage and Justice, the twins who looked nothing alike, but who seemingly shared the same brain. There was Brandon Stillwater, a guy Justice had been dating for over a year now, but she always waved away any questions about their future together. She never flat out denied there was one, but she certainly wasn't confirming anything either. Charity couldn't help wondering if Justice was subconsciously waiting for Courage to find a man of her own before committing to Brandon, and she couldn't help feeling sorry for the older twin if that was the case. As far as she knew, Courage hadn't dated anyone since high school, and the way she behaved indicated that a love life was a low priority, at least for now.

Perhaps Charity could redirect attention to Prudence. But one glance at the girl down near the end of their row had Charity shaking her head. Pru looked like she'd just stepped off the cover of Faerie World or Gypsies R Us, with her fluttering clothes and languid hand gestures. She played up her pixie-like features with artistic and often rather startling makeup, while other times, she wore none at all. There was always some kind of flower or leaf tucked into her hair or spilling out of a pocket, and she'd been known to show up on occasion in completely inappropriate footwear, and sometimes, none at all. Dirty, scuffed-up work boots under a fancy dress at church, high-heeled sandals at the park—but of course, her heels never seemed to sink into the soft ground as she walked—barefoot at a town meeting, simply because she'd forgotten to put shoes on before climbing in the back seat of the family station wagon. The thing about Prudence, though, was that the girl had a deep capacity to love and be loved. It was evident in the way she embraced everyone around her, in how she poured herself into every encounter with her customers at Trilby's Blossoms and Books, and how she worked her magic into the herbal remedies she concocted for anyone in need of her services. Something had happened to Prudence her senior year in high school, though; something that had changed her, that had grounded her, and not necessarily in a good way. All the girls knew it, and although Pru insisted it was simply because she'd grown up, they all knew better, Charity and Faith especially. The two oldest sisters had both lived with the loss of their true loves, and they recognized it in Prudence. The girl moved through life as though her heart were broken beyond repair.

No, Prudence would not be marrying any time soon.

And neither would Abby if any of the Goodacres had anything to say about it. She was too young. She was too flighty, too antsy. Abby had places to go, people to see, life to experience, and although none of them wanted to see her go, it was as though they were simply waiting for her to spread her wings and fly the coop. Nashville, at this point, was the likeliest destination, where Abby hoped to woo the world with her songs. A small-town girl with a great big voice, and the ability to sing her way into the hidden places of the heart.

That leaves me, Charity frowned as she mentally came full circle back to herself. The old biddies wouldn't leave her alone, would they?

From the row behind them, she heard Frank murmur something to Binks, and the old man chuckled in response. This was Frank's first Sunday back in the hollow, and Charity was certain Pastor Treadwell would make some kind of announcement from the pulpit. She'd caught sight of him out front as they made their way inside the sanctuary; well-wishers had surrounded Frank, Binks, and Cord, and Faith had latched on to Charity's arm, tugging Jasmine along with her, to escape the masses. Faith, bless her heart, wasn't a social butterfly, and any kind of social gathering—even the ones she hosted—made her a little claustrophobic, so they slipped away and inside the church, leaving the men to deal with the masses. Now Frank sat in the seat that had once been filled by his father, Judge Flanner, with Jordan Binks at his side. Binks wasn't much of a church-going man, although he claimed to be a God-fearing one, and Charity knew the old man's presence there was likely due more to his paternal pride in Frankie Flanner than for a pressing need to hear Reverend Treadwell preach the Word.

Frank had yet to acknowledge her with anything more than a meeting of the eyes and a quick smile, but she felt his presence behind her as though he rested his hand on her back. How was she going to get through a whole hour of sitting still with him all but breathing down her neck? She reached up to run her fingers along the hairline at the back of her head, glad she'd decided at the last minute to wear her blonde curls down. Having her neck exposed would have only heightened the sensation, she was certain.

An hour later—had it only been one hour?—the last note of the closing hymn rang out, and Charity breathed a deep sigh of relief. She hadn't heard a single word the pastor spoke, and if not for the bulletin in her hand, she would have had no idea what passage he'd read out of. At least she could go over that quickly before dinner, just in case the topic of the message came up in conversation at the table. They often chatted about the pastor's teachings, discussions that were lively and challenging as they unwrapped what it meant to believe in God in the day and age they lived in.

Cord and Faith slipped out the end of the pew down the side aisle, towed by Jasmine who was anxious to hunt down Yvette. The Valiente family would all be coming over in an hour for Sunday Dinner, but the girls could hardly bear the hour spent sitting in the same room together but separated by the chasm of the church aisle. The twins ducked out after them, and Charity started to follow, wanting to get outside for a breath of fresh air, needing to put a little space between Frank and her awareness of him.

"Would you like to join us for Sunday Dinner?" she heard her father say, and she turned to find him leaning over the back of the pew to shake hands with Frank and Binks. "We'd love to have both of you at our table."

"Oh, do," Prudence joined in, sidling closer to shake hands with Frank before reaching over to hug Binks. "Mr. Binks, it is so good to see you." She grabbed one of his hands in both of hers, then ran her thumbs over his knobby knuckles. "Looks like I need to get over there with some more of my liniment, don't I?" Before he could answer, she glanced over at Frank again. "You don't want to miss today's meal. Charity has a couple of fat chickens ready to go in the oven at home, and there will be plenty of food to go around."

Charity felt her cheeks grow warm at the praise, but then in an apologetic voice, Frank said, "Binks and I have already accepted an invitation to dinner at Pastor Treadwell's home." The disappointment that washed over her surprised her.

"Church hierarchy," Jed declared. "Dinner with the reverend comes first. We're neighbors, son. Your parents were fine people and good friends to us. You are welcome in our home any time you find yourself without a table to sit at. You too, Binks, but you already know that." Turning back to Frank, he added, "I mean it, son. Welcome home."

"Can I take a rain check? Phil and Leslie Braxton invited me to dinner next Sunday, then Edith and Pete Jurgen have asked me to join them the following Sunday. Would the one after that be okay? Three weeks from now?" Frank asked with a hopeful grimace.

"Just a word of warning, Frank," Hope spoke up as she leaned in to give hugs to her family. "Edith is actively seeking a husband for her niece, Bethany, but you should know that Bethany already has a thing for a guy her aunt isn't so keen on. Julian Bay—he's a great kid who happens to have the misfortune of coming from a coal mining family." She lifted her fingers in air quotes around the word misfortune.

Frank grinned. "So that's who that was. A young woman started toward us while we were talking, heard Edith invite me, then turned and walked away after rolling her eyes at us. I couldn't decide if I should be offended or not."

Levi reached around his wife and shook Frank's hand. "Good to see you again, man. Welcome home."

"You're a busy man, Franklin Flanner, Jr.," Jed said with a chuckle. "Our Charity is the finest cook in the hollow, so it's probably better you eat everyone else's food first."

"Daddy's right," Prudence said, slipping an arm around Charity's waist. "She'll ruin you for everyone else's cooking."

Frank turned to Charity and held out his hand to her. "If you don't think you'll be tired of me invading your kitchen before then, I'd love to join you."

Charity shook his hand, but when he didn't immediately release hers, she nodded, realizing he was waiting for her to answer his question. "Of course, Frank. Like Daddy said, you're welcome in our home any time. If you don't think you'll get tired of my cooking, that is."

"Not likely," Frank replied, still keeping her hand in his. "I'm looking forward to trying, though," he added with a chuckle.

"Good luck with that," Prudence said with a bright laugh. "You're far more likely to fall in love with her because of her cooking than you are to get tired of it."

SIXTEEN

Dinner with the pastor and his wife was a pleasant and casual affair. His secretary, Trudy Huckster, and her husband, Alfred, joined them around the table, and talk moved fluidly from the old days when the Flanners still held court in Plumwood Hollow to current times with Cord Overman at the helm at Whispering Hills. "It's so good to have you boys back home together, even if it is short term," Patty Treadwell told him. "You must be so proud, Jordan." She was the only person Frank knew who called the old foreman by his first name, but then, they'd been friends growing up.

So much had changed in the fifteen years since Frank left to fight for his country, and yet, life had a way of coming around full circle. Here he was, sitting across the dining table from the man who'd been his family's spiritual leader all Frank's growing up years. Binks sat on one side of him, enjoying Patty's delicious apple cobbler and ice cream, the ranch foreman who'd taught Frank to sit a horse, and on his other side, Trudy and Alfred. Trudy kept dabbing her eyes whenever she looked at Frank, and every so often, she'd reach over and lay a chubby hand on his shoulder or forearm in an achingly maternal gesture.

Near the end of the meal, Reverend Treadwell asked the tough questions, and by then, any awkwardness that might have arisen was eliminated by the easy camaraderie that had been re-established over good food. As Frank explained his situation, Trudy sniffled sympathetically in her seat beside him, and once again, Binks' eyes welled up, but this time, he remained at the table and listened carefully.

"I taught you to get on a horse the first time, boy. I'll help you get back up there this time around, too." Binks nodded solemnly, his steel wool hair bobbing along with his head movement. "We'll have you and Hidalgo back at it in no time."

Over and over, Frank found himself moved by how much the community of Plumwood Hollow seemed to genuinely care about him. He'd been gone for so long, yet folks readily welcomed him back into the fold like they'd been waiting for his return all along. And not just at church where everyone put on their Sunday best behavior. The Maddox brothers had treated him like a pal from the old days. Phil Braxton, who stopped by the ranch to deliver an order of shingles from the hardware store, had greeted Frank enthusiastically. At Nesbits Grocery where Russ Timmons still worked the first checkout lane, the barrel-chested man came out from behind his register to give Frank a careful hug.

People asked all the same questions, of course. What happened? How long do you plan to stay in town? What do you make of all the things that Cordell Overman has going on at the ranch? But folks were warm and considerate and didn't press him for more information than what he was willing to give.

Except for Jenny Stuben, who caught up with him in the church foyer after the service. Jenny hadn't changed much in the years Frank had been gone. She still had her cheerleader looks and that killer smile, but he was pretty sure the last time he'd seen her, her hair had been more the color of dirty dishwater, and her teeth hadn't sparkled so brightly in the midmorning sun. She also still had her irrepressible lack of subtlety, and after hugging him tightly against her ample bosom, instead of letting go, she murmured in his ear how sorry she was to see such a tragic thing happen to such a wonderful man, and if he needed any cheering up, just to give her a call and she'd come right on over and do whatever she could to comfort him.

If it had been anyone else, Frank would have been appalled at what appeared to be a blatant proposition, but being Jenny Stuben, he just thanked her, patted her shoulder, and waited until she released him. Because with Jenny, it might have been an inappropriate offer, but it was just as possible that she was genuinely concerned for him and wanted to do her part to be neighborly. One could never be quite sure with her.

By the time he and Binks started back to the ranch, Frank's leg had begun to ache. He needed to elevate it and get some ice on it. Between packing, meetings, driving back and forth between Fort Campbell and the hollow, he'd done more activity in the last week than he had in a month. As much as he wanted to jump right into things at the ranch, he couldn't forget that he wasn't cleared medically to return to normal daily activity, not by a long shot. If he weren't careful, he'd end up back in Dr. Broderick's office a lot earlier than November.

On the drive across town, they came up with a schedule for Frank getting back in the saddle. Both of them confessed to being better in the mornings before fatigue set in, so they agreed to meet over breakfast first thing Monday, then head over to the barn to get started.

"I'm ready for a Sunday afternoon nap," Binks told him when Frank pulled up in front of the foreman's cabin to let him out. "But if you're up for supper tonight, you're welcome to come by my place for a bowl of chili and a couple of pieces of cornbread."

"You still making your famous cornbread, old man?"

Binks nodded proudly. "I sure am. Serve it with real honey straight from Miss Prudence's hives next door. Can't beat it."

"I'll be there. And I discovered a small container of lemon bars in the fridge. There's a note on the door that says I can eat anything on the top two shelves, and those bars were on the top shelf calling out to me. I'll bring them with me."

"Sounds like a plan." Binks climbed out of the passenger seat of the Challenger, the low seat slowing him down only a little. "Mighty fine car, son. Thanks for the ride."

The house felt over-sized and terribly empty when Frank pushed open the back door and wound his way through the kitchen. He'd brought the lighter weight forearm crutches with him this time, and although they weren't quite as conspicuous and gave him a little more freedom with his hands, they didn't give him quite the stability the under-arm crutches did. He peered into the front room and stopped to appreciate the panoramic scene. The huge picture windows with their curtains drawn back offered a spectacular view of the front lane leading up from Carpenter Road. At this time of year, the grass was green and lush, the trees in full leaf with branches raised like worshiping arms to the afternoon sun. Light streamed into the room, giving a warm glow to the furniture and the hardwood floor. The massive stone fireplace taking up one wall beckoned invitingly, even though it was the middle of summer. Cord really was working miracles with the property, and Frank felt a surge of pride in his cousin's vision for the ranch. Who would have thought the old place could look so elegant and serene? So... pastoral.

Upstairs in his room, he stretched out on his bed and propped a couple of pillows up under his leg. He'd changed out of The Beast to The Beauty, the diminutive nighttime support brace, and gingerly tucked the cold gel pack around his swollen ankle. He'd overdone it; when it swelled that way, it was a sign that he needed to take it easy.

He dreamed of Afghanistan again. The fear was there—that looming awareness of an unseen enemy—but nothing materialized out of the darkness this time. The stars sparkled like crystals in the inky dome of the sky overhead, and Frank found himself thinking about Jesus, something he often did in those still moments in the desert. The notion that the God of the universe, the one who created both the sand and the night sky, who placed each of those stars exactly where he wanted them, had once come to earth as a man, and had stared up at this same sky from another desert not too far away from where Frank lay. Somewhere across camp, someone started calling his name. Binks? When did the old foreman enlist?

"Frankie? Cornbread's ready."

Frank awoke with a start, his old bedroom filled with long shadows.

"Frank? You all right up there?" Binks' voice rang with a note of concern.

He glanced at his phone on the nightstand, surprised to see that it was well past when he'd promised Binks he'd be by. He sat up quickly, hating that he'd caused the old man to worry. "Coming!" he called out, easing his leg off the mattress and resting his heel against the floor. The swelling had gone down a little, and for the first time in quite a while, Frank felt rested.

By the time he headed downstairs, Binks had set up the meal at the worktable in the kitchen. "I brought the food over here when you didn't show. Figured I'd kill two birds with one stone. I could check on you and save us some extra time by bringing it with me."

The cornbread was just as delicious as Frank remembered it. Prudence's honey was—quite literally—icing on the cake.

"That girl and her bees. She has a way with plants and creatures. You should see her with that horse she rescued. A big, beautiful Andalusian. Follows her around like a smitten pup."

Frank's eyebrows rose. "A rescued Andalusian?" His leg was propped up on a stool beside him, and he shifted it to a more comfortable position. He was extra careful with it tonight, hoping it wouldn't slow him down in the morning.

"You ask her about it someday. She likes to tell that story," Binks said with a chuckle. "I swear that girl is part fairy, what with the way she flits around like she's half in another world. And she makes the best liniment for my arthritis. I'm telling you; her touch is magic."

"I think you're half in love with that girl, Binks," Frank teased.

"Half? Laws, no." Binks grinned like a schoolboy. "I'm just as smitten as that horse of hers. I'd follow her around like a pup, too, if it didn't get the police called on me." He grew serious after a moment. "Miss Prudence is a rare treasure, Frankie, and don't you forget it. Someone did that girl wrong at some point; someone who didn't realize that child's worth." He swallowed the last dregs of coffee in his cup. "She's a fine young woman, just like the rest of those Goodacre girls."

"I barely remember her," Frank admitted. "She was pretty little when I left; maybe still in elementary school, I think."

"But you remember Charity?" There was a mischievous sparkle in the old man's eyes.

Frank grinned slowly. "I do," he said, nodding his head. "Pretty little blonde thing back then, too. She laughed a lot, but it wasn't that irritating giggle, you know?"

Binks chuckled. "Hoo-boy. That girl has a laugh, that's for sure. Don't matter what she's going on about, either; you hear that sound, and pretty soon, you're laughing along with her. It's contagious all right." He leaned forward; his gnarled fingers wrapped around his empty mug. "Since her man died out in the desert a couple of years ago, we've heard a lot less of that laugh around these parts. But I have a feeling, young squire, that you might be just what the doctor ordered for that sweet lady. I may be old," he said with a bold wink, "but I'm not too old to have picked up on that little bit of chemistry that snapped and crackled between you two after church this morning."

Frank shrugged noncommittally. "I've been back less than forty-eight hours, man," he said with a soft chuckle. "Don't you think it's a little early to be playing matchmaker?"

Binks pressed his lips together in a firm line and shook his head slowly. "I am not playing matchmaker, son. I'm just saying it like it is." He reached up and scratched his jaw. "Listen to me. Some things in this life are not worth risking. You should think about that with your foot. Don't let pride hold wisdom prisoner. I'm not saying one way or the other what you should do about that, you hear? But some risks aren't worth taking," he reiterated, picking up his mug to take another sip, forgetting it was empty.

"More coffee?" Frank asked, sliding the carafe toward Binks. The foreman's words resonated in Frank's gut, and he knew that a big part of his resistance was the very pride Binks referred to.

"Not tonight," the old man said, moving the cup toward the middle of the table and linking his fingers together instead. "But Frankie, there are also some things in this life that aren't worth putting off for a better time." He paused, as though carefully considering his words. "I know you two have hardly spent more than a couple of hours together, but when that magic is there, you reach out with both hands and take hold of it. You two share something that no one else in our little community understands. You both have lived through tragedy in Afghanistan, and don't think for one moment that Ms. Charity hasn't experienced what you have. She might not have been there in person, but she was there in spirit, in every step young Theo took, in every move he made while he served God and country in the desert. She, of all people, knows what you're going through. She's lived it, son. You think you might lose a leg? She thinks she's lost her heart."

Frank lowered his gaze to his cup, letting the words settle around him as he listened. He hadn't thought about it that way, that was for sure.

"But guess what." Binks' tone softened. "You both have it in you to move forward. Not to forget, mind you, and certainly not to put the past behind you. It's the past that makes us what and who we are today. With or without that bum leg, son, you're a whole man. But you know that; I'm not telling you anything new. Your Daddy and Mama raised you right, boy, so don't go selling yourself short." He thrust his chin in the direction of Seven Virtues Ranch. "And that little lady? She's got more heart than most people I know. She just needs someone to remind her how to use it."

SEVENTEEN

Charity saw very little of Frank the following week. She was admittedly disappointed, and she couldn't decide whether she should take it personally or not. It almost felt like he was intentionally steering clear of her. Was he worried that he might get in her way? Maybe he needed to be reminded that she was accustomed to working around a roomful of people—even with a few less sisters and one less niece in the house, there were still six people wandering in and out of the Seven Virtues kitchen at any given time. And that's if no one brought friends or boyfriends home. It could get really chaotic then, and as big a kitchen as they had next door, it was tiny compared to the one at Whispering Hills.

Truth be told, she'd allowed herself to imagine what the mornings might be like with Frank staying at the big ranch house, and the picture she'd painted could only be described as a modified version of domestic bliss. Which was silly, since the only reason she was in the big service kitchen was for work. Regardless, she'd pictured it differently than the way it was turning out to be.

In her mind, she'd get there first thing in the morning, put on a fresh pot of coffee, and pop a pan of blueberry muffins or cinnamon scones in the oven. Then just as she pulled them out, Frank would appear in the doorway, a warm smile on his face, still a little rumpled from a good night's sleep. "Smells good in here," he'd say in his slightly raspy morning voice. "Mind if I join you?" Charity, of course, would blush becomingly, and welcome him into her domain. Then the two of them would pull up stools to the butcher block table and have coffee and fresh-baked pastries.

Or she'd arrive midmorning with apple cinnamon muffins from home, start a fresh pot of coffee brewing while she put together a fruit tray or some other healthy snack. Frank would make his way in from outside, perhaps Binks, or even Cord and Faith in tow, and they'd all gather around and talk about how their days were going, laughing and teasing and toasting their glasses like they did in television commercials.

It was ridiculous; she knew it, but she couldn't seem to stop the endless scenarios playing over and over in her mind each morning.

On the rare occasions Frank did happen to come through the kitchen while she was there, he rarely spared more than a moment or two to greet her. To give him due credit, he always took the time to thank her for the wonderful leftovers she stocked the refrigerator with. He seemed sincere in his gratitude, and he wasn't rude by any stretch of the word, but he didn't visit with her. Maybe he'd only had coffee with her out of a sense of obligation because of what had happened in his room. Perhaps he'd felt compelled to sit across from her that strange Monday morning just to make sure she was all right.

By the end of the first week, she did not doubt that Frank was avoiding her. When she sat down alone for a midmorning break in the front room, it suddenly occurred to her that when Frank walked into the middle of the conversation that she and Faith were having last Monday, he'd politely requested his breakfast to go. It was Faith who'd convinced him to sit and have his meal in the kitchen with Charity; Frank had been clearly reluctant to do so.

What a blind fool. Charity smacked her forehead with the palm of her hand. He'd been coerced into that visit, that was all there was to it.

Okay. So, the guy was a career military man. He was here at the ranch for because he needed to clear his head. A mental wellness leave or something—Theo had talked compassionately about guys who took them. Frank had told Cord and Faith in no uncertain terms that he wasn't interested in a free ride, that he wanted to work and plug in. Which translated, Charity presumed, into something along the lines of, "I'm not interested in any female distraction right now. I've got to focus on my leg and my head."

Fine. Charity wouldn't take it personally, but she wouldn't go out of her way to be available to him, either. She'd continue leaving leftovers, greet him politely when he came through, serve him at lunch as though he were just another one of the guys, and head on home at the end of the day like she'd done countless times since taking this job.

They didn't say much to each other in church on Sunday. She noticed his hollow cheeks and bleary eyes, though, and wondered if he was all right. But after the service, he engaged quickly in an animated conversation with some of his old friends from high school, and Charity slipped away before she inadvertently got included in the group surrounding the pews they were in.

The second week was a blur of activity as the folks from whom Cord had purchased the Quarter Horse business arrived with three enormous trailers of the most gorgeous Quarters Charity had ever seen. Those horses made her fat little Nutmeg looked like a country bumpkin, even though she was a lovely little purebred, too. Dennis and Nancy Bastion had brought with them eight additional staff members to help with the horses, not the two or three that had been planned for, and Faith frantically hired Charity to cover breakfasts as well as lunches. The two of them scrambled to make up rooms in the big house for all those people. Fortunately, the majority of them were couples, so Frank had been able to keep his room, but she didn't blame him for lying low.

They seemed to fill every corner of the house all day long, and it quickly dawned on Charity that the Bastions had, indeed, brought only three staff members. But those three had brought friends and spouses along as though they were on vacation—presumably with the Bastion's permission—and the whole group treated the ranch house like it was a bed and breakfast. On Tuesday afternoon, one of the women—Brittany? Barbie?—stuck her head in the kitchen where Faith and Charity were having a quiet conversation, and said, "Um, the trash can in the bathroom is overflowing, and no one has come to take our laundry. Can you look into that?" Faith broke down in tears, and Charity shooed the shocked girl out of the room, assuring her that someone would take care of the trash, but that the washing machine wasn't available for public use.

Through clenched teeth that she tried to mask as a smile, she said, "There's a cute little coin-operated Laundromat downtown, though. It's only a dollar a load. They even have a vending machine with detergent and fabric softener if you didn't bring any of your own."

"I don't do my own laundry." Barbie had actually stuck out her bottom lip.

"Then there's a dry cleaner, too. You'll have to pay extra for next day service, though." And with that, Charity had patted the girl's shoulder none too gently, then ducked back into the kitchen to escort Faith outside to her little truck. She drove her sister home and told her to call it a day, then returned to the big house to finish prepping for breakfast the next day.

Wednesday morning, Charity arrived to find the kitchen in complete disarray, dirty dishes and glasses scattered about, and the pantry door standing open, its shelves looking like they'd been ransacked. The inside of the refrigerator wasn't much better. Most of the cheese she'd purchased for the whole week was gone, the telltale platter of wasted crackers and cheese slices left over from the night's binge still sitting in the middle of the butcher block table, the four gallons of Florida orange juice she'd put in the refrigerator to chill for breakfast all open and every one of them more than half gone. In the trash, she discovered one empty ice cream tub—a gallon of soft-churned vanilla she'd planned to serve on waffles Thursday morning—the skin and seeds from two dozen avocados she'd been saving to make guacamole for the South of the Border meal she had planned for noon today, and an enormous—and empty—Vodka bottle. "Screwdrivers? Really? How old are you?" she wailed, not caring if anyone heard her.

"Whoa. What happened here?" Frank came into the room from the back porch, his clothes rumpled and his eyes a little puffy from sleep. He had his nighttime brace draped around his neck, his regular one already buckled on.

"Take a guess," Charity ground out. "Can you believe this? How am I supposed to make breakfast with my kitchen looking like this? Half my supplies are used up, too." Then she turned a narrowed gaze on him. "Where were you? Didn't you hear any of this going on?"

Frank held up both hands in surrender. "Don't look at me. It was so noisy here Monday night that I couldn't sleep. I crashed at Binks' cabin last night."

"Great," she muttered under her breath. "You bailed, and they celebrated." Then she clamped a hand over her mouth. "I'm sorry," she said, her words muffled behind her hand. She lowered it and eyed him apologetically. "That didn't come out right. I didn't mean they celebrated because you left."

Frank chuckled and waved away her apology. "I understood. If I'd been here, this wouldn't have happened, believe me, Charity." He straightened his shoulders and removed the night brace from around his neck, placing it on the seat of one of the stools. "Listen. I'm not fast, but I can help you get this cleaned up."

"It's not your fault, Frank. Nor is it your responsibility." She sighed heavily and started gathering dirty dishes.

"Nor is it yours, Charity," he said, peeling off the flannel overshirt he wore to reveal a short-sleeve Army t-shirt underneath. He folded it deftly and set it on top of his brace. Then he made his way to the sink and started rinsing the first of the dishes. "This will be my station. You bring me stuff; I'll wash and dry. As soon as we've put things back together, I'll help with breakfast, too. I do know my way around the kitchen; I'll have you know."

She hesitated, hating that she had no choice but to take him up on his offer. Not because she didn't want him in the kitchen with her—hadn't she been pining for just that all last week?—but because she knew full well that he was only going to stick around out of an overactive sense of duty. But need him, she did. There was no way she could get the mess cleaned up, the dishes washed, the fridge and pantry put back to some semblance of order, and then cook up enough breakfast for a dozen people. Granted, half of them may not even show up, if the empty bottle of liquor meant anything, but she still needed to make sure there was enough for everyone in the house, as well as for Terrell Jackson, the new horse guy, Cord and Faith, Binks, and Frank. Charity didn't feel like eating, not after seeing the devastation, the invasion, of her sanctuary.

Today, she was going to lay down the law. Oh, she'd do it nicely, the way she always did things—except, apparently, where Frank was concerned—but there would be no doubt in anyone's mind that her kitchen was off limits. No exceptions.

Frank saved the day. Not only did he stick around until the kitchen was spotless, but he also pulled a stool up to the counter so he could give his leg a break while he fried five pounds of bacon on an electric griddle, and then thinly-sliced a couple of cantaloupes, honeydew melons, and pineapples for a fruit platter.

"I'm surprised they didn't use my pineapples for their mixed drinks," Charity grumbled, but Frank laughed her complaint off and reminded her that the guests were probably pretty intimidated by the prickly skin and serrated leaves. "I seriously doubt they even knew what they were," he added with a smile.

While Frank took care of his tasks, Charity shredded potatoes she'd baked the day before, and made heaps of hash browns that she spread out on cookie sheets in the oven to crisp up. In a large bowl, she quickly cracked eighteen eggs, added about a cup of chicken broth, then whipped them gently until all the yolks were broken and the broth mixed in. She ladled a generous amount of the bacon drippings from Frank's griddle into a bowl, added a dash of curry pepper to it, and stirred it up before slathering the insides of three muffins pans with it. She filled eighteen of the muffin cups with the scrambled eggs and cracked individual eggs into the remaining eighteen, then slid the pans into a convection oven to bake.

"Wow. That's brilliant. Good idea for a big group," Frank said.

"Thanks," Charity said, shooting him an appreciative smile. "It's great for camping, too. You can do this right over an open flame if you keep the fire burning evenly. I crack all my eggs into one Mason jar and keep it in the cooler. Then in the morning, I shake the jar up and pour them into the muffin tins. Easy meal, easy cleanup."

"Brilliant," he said again, and Charity turned away so he wouldn't see how good his simple compliments made her feel.

In short order, the breakfast was ready, the formal dining table set for twelve, and a few minutes before eight, she sent Frank upstairs. "If you don't want to have to interact with the other guests, you might want to run for cover now before they all start stumbling down the stairs. You've earned it."

Frank reached for her hand and stopped her before she could push open the swinging door that led into the dining room. "I'm not a guest, Charity. I wish you could come upstairs to my room with me, because you've earned it, too."

"Whoa." Cord, with Faith close on his heels, pulled open the screen door from the back porch and entered the kitchen. "Cuz. Crossing a line there, man. She works for me." He shot a concerned glance at Charity, but behind him, Faith was pressing her lips together to keep from laughing.

No matter how hard she tried, Charity could not stop the flush that burned up her neck and lit her cheeks on fire.

"Wow," Frank muttered, closing his eyes in apparent dismay. "I really put my foot in it, didn't I? I did not mean that the way it came out. Forgive me, all of you." He ducked through the swinging door shoulder first and made a beeline for the stairs. The sound of muffled voices could be heard from the floor above, but there hadn't been anyone waiting at the big dining table yet.

"What just happened here?" Cord asked, a flash of something that might have been anger sparking in his eyes. "Did I just hear what I think I heard? Charity?"

"No," she moaned, covering her face with her hands. "No, of course not."

"Come on, Cord," Faith said, her voice tight with the effort to hold back her laughter. "Calm down. It's your cousin, honey. You know he would never—"

"I know no such thing," Cord interrupted. "I've been surprised by nicer guys, okay? You'd be amazed at some of the harassment I've seen out there, and I'm sorry if I'm jumping to conclusions, but that was—"

"Cord, stop." It was Charity's turn to interrupt. "Let me tell you about this morning, okay? Please sit." She pointed at the worktable. "No one is downstairs yet, so we have a few minutes." She propped open the swinging door with a doorstop just to make sure they'd see or hear anyone. Then she poured Cord and herself a fresh cup of coffee, made a mug of Prudence's hibiscus herbal tea for Faith, and explained to them in great detail about the utter chaos she'd stepped into at six o'clock that morning. She told them about Frank's appearance, how he'd helped her without a single complaint or unkind remark—except perhaps for the pineapple thing—and finished up with, "I told him he'd earned the right to disappear upstairs to his room. And you heard his response."

Faith wasn't even attempting to hide her mirth. She poked her husband in the shoulder. "You need to go apologize to that man, Cowboy. He must be mortified thinking you believe him to be that kind of guy, especially after he was such a gentleman."

"She's right," Charity agreed, shooting Cord a wounded look, although it was a little difficult to pull off since Faith's laughter was starting to get to her. "It was bad enough that he said what he did," she said, the corners of her mouth turning up. "But then you took it—" She chortled quietly. "And ran with it." She covered her mouth to keep from laughing out loud.

"Go talk to him," Faith said, nudging her husband. "And then come right back downstairs and talk to your guests. It shouldn't be Charity's job to lay down the law. And if you don't, I will, and you do not want that." Faith bobbled her head the way her daughter did when Jasmine was getting sassy. "I am pregnant, remember? They could set me off, and I won't be responsible for what happens."

"No, we do not want that," Cord said with a resigned chuckle. "You two try to keep a cool head in here. I'll be back shortly."

The moment he stepped out of the room, the girls collapsed in giggles. "Oh, my lands, Charity. That was awful and hilarious and absolutely terrible for poor Frankie. He's probably upstairs packing his bags, thinking we want him out before noon."

"The look on Cord's face," Charity gasped between guffaws. "You have a keeper there, Faithy. I mean, he was right to question that statement, you know? Can you imagine if Daddy had walked in on that?"

"Lord, no. I don't even want to think about that." Faith shook her head, but then she grew serious. "Charity, I am so sorry about this morning. I'm glad Frank was here, but you still shouldn't have had to deal with that. You should have called Cord immediately."

Charity shrugged. "It was okay, really. I mean, it looked a lot worse than it was, and Frank being here made it a lot easier to stomach. I'm more upset about the waste than anything else now. Not only did they plow through all my avocados and cheese—"

"I hope they are all lactose intolerant and have serious stomach problems now."

"No!" Charity waved both hands in front of her. "Stop, no! Who do you think is going to have to clean up after that? It's already going to be awful because of the alcohol. That's a huge bottle of booze, Faithy, and unless they brought it here half empty, there will probably be far fewer guests at the breakfast table this morning." She leaned to the right a little so she could see through the propped open door. "So far, we're it."

"This can't happen again," Faith declared, her brow furrowed in anger. "It never ceases to amaze me how some people can act so entitled. Cord paid good money for their horses and their business name, so it's not like we owe them anything. This whole week is over and above anything we talked about." She took a deep breath, then let it out slowly. "Cord will set them straight, I'm sure of it. I really don't want to talk to them about this; they come from money, and my sweet husband knows their language. I do not."

"Thank God," Charity said.

"So, tell me."

"Tell you what?" Charity eyed her sister suspiciously, not liking the way Faith suddenly leaned in, her eyes lighting up with piqued interest.

"Tell me about your morning with Frank." Faith waved a hand around in a circle in front of her. "All this. I mean, you guys just spent two hours together. What did you talk about?"

"Oh, my goodness, woman. You make me crazy." But Charity found herself telling her sister anyway. "For the first hour, I raged about your house guests," she began, even though it wasn't true.

"No, you didn't." Faith shook her head and rolled her eyes. "Spill."

EIGHTEEN

"I'm sorry," Cord said after pulling the bedroom door closed behind him. "I was out of line."

Frank was seated on the edge of his bed, his head in his hands. "I'm the one who was out of line. I just said the first thing that came into my head. Didn't even think twice about the way it would sound." He met Cord's eyes. "Doesn't matter what I meant; it matters what I said. I know that. It's my job to know that. Do you know what could have happened to me if that had been anyone down there other than your sister-in-law?"

Cord chuckled. "You're not in the Army here, Cuz. So, you said something out of line. Get back in line, that's all." Cord crossed to the bedroom window and peered out. "You have the best view in the house from up here," he said.

"That's why I moved to this room when I was a kid. Remember I used to have the big one across the hall? It looks out over the front of the house, which is nice enough, but not compared the one you're looking at."

"You can see all the way out past the lake. I think I see a couple of cows. Wow." Cord turned back to face him. "So, are you going to come downstairs and eat with us?"

"Nah. Charity and I ate already. We wanted our breakfast hot." Frank grinned at his cousin. "Besides, these are your people, not mine. Unless you can give me a really good reason for spending time with them, I'd rather keep to myself."

Cord grimaced and shook his head. "Can't come up with a single reason, good or bad."

Frank chuckled. "Guess you're on your own. And don't subject your wife to too much of them, either. I was here Monday when they were busy getting themselves settled in. I don't know how much Faith told you, but they ran her ragged. No one needs to be treated that way, especially not the pregnant lady of the house."

"She didn't tell me." Cord's tone went still and ominous, a sure sign that his blood was beginning to boil. He'd always been that way; Frank knew to run for cover when his cousin's eyes went dark like that.

"Well, I'm telling you," he said. The people in the other rooms had earned a little of Cord's wrath. "I'm also telling that I'll be sleeping here the rest of the week, or however long they're here. They wouldn't have been able to pull that stunt downstairs if I hadn't bailed."

"They shouldn't have pulled it, period," Cord ground out. He turned toward the door, but he paused before opening it. "Listen, I know I embarrassed you downstairs. But you should know that Charity defended your honor loud and clear. She said a lot of nice things about you." Then he pulled the door open and stepped out into the hall.

Frank had no desire to follow Cord downstairs for the conversation that was coming, but once the hall cleared, he might just prop the door open to listen.

"Nah," he said aloud, then carefully lay back on the bed, lifting his leg up to prop it on the footboard. He'd rather lie there and think about Charity and the last two hours they'd just spent together.

They'd talked of nothing and everything. They talked about food and cooking—a lot of cooking stories, that was for sure. They talked about camping and laughed about how different Frank's experiences were with a bunch of guys compared to Charity's with her father and all her sisters. "You make it sound like an elegant tea party in the wilderness," he'd teased. "Did you ever get dirty? Burned? Stung?" Charity had laughed, making him crack up, too, and had assured him that yes, the girls had all gotten dirty, burned, and stung multiple times on their excursions.

Charity regaled him with stories from high school after he left. "You were a big deal around here, Frank. Did you know that? People called you Captain America." She'd smiled over at him, then reached out to brush the backs of her knuckles across his temple. "With your hair like this, you look a little like Steve Rogers, you know. You probably look pretty good in a uniform, too, don't you?"

Her touch had sent a flood of heat coursing through his veins. Her teasing words and that pretty smile made it difficult to catch his breath.

She asked him a few questions about the Army, but they didn't linger there. He figured she was asking to be polite, but it probably stirred up hard memories for her. She talked about trying to decide what she wanted to do in the future. "I won't always be working for Cord this much; at least I don't think so. The Maddox brothers will eventually move on to another job, and there won't be anyone left to feed."

"What about Cord and Faith and their kids? Binks?" He wanted to add his name to the list, but that might be a little premature. "And now the new guy, Terrell, right? Who will feed them?"

Charity shrugged noncommittally. "I don't know. I suppose they'll all have to start cooking for themselves again. I mean, I can't lean on Cord forever."

"Lean on Cord?" Frank asked. "What do you mean by that? From what I can see, he—along with everyone else on this ranch—leans on you."

"He created this position for me, knowing I was looking for work." She said it softly, almost like she was embarrassed about it. "He could have hired anyone with a lot more experience than I have. I'm sure it had something to do with Faith being my sister, you know?"

"No. I'm sure it didn't." Frank turned so he was facing her. "Charity, Cord hired you because folks in the hollow recommended you to him. He hired you because you can cook." He didn't like to hear her sell herself short. "And you've proved to be a really good investment. Those guys out there?" He pointed in the direction of the mess hall. "They rave about your food. That's why he hired you."

"Thank you," she finally murmured. "That's good to know. I've always wondered if—"

"Stop wondering, okay?"

They went on to talk about her catering ideas, but she seemed less enthusiastic than he would have expected her to be about it. He didn't question her, but he got the sneaky suspicion that Charity was considering starting a catering business because people told her she should. Did she even know what she wanted to do with her life?

He regaled her with stories about him and Cord growing up. "He was trouble with a capital T, that brother-in-law of yours. Reverend Treadwell used to say Cord was working on his testimony."

By the time they settled around the worktable to eat their breakfast—"This feels like we're the kitchen staff in one of those old British manor house shows."—Charity seemed to have gotten over the worst of her frustration over the condition she'd found her kitchen in, and she couldn't seem to stop smiling.

All in all, it had been one of the better mornings he'd had in a long time. Especially after last week.

Last week had been excruciating. At the end of each morning session with Binks, it was all Frank could do to keep his chin up as he hobbled through the kitchen on his way to his room. He'd taken to timing his comings and goings around Charity's schedule, purposely waiting until she was over at the mess hall before hauling himself, trembling and nauseated, into the house. He didn't want her to see him so vulnerable and weak. It was his pride, sure, but it was more than that. She'd worry, and he didn't want her to do so needlessly. He knew it would take some time before he was back in the saddle enough to take over for Faith; he just needed to get past the initial transition, and then things would be better, he was certain.

By Wednesday, he'd gotten up on Hidalgo's back, but because his brace was an immobilizer, once he was on the horse, it stuck out an odd and uncomfortable angle. It had been impossible to find a comfortable position to sit in. He'd ended the session early, having twisted his leg awkwardly during a dismount. He'd felt a sharp twinge in his ankle that had scared him, so he'd skipped lunch with the rest of the crew, and instead, made a sandwich while the kitchen was empty, then spent several hours in bed with his leg elevated and iced. On Thursday, he'd traded out The Beast for The Beauty, the smaller and lighter brace much more adaptable to being in the saddle, but it gave only minimal support. By the time he wrapped things up, he'd dug his bottle of Percocet out of the bottom of his duffel and allowed himself to take one. He'd fallen asleep and had missed lunch again, but the relief from his pain had lingered long enough for him to feel almost human again by the time Binks came by to check on him. Frank convinced the man to stay for dinner, and the two had feasted on fried chicken and mashed potatoes, green beans, and some kind of chickpea salad with fresh vegetables, feta cheese, Greek olives, and a mouthwatering vinaigrette dressing. The meal had been made complete with a thick slice of layered banana cake topped with cream cheese frosting. Frank had taken another pain pill before bed and had slept like a rock until about five a.m. on Friday. He'd endured another hour of torture before he gave up and went back to hide in his room, a puke bucket close at hand.

He'd tried again Saturday morning, but Binks put an end to it when Frank doubled over and emptied the contents of his stomach before he even managed to get on the horse. "Enough, boy. This ain't right. You take it easy for the next coupla days, you hear? We'll see how things are, come Monday."

Frank hadn't argued. He wound up spending the day in the big armchair in front of the large windows that overlooked the long, sloping front lawn and the drive that led up the house from Carpenter Road. The chair was remarkably comfortable, and with the matching footstool drawn close to prop his leg on, he'd dozed off and on until evening, appreciating the changing scenery outside the window as the sun rose and fell. Appreciating the fact that he didn't have to climb up and down stairs to find himself something to eat that his stomach wouldn't reject.

He wasn't feverish, not that he could tell, but his pain was almost unbearable, and Sunday morning, he took another pill to get him through church where he wouldn't be able to keep his leg elevated, followed by dinner at his old friend's house.

Monday morning, he didn't think twice. There was no way he was going to try getting back on Hidalgo without a little pharmaceutical assistance.

Then the Bastions and their minions arrived, and the whole ranch seemed to be turned on its head.

"And what did I do?" he muttered to himself. "I abandoned ship, leaving Charity to deal with the unruly masses." Thinking about this morning, however, put a smile on his face. "And then I redeemed myself," he said. "And I will continue to redeem myself every morning for the rest of the week."

He wasn't just going to sleep there at night to keep the guests from invading her kitchen. He would also go down around six each morning and offer to help with breakfast. Hopefully, it would help her day go better, and it would certainly make his day, starting out each morning side by side with Charity.

NINETEEN

Friday morning, the Bastions, their team of little helpers, and their empty trailers pulled down the long driveway and back out onto Carpenter Road. Charity could have sworn the whole ranch breathed a collective sigh of relief.

Things got a little better after the morning when she'd walked into the middle of a nightmare in her kitchen. The only people who made it to the breakfast table were the Bastions and their three assistants, and although Cord had kept his cool, there'd been an edge in his voice that brooked no argument or excuse for any of the bad behavior of the group. Dennis had, in fact, apologized profusely to Cord, although his wife, according to Cord, sat in a silent rage while her husband gave her a talking down in front of her staff. "But from the way it sounds, she's the one who extended the invitation to everyone, referring to this delivery as their last huzzah, and she was the one who suggested the party. Later that day, Charity had come into the kitchen to find an envelope on the inside of the swinging door. It was addressed to her, so she opened it and discovered it to be full of cash with a note clipped to it. "This is for your trouble. B" was all it said. Because she didn't care what the Bastions thought of her, she kept the note, wrote the exact dollar amount she'd received on the envelope, signed and dated it, then hand-delivered the whole thing to Faith. For their troubles.

Charity had also insisted that Faith take Thursday off. "Put your feet up, Faithy. Get some rest. Go hang out with Jasmine in Bowling Green. Anything. Just don't come to the house, no matter what, okay?" She only agreed after Charity called home to see if any of the girls might be available to help out for a little extra cash. Courage, bless her heart, had the day off, and agreed to come over and help. While Faith disappeared for the day, Charity and Courage played hostess to the Bastions, their "people" as they liked to refer to them, and Terrell Jackson, the new director of the Quarter Horse breeding program.

To Charity's surprise, Courage offered to come back on Friday and help, too. She wasn't about to second guess her sister's motives, but she didn't miss the sidelong glances the twin was angling at the new director.

Frank had also surprised her early Thursday morning by showing up unannounced to help her with breakfast preparations. Once again, they'd spent a couple of hours working side by side and getting to know each other while they put together breakfast casseroles and assorted side dishes.

She wasn't surprised at his appearance on Friday morning, but she was just as pleased.

That same afternoon as she was putting the last of the pots and pans away, Frank practically sauntered in through the back door—if one could saunter on crutches. He startled her so badly she dropped the pot lid she was drying into the sink, and it clattered loudly before she scooped it up again and clutched it to her chest. Her heart pounding, she whirled around to face him, but Frank didn't seem to notice her dismay.

"Hey, Charity," he said, casually pulling out a stool at the worktable without waiting for an invitation. "Do you ever leave this kitchen? Other than to go next door to the mess hall, I mean?"

She leaned against the counter to study him, her pulse still racing to recover from his unexpected arrival. She didn't like his tone. It was almost like he was making fun of her or goading her or something. Sure, maybe she was a little tired after the week, but she wasn't imagining it, was she? Before she could stop herself, she retorted, "Yes, First Sergeant Flanner, I do. I go home to Seven Virtues Ranch, to the peace and quiet of my own room, the gentle company of my father, and the sweet conversation of my sisters."

"Ah," he said, the single word heavy with meaning, but Charity was having a difficult time understanding what he was getting at.

"Why do you ask?" It seemed such a ridiculous question; surely, he knew exactly where she went after closing down the kitchen.

He grinned sheepishly. "I just wanted to make sure you were actually getting out of here each night. "

"Really?" Charity frowned. "Why didn't you just say so?" She shook her head and pushed away from the counter to start gathering her things. This conversation was getting weird, but he'd been so much help this week, she didn't want to be rude. "Look, I'm wrapping things up here for the day, Frank. Is there anything I can do for you before I leave? Would you like me to put on a small pot of coffee for you? There are leftover blondies from lunch if you'd like one." She eyed him directly, attempting to keep her expression neutral.

"No, no," he said, lacing his fingers together and resting his forearms on the table. "I was wondering—since you do, apparently, leave this place in the evenings—if you'd like to go out for dinner this evening. With me," he added, as though he needed to clarify. "You spend all your time taking care of everyone around here. How about I take you out somewhere nice and let someone else cook for you?" He nodded his head toward the back door. "Besides, I haven't had the chance to show off my ride to you. Have you taken a look at the beauty parked out back?"

He sounded a whole lot like he used to back in high school, like that kid who had the world by its tail, who wasn't afraid of anything. A cocky kid who was confident he'd only get a yes from a girl like her.

Except that he wasn't that kid anymore. She knew that. The Frankie Flanner from the past would never have spent the first two hours of the morning helping her clean and cook for a bunch of ungrateful house guests. The fact that he was here now, asking her out—was this a date? She hadn't been on a date since, well, since Theo. "Um..." she breathed out, suddenly quite nervous. "Uh, no, I don't think so," she said. "I need to go home and make dinner for my family. They're expecting me. I've already got a chicken in the slow cooker, so..." she said, waving a hand aimlessly in the air. "I—I have plans."

"Kinda validates my concerns," Frank said candidly. "Don't you ever take a break? Doesn't anyone ever cook for you?"

"I love what I do," she shot back, picking up the towel and folding it absentmindedly. "I love cooking. I love feeding people."

"I can tell," he said without a trace of cynicism. "And believe me, you know your way around a kitchen. I swear I'm putting on a couple of pounds a week just eating your food. If cooking were a spiritual gift, Charity, you'd be the holiest woman I know."

An unexpected laugh burst out of her, and she covered her mouth with both hands too late to catch it. Frank grinned appreciatively at her from across the table.

Faith often said something along those lines, but coming from Frank, the words sounded marvelously endearing.

"I mean it, you know," he said when she lowered her hands. "You know that adage about a way to a man's heart is through his stomach?" He paused, as though waiting for her to respond. She couldn't; she had no clue where he was leading with that question, and she wasn't quite sure she was ready to follow him blindly. When she only stared down at her folded towel on the table in front of her, he continued. "Prudence was right, Charity." His tone softened even more, and she lifted her gaze to his, those hazel eyes making her think of mulled apple cider. "Having eaten your food every day for the last two weeks, I'm definitely not getting tired of it."

She heard her sister's lyrical words to Frank from last Sunday play through her mind. "You're far more likely to fall in love with her over her cooking than you are to get tired of it."

TWENTY

She'd turned him down. He'd been so sure she was experiencing the same jolt of pleasure between them that he was.

Apparently not.

Frank had been looking forward to spending an evening with her. He'd been planning it all week. He'd take her over to Muldoon where they wouldn't be bombarded with folks either of them knew, where they could sit at a table for two and get to know each other. It wasn't so much about finding a place where the food was top notch; he had a feeling Charity could out-cook the majority of the chefs this side of the Mississippi. No, he wanted to get away with her, to head out of town in his little muscle car with the pretty woman in the passenger seat beside him. He wanted to show her that he was more than just a messed-up soldier boy come home to lick his wounds. With his leg tucked out of sight under the table, and her sitting across from him, he could look into those sky-colored eyes in search of the heart that was hiding inside her. Because the more he'd thought about what Binks had said, the more he agreed with the man. Maybe Frank's reasons for coming to the ranch when he did had just as much to do with Charity's heart as it did with his foot.

"Now there's a romantic notion," Frank muttered dryly as he mounted the stairs to his room. It was nice to have the house to himself again, and not have to worry about who he'd run into, sometimes literally. He hated the stares he could feel long after he passed someone, the pity, the random offers of help that were all about appeasing consciences and had nothing to do with whether or not he needed assistance. He was getting much more adept with the forearm crutches, but he had the feeling it had more to do with his growing confidence in himself than anything else.

Frank was glad the week was over, not because it had been so busy, but because he hadn't been busy enough. He'd had too much time to sit around and think about his leg. He'd looked forward to the early mornings with Charity mostly because he got to spend time with her on her turf, but also because he had something to do. Outside of those two or three hours, he'd spent a lot of time sitting in the shade with Binks and Faith, watching the new horses acclimate to their surroundings and accommodations. In the end, it had been for the good. His leg had gotten some much-needed rest, but he was ready to get back on the horse again and get things moving along.

His leg wasn't any better, though. He didn't have to be a surgeon to know that. He'd had a few short sessions with Binks that week—aided and assisted by the relief his Percodan brought. His physical therapist often begged him to take his pain meds before therapy so they could get more done, and as far as he was concerned, his work with Binks was the equivalent of PT. Friday morning, after spending a couple of hours with Charity, he'd had the first session he could feel good about since arriving at Whispering Hills.

Frank hated that he'd resorted to taking the opioids again—he'd used them religiously for about six weeks after he'd come through his first surgery, but when he realized he was practically setting his clock by them, and then tried to wean himself off them, he'd come face to face with how addictive the narcotics were. He'd used them sparingly since, and every time he started up again, he felt the medicated haze settle around him. The stuff didn't produce euphoria so much as a sense of mellowness, almost as though his brain could suddenly handle the pain after all, so there was no need to stress about it. It was always a little unsettling after the fact, but Frank was confident that in another week or two at the most, he could go back to managing his pain with over-the-counter meds and ice.

That said, he'd heard too many horror stories about narcotics addiction to fall victim to it. There was a right way to use the medication, and there was a wrong way, and he was determined to be on the positive side of the statistics. So, to keep himself accountable, on Friday afternoon, he knocked on Binks' door. When the old foreman invited him in, Frank had simply handed him the bottle of pills and explained how he wanted to use them.

Binks had nodded solemnly. "I got you covered, son. One before we work, one after, and one at dinner if you need it."

Frank had been so relieved to share the burden of the pills with someone else, that he'd all but burst into the kitchen to ask Charity out to dinner.

Then she'd turned him down.

But he'd seen the flicker of interest in her eyes when he'd asked. She'd been on the verge of saying yes, he was certain, but something had changed her mind, and he had a good idea what—or who—it was. Theo Banner.

Except Frank wasn't worried about a dead man. Especially not a dead man of integrity and honor, one who was held in such high esteem by his family, friends, and colleagues. A man who, according to Cord, Faith, and Binks, had loved his wife immeasurably, and had been loved by her in return.

Because that meant the lovely Widow Banner knew what a good man looked like.

That meant she would eventually recognize those things in Frank.

TWENTY-ONE

MONDAY MORNING, CHARITY ARRIVED at an empty house. She'd come early, hoping to get a jump start on cleaning for a couple of hours before having to start on lunch. She didn't want to wake Frank if he was still sleeping, so she moved quietly around the big rooms of the first floor, setting furniture back in the places they belonged, picking up trash and the odd dish she found abandoned here and there. Evidence the guests had continued to take advantage of her kitchen when no one was around to stop them. The thought annoyed her, but she put it from her mind, remembering to be glad those people were gone, never to return.

Fortunately, the guests hadn't spent a whole lot of time in the downstairs rooms, and by nine o'clock, she was ready to start the vacuum cleaner, but she hadn't heard a peep from upstairs. If he was still sleeping, it was because he needed it. Maybe she should go upstairs and start on some of the bedrooms; she could always vacuum when everything else was finished. Secretly, she also hoped Frank might hear her rustling around. She'd be happy to take a break and whip up an omelet for him.

At the top of the stairs, she peered down the hallway. The doors to all the rooms stood open, some wider than others, revealing various stages of disarray in each one.

Frank's door stood slightly ajar, too.

She eased down the hall, holding her breath, not bothering to look in the rooms she passed. They would look like her kitchen had last week, she was certain, and a woman could only handle so much chaos at a time. She tapped on Frank's door, but there was no answer.

"Frank?" she called out. "You in here?"

There was still no answer, and Charity felt an eerie sense *of deja vu* wash over her. She'd handle things differently this time. She knew him better, and he knew her, too. Surely, she could handle this.

She nudged the door with her foot, pushing it hard enough for it to swing all the way open, eliminating the possibility of him hiding behind it. The room looked empty once again. She dropped to her hands and knees and peered under the bed, but there was nothing under it, either.

Finally, she got to her feet and made a slow, analytical perusal of the room. Freshly—and frighteningly neatly—made bed, sleeping brace placed carefully at the end of the bed near the footboard. Frank wasn't there. He wasn't hiding under the bed or in the closet. He'd put his room to right and left the house sometime that morning, not even bothering to stop in to say hello or welcome back or whatever else she'd hoped for that morning. Where had he gone?

They'd spoken briefly at church, but he hadn't mentioned anything about an early morning project.

Maybe he'd had trouble sleeping and had gone straight to the barn... to his car. She hurried to his bedroom window and looked down at the small gravel parking area near the back porch. His car was gone.

"Well. No reason not to run the vacuum cleaner," Charity said in a bit of a huff. By ten o'clock, she was sweating, angry, and disgusted beyond measure by the condition the guests had left the rooms. She was put out by Frank's absence, too, but she was willing to give him the benefit of the doubt. After stewing over it for a while, she'd reminded herself that he owed her nothing, that she, in fact, owed him for all the help he'd been to her.

"Besides," she told herself. "He'll explain it when he gets back. You know he will."

But Frank wasn't at lunch, and she wasn't about to ask anyone where he was, especially not Cord or Faith. Cord would tell Faith she'd asked, and Faith would tease her mercilessly about her interest in the man and his comings and goings.

By five o'clock, Frank still wasn't home, and she had to get going if she was going to feed her family. She sent up a silent prayer for safety for Frank, hoping he was all right, wishing now that she'd dared to ask Faith about him. What if no one knew he was gone, and something had happened?

She slept fitfully that night, waking herself several times from uncomfortable dreams, and each time, she sent another prayer heavenward for this new man who haunted her dreams.

She hadn't dreamed about Theo in weeks.

TWENTY-TWO

"I BELIEVE YOU'RE GOING about this the right way, Sergeant Flanner," the doctor reiterated. "Per your request, I'm giving you an in-depth list of pros and cons of both options, and I've included legitimate sites online where you can do some of your own research. Please do not randomly search for answers on Google, okay? Everyone and their mother will tell you something different. This is your leg and your future."

Frank nodded, appreciating the man's candor. "No Googling death by amputation," he said with a chuckle. "Check."

Dr. Broderick smiled, then grew serious. "Sir, I need to make something very apparent before I can let you go back to the ranch with a clear conscience."

Frank tensed in his chair across the desk from the surgeon. "Please do," he said.

"If you were to ask me—and you haven't, so I assume that you don't want to know my answer, which means I'm already overstepping my bounds. But like I said..." He paused and picked up a pen from his desk, studying it carefully for a few moments.

"Like you said," Frank prompted. "Clear conscience. I understand. Please proceed."

"If you were to ask me what I would choose if I were in your place," Dr. Broderick said, meeting Frank's eyes again. "Knowing what I know and having seen what I've seen with cases similar to yours, I would, without hesitation, choose amputation. Sooner, rather than later."

Frank held the man's gaze for several long moments. He knew he should say something, but no words came.

"If you choose to try to keep the leg, you have my assurance that my team and I will do everything in our power to help in that endeavor. But if you choose to amputate, your prognosis will be immeasurably—yes, immeasurably—better, your journey to recovery will be much more expedient, and because of your excellent health and strong motivation to succeed, there is every reason to believe that you will live a full and productive life. There is no guarantee you'll be able to return to your duties prior to this accident—I know that's your goal, and I am sorry I can't give you that kind of assurance—but I believe you will be exponentially better off with a prosthesis than with what remains of your leg." He laid the pen down and folded his hands on his desk. "Sir, it is my professional opinion that choosing not to amputate is only putting off the inevitable. I believe that you will eventually end up back here again at a later time, no matter how hard we try to save your limb."

Frank nodded slowly. "Thank you for being so candid. I appreciate it." Up to this point, Dr. Broderick had made it sound like the decision to keep the leg or not was more of a matter of preference than one of sound medical judgment. Now, hearing his surgeon—a man who had become something of a friend over the last several months—tell him so succinctly what he recommended was a bit of a wake-up call.

"I'm officially recommending amputation as of today, Sergeant Flanner. Against my better judgment, I'm willing to give you three more months before we need a decision on how we're going to move forward one way or the other. That's if you last that long. Your leg isn't showing any signs of progress, Sir, and although you look remarkably better, yourself, I'm concerned that if we wait too long, you'll end up suffering needlessly."

"I'd like four months, Dr. Broderick," Frank said quietly. "Preferably five."

The doctor nodded. "I understand. But I'm looking at your leg, Sir, and I don't think you're going to get another five months with it like it is. So, we're going to have this conversation again in October if you last that long, and that will give us enough time to schedule your surgery in plenty of time so you can be home over the holidays. If your leg holds out, you'll get your four months, maybe more." He leaned forward and eyed Frank sternly. "You must continue to come to see me every two weeks between now and then, Sir. I don't know what you're up to, but you don't look like you're sitting around doing crossword puzzles and sipping juice cocktails. Your color is good, you've put on a little weight, and I'm thrilled to see you using the forearm crutches. That is all good progress in my book, but it doesn't have much to do with your leg, and that's the priority for me."

Frank nodded, hating that he wasn't being forthright with the doctor, but confident the man would forbid him to get on a horse, no less ride it daily to round up three hundred head of cattle. "Every two weeks. I'll be here."

"However, if you want to proceed before October, all you have to do is call me or let me know during one of your visits."

"Not likely, but yes, of course," Frank said.

"This kind of below-knee amputation is quick and efficient and effective, Sir."

"I'm sure it is," Frank said wryly. The doctor was right; Frank hadn't asked because he already knew what the good doctor would say. "Again, I appreciate you being straight with me, and to be honest, I think I already knew you'd say just that."

Dr. Broderick studied him as he spoke, but said nothing, so Frank continued.

"I haven't quite put this into words yet, and saying so now feels a little like diving into a frigid lake in winter, but this leave I'm taking is more about learning how to live without my leg, then trying to decide if I can keep it. I think I've known for some time that losing it was inevitable." Frank broke the eye contact first, dropping his gaze to his doctor's folded hands. The hands that would eventually wield the tools used to remove the lower portion of Frank's leg. He had to look away, lest he be sick all over the desk.

Dr. Broderick still said nothing, but he nodded slowly, the lines in his forehead smoothing out in what could only be relief.

"I need this time to come to terms with this, Doc." He was beginning to feel antsy, agitated. He needed to get out of the office and breathe some fresh air.

"I understand," the doctor said quietly. "Use it well." He slid a folder across the desk toward Frank. "Here's your list. Read over it carefully, and when I see you again in two weeks, we can address any questions you might have. We'll take this a day at a time, Sir."

"Thank you, Dr. Broderick. You're a good man." Frank tucked the folder into the canvas messenger bag he wore, then he stood and shook hands with the doctor. "See you in a couple of weeks." Slipping his arms into the brackets on his crutches, Frank left the office without looking back and headed out into the late afternoon sunshine as fast as he could manage without tripping himself up. He made it across the parking lot to his car, his breaths coming in short, shallow gasps, his pulse racing. He practically threw himself into the driver's seat, angling his crutches into the passenger seat, and jerked the door closed behind him, almost catching his braced foot between the door and his seat in his hurry.

He sat there like a stone for several minutes, the warmth of the car settling around him. For a few moments, he thought he might be able to pull himself together after all...Then the gut-wrenching sobs began, rearing up and tearing out of him as he gave in to grief, to loss. To surrender.

As he'd sat there listening to his doctor spell out what Frank already knew, he'd had an epiphany. He wasn't fighting to keep his leg. He was fighting to keep his men alive, to make their loss, their sacrifice, count for something. By letting them take his leg, Frank was symbolically letting the war take his men.

Saying yes to today meant saying no to tomorrow.

It was all so final.

Permanent.

Terminal.

Forever.

TWENTY-THREE

Charity lay wide awake and restless in the hour before dawn, and finally, when the sky began to lighten enough that she wouldn't need to turn on the lights in the kitchen, she got up and headed that way. To her surprise, Daddy was already awake, too. He sat at the table reading his Bible, his brow furrowed as though deep in thought.

"Morning, Daddy," she said softly as she came around the table to kiss the top of his head. "What are you reading that has you so concerned?" She touched the knot of wrinkles between his brows, then turned to peer down at his Bible.

"I wasn't reading," Jed said, smoothing the open pages with his palms. "I was praying. For you and your sisters. I woke up unsettled this morning and couldn't go back to sleep. Figured I'd take the time to do something productive."

"So, you're praying."

"So, I'm praying." He pointed at the coffee carafe. "It's fresh if you'd like some, seeing as how you're up early, too." He slid his cup toward her. "Top me off, too, would you?"

She brought the coffee back to the table and sat down close by. The dark brew was delicious and strong, so aromatic it practically cleared the cobwebs from her mind with the smell alone.

"What's got you rising before the chickens, Charity?" her father asked gently.

She didn't even hesitate. "Frank Flanner."

"Hmm." Jed was notorious for withholding his thoughts until he'd had a chance to ruminate over them.

"I'm kind of worried about him, Daddy. He wasn't there when I got there in the morning, but he didn't leave a note or message telling me he was going anywhere. I know, I know. He doesn't owe me anything," she said, lifting a hand to stave off her father's words. Except there were none to stave off. He simply sat there listening. So, she continued. "I expected him home all day, but I didn't want to ask anyone lest they think I'm interested in him." She rolled her eyes at her father's hesitant smile. "Of course, I'm interested in him. But that's not the point."

"I see," Jed said, nodding slowly.

"The point is that we worked together all last week—well, almost all—and he's come downstairs to help me every morning for a couple of hours. Then yesterday, he just up and leaves without any kind of an explanation. He was gone all day, up until five when I left. It just seemed so out of character for him; I believe he would have told me if he was going to be gone so long." She sighed and added, "It doesn't make sense, and I'm worried about him."

Jed reached out and placed one of his hand over hers where it rested on the table between them. "Let's pray for him. Right now, shall we?"

Charity nodded, her eyes filling with tears. She was so grateful for her father and his strong abiding presence in their lives. She turned her hand over and clung to his, then bowed her head and let her father's words usher a little peace into her soul.

After he said "Amen," Jed lifted his head and smiled adoringly at her. "What are you doing still sitting here with your old dad, sweetheart? Go on, now. Go see if that boy made it home last night."

When Charity entered the kitchen to find Frank already sitting at the butcher block table, a pot of coffee still gurgling through its brew cycle, she was struck by a wave of relief so strong, that she had to pull out a stool and sit before her legs gave out. She covered it up by making a show of setting her purse down on the table and complaining about its weight, but when she looked over at him, her heart sank. His eyes glistened with moisture, his jaw shadowed by growth, and there were circles under his eyes that told her he'd slept less than she did. Something was wrong.

"I missed you yesterday," she said, not quite sure where to begin. To her dismay, a single tear welled up and over his lower lid to slide over his cheekbone and down the side of his face. "Oh, Frank. What is it?" She shoved to her feet, somehow finding an extra measure of strength, and circled the table to his side. Without waiting for an invitation or asking permission, she stepped over the braced foot resting on the rung of another stool, so she was standing between his legs facing him. She cupped his face in her hands and brushed the moisture away with her thumbs. "Hey," she said, her voice gentle and soothing, the way she spoke when she was trying to comfort Jasmine. "Let me help. What can I do?"

He said nothing, just closed his eyes, but he slipped his arms around her waist as he drew her to him. Then he lowered his head against her, his cheek and ear pressed to her chest right over her heart.

It was intimate and tender, yet as innocent as a child, and after the briefest hesitation—she hoped he hadn't noticed—she slid her arms around his shoulders and rested her cheek on top of his head. She felt him draw in a ratcheting, deep gulp of air, then let it out slowly, shakily, his breath warm against the neckline of her shirt. She slid a hand up to cup his head, holding him tenderly to her the way a mother would her child. "It's okay," she murmured, knowing that whatever was wrong, it wasn't okay. "I'm here."

TWENTY-FOUR

IT DIDN'T MATTER WHAT her words were. What mattered was that she was there. She'd come before the sun, and he wasn't alone anymore. He could hear her heart beating sure and strong beneath the frame of her ribcage, and the steady rhythm soothed him. Her palm, cool against the curve of his head, her thumb stroking his cheek as she held him to her. He had a vivid memory of being held like this as a child, but he didn't try to shake it. Instead, he drew on the comfort he'd been offered back then, too, and he missed his mother fiercely.

Charity shifted her weight, the subtle movement making him suddenly and acutely aware that he held a beautiful woman in his arms, that she cradled him against her, and her words, soft and soothing, began to sound soft and sultry to his messed-up head. He slowly straightened, lifting his head from her and loosening his grip around her waist. He didn't let go of her completely—he couldn't quite yet—but he did bring his hands around to take hers. He stared at his leg in the bulky brace, and the thought came to him, fleeting though it was, of how different this scene might have played out if The Beast wasn't there to hinder him.

The destroyed leg and the immobilizing brace brought him down, humbled him, took him out at the knees for real.

But it also brought him to Whispering Hills when he'd made no plans to ever return for anything more than a short visit now and then. It had brought him to her. Would she let him in? Would Theo step aside and allow Frank access to Charity's heart?

"Thank you," he murmured, squeezing her hands gently, his thumbs brushing back and forth over the backs of her wrists. He finally looked up at her and smiled, glad he was no longer teary-eyed. Tired, grieving, yearning, yes. But at least he wasn't crying anymore. "I'm glad you're here this morning. I was dreading facing the next couple of hours alone."

"I'm glad you're here," she said, her brow furrowing as she studied him. She didn't stand much taller than he was with him sitting on the high stool, but he still felt a little vulnerable. "I was so worried about you yesterday. Why didn't you tell me you were going to be gone? Where did you go?"

He frowned and leaned back a little. "I asked Faith to be sure and tell you. I had two doctor's appointment back at Fort Campbell, so I had to head out early, and then I didn't get back here until after dinner last night. She didn't tell you?"

Charity sighed and shook her head. "No, and I didn't ask. I should have asked." She grimaced and gave him a goofy grin. "I didn't want anyone to think I was stalking you or anything, so I just let myself worry all day instead. Smart, huh?"

Frank chuckled softly, the act of laughter, however tentative it was, making the shrouds of worry and fear start to slip from his shoulders. "I should have left you a note. You like notes, I can tell."

Charity nodded, still smiling. "I do. I love notes. And at this point, I'd say don't trust my sister on things like this. I'm not saying this to be cruel, but she's got major pregnancy brain syndrome. She's downright dingy these days, and believe me when I say that Faith Goodacre Overman is not a dingbat."

"Is that a real thing?" Frank asked, completely ignorant when it came to pregnant women. They were walking miracles, that was all he knew, and miracles weren't meant to be understood, right? That's what made them miracles.

"Well," Charity giggled. "It is a thing, but I'm sure it has some classy, medical term. I don't think the doctors and nurses call it pregnancy brain."

They were silent a few moments, then she pulled her hands from his and lifted them to cup his face again. "Frank. What happened yesterday? Did you get bad news?"

He debated making something up. For the first time since his visit with Dr. Broderick, he'd stopped focusing on his leg. Now her questions brought the topic back to the foreground of his thoughts. Instead, he said, "I didn't hear what I wanted to hear, Charity. I'd hoped these two weeks would have made a noticeable difference in my leg, but there's no change."

"And that's what upset you?" It wasn't going to be that easy, apparently.

"Not exactly. Here's the thing, Charity. I need a little time to think things over, to process everything I've been told. I'm not quite ready to share all of it yet, but when I am, would you be willing to be my sounding board?"

"Of course," she murmured. "Absolutely." She smiled and waved a hand around the kitchen before returning it to his face. "You'll know where to find me." Then she leaned forward, kissed his forehead, and stepped away from him. "Can I make you some breakfast?" she asked.

Over the course of the rest of the week, they spent several hours a day together. She only came one other morning for early breakfast, but she was always in the kitchen when he finished his riding sessions with Binks. She greeted him with a warm smile, a bag of ice, and a snack that would have made his doctor proud. Multigrain muffins with fruit, zucchini bread slathered in raw almond butter. Sometimes he was too miserable to sit and eat it like a civilized person downstairs, and on those days, she followed him up with a plate in her hands, waited until he was comfortable, helped him settle the ice on his ankle, then handed him the plate of food. "Eat," she'd say every time. "I'll come to get your plate later."

When he wasn't in bed, he'd offer his help in the kitchen or in the mess hall, and after lunch, he'd escort her back to the ranch to do clean up duty with her. On Saturday morning, he accompanied her to the grocery store, glad to get out of the house, and glad to have someone like Charity to be out of the house with. It was a peaceful—albeit painful—week, but as the days went by, he found that he was growing more and more attached—reattached?—to Plumwood Hollow, to Whispering Hills Ranch, and in particular, to one sweet Charity Goodacre Banner from Seven Virtues Ranch.

TWENTY-FIVE

Sunday morning dawned hot and humid, and by the time Jed herded his ladies out the door, Charity felt like a limp dishrag. She prayed that someone had remembered to come early to turn down the air conditioner at church, but she'd tucked her pretty sandalwood fan in her purse, just in case. It wasn't one of those cheap versions they sold on Amazon or any other big box stores where you got a dozen for ten bucks. Theo had picked this one up at a street market in Afghanistan, and every time she opened it, a heady rush of Middle Eastern aromas made her close her eyes and breathe in appreciatively. The cutout carvings were intricate and delicate beyond belief, and the creator had woven three narrow, rose-hued ribbons into the pattern. A silk tassel hung from the hinge and tapped elegantly against her wrist when she used it.

Charity was already seated when Frank slid into the pew behind her, Binks in tow. Three weeks in a row for the old guy, she mused to herself. She suspected this week his reasons had more to do with the Goodacre Sunday Dinner than what the reverend might offer from the podium, but the Good Lord worked in mysterious ways. If the adage was true as Frank claimed it was, and the way to a man's heart was indeed, through his stomach, then why wouldn't Jesus use Charity's cooking to get Jordan Binks into church on a Sunday morning?

She felt a hand on her shoulder and turned just enough to catch Frank's eye. "Hey, Charity. You still okay with a couple of bachelors crashing your Sunday Dinner?" he asked, leaning forward as he settled his braced leg more comfortably in front of him.

"Absolutely," she said with a nod, then turned to shoot Binks a smile, too. "You boys look nice today."

"Thank you, ma'am," they said in unison, making her laugh softly. Beside her, Prudence giggled, then turned to greet the men.

This week Reverend Treadwell spoke on gratitude, but his message wasn't a reminder to be grateful. Instead, he talked about how easy it was to become complacent when life was good. "Gratitude is not being thankful that you've got it made," the pastor explained. "It's learning to be thankful no matter what your circumstances. Easy, hard, joyful, painful. Like the apostle Paul, we must learn to be thankful in all things. It's easy to sit back on our haunches and appreciate all that the Good Lord has done when your life is overflowing with good things. Real gratitude reveals itself when you can thank him for sustaining you through the loss of a loved one, the terminal diagnosis, the sleepless nights with a colicky baby."

"Amen," some weary-sounding woman murmured from a few rows back, garnering understanding chuckles from several folks in the congregation, including the reverend himself.

It was a good reminder for Charity to be thankful for all that she'd had in her marriage to Theo, in spite of the fact that she'd lost him so soon. It was also a wake-up call for her not to sit back and let life and possibilities pass her by because she wanted to rest comfortably in the memory and security of that relationship. It didn't mean she needed a new man in her life, no. But perhaps it meant that she needed to step out of the security of that complacent comfort zone and see what else God had in store for her, whether it be a new romance, a new career, a new home, or something completely out of left field.

After the service, Charity stopped to talk briefly with Reverend Treadwell, thanking him for his timely message. The pastor gripped her hand in both of his and studied her with a warm smile. "You look especially lovely today, Ms. Charity. There's a new light in your eyes, I think. You still enjoying your work at Whispering Hills?"

"I am," Charity confirmed. "Cooking for people makes me happy."

"Makes us happy, too," Cord said from behind her, resting a hand on her shoulder. "Talk about gratitude, Rev. We are truly grateful for this lady and her culinary skills."

"Hear, hear," Binks and Frank chimed in. Charity glanced over her shoulder and smiled at the men lined up to shake hands with the pastor. She was grateful for each one of those faces, she realized, and in three completely different ways.

Dinner around the Goodacre table was loud and boisterous and messy. Jasmine knocked her glass of lemonade over into the bowl of mashed potatoes, but fortunately, they were nearly gone by then. Daddy dribbled gravy down the front of his Sunday shirt, but that was nothing new. He claimed it was evidence that he'd enjoyed his meal. Abby regaled everyone with tales of guys who came into the parts store looking for the most ridiculous items.

"They hang around, walking the aisles, acting all confused and bewildered over why they can't find what they're looking for. So of course, like the fine customer service rep that I am, I finally go over there to see if I can help. I have never heard so many made up parts names in my life. I swear people think I'm an idiot. And then they have the audacity to ask me out, because hey, if I'm stupid enough to look up the parts number for an inverted cyclical manifold modifier, then surely, I'm stupid enough to say yes, right?" She rolled her eyes, but the smile on her face indicated she wasn't wholly unappreciative of the attention.

Hope, Levi, Yvette, and Nona Valiente joined them for dessert—they'd had some friends of Levi's visiting from New Mexico all week, and they'd taken them to the airport that morning. Yvette and Jasmine flew into each other's arms like they'd been separated since birth, and their parents permitted them to take their plates of peach cobbler outside. "I swear those girls would agree to be sewn together at the hip if we let them," Faith said with a laugh. "It's a good thing you married Mr. Mostacho, Hope. Otherwise, we'd have to kidnap that girl and adopt her as our own." Levi had the finest mustache, bar none, in Plumwood Hollow, and the girls said his superhero name was Mr. Mostacho. No one knew quite what his superpower was—Hope insisted she did, then wiggled her eyebrows so that everyone plugged their ears and closed their eyes, lest they get too much information out of the newlyweds—but they all knew that the man was the best thing that ever happened to their beloved Hope. For that, he deserved to wear a cape. And an epic mustache.

Finally, Jed excused himself, explaining that he never missed a Sunday afternoon nap, and that was the cue for everyone else to wrap things up. The girls made quick work of the dishes, shooing the guys out onto the back porch to talk about whatever guys talked about, and Nona told them some funny stories about Levi growing up as a Mexican cowboy on the vast open plains near the Texas panhandle. Hope glowed with love for her man, beaming over the bits and pieces of his life his mother shared with them.

Charity watched her sister with gratitude once again, thankful that Hope had found such happiness. Thankful that both Faith and Hope, in very different ways, had gotten a second chance at love.

For a fleeting moment, she wondered if she, too, might get a second chance at love. But there was that painful flood of guilt again, the ache for Theo, for the way things were. If only she could go back in time. If only...

There was no gratitude in the 'if only' mindset, was there?

Once the kitchen was spotless, they all trooped out to the sprawling back porch to join the guys. Binks was dozing in a deck chair, slumped down so low it looked like he might just slide right out of it onto the floor. Frank, Levi, and Cord were deep in conversation about cattle, and the vast difference in quality between grass-fed and grass-finished beef.

"Okay, boys," Faith began, moving to stand behind Cord. She leaned down and planted a kiss on his temple. "Your baby mama needs her Sunday afternoon nap, too, Cowboy," she murmured suggestively. There was nothing subtle about how Faith felt about her handsome husband.

Without another word, Cord rose, offered a hand to Frank to help haul him up out of his seat, then turned to shake hands with Levi, who'd also risen to his feet.

Prudence crouched down next to Binks and laid a gentle hand on his forearm where it hung off the armrest. "Mr. Binks?" She spoke softly, a little above a whisper, but the man came to with a start. He had the good sense not to be embarrassed, though.

"You young whippersnappers just wear an old man out. I can't keep up with you." He took his time getting his feet under him, letting loose a jaw-cracking yawn once he was upright. "Boy, take me home. Jed Goodacre has the right idea." He turned to Charity. "I'm sure glad you're my neighbor, Ms. Charity, and even gladder Cordell Overman had the good sense to hire you on. You are a culinary goddess, I do believe. Once a man eats your food, he's doomed to worship at your feet for the rest of his life. Isn't that so, Frankie?"

Frank nodded beside the man and shot a playful wink at Charity. "You know what they say, Binks. The way to a man's heart...." He let the rest of the adage go unspoken but didn't take his eyes of Charity.

"Oh, yes," Binks chuckled, patting his little gut that stuck out just beyond the belt buckle on his jeans.

Charity blushed—she hoped it was becomingly—at Frank's choice of words. She knew he secretly referred to their conversation from the other day, and she hoped everyone else attributed it to the compliments being sent her way. She waved an all-encompassing hand at her sisters. "Everyone helps with Sunday Dinner," she said. "This is a team effort."

"Our lives are a team effort, aren't they, sweetie?" Cord said, pulling his wife close to his side. "Frank?" He looked pointedly at his cousin. "We're glad you're here, man. You shouldn't be going through this season alone, and I, for one, am glad you chose to spend it with us."

"Amen, Big Brother," Prudence interjected softly.

"This group here?" Cord continued, gesturing around the circle with his free hand. "We're your family. We're your team. We've got your back."

"And your foot," Abby chirped from where she sat in the porch swing nearby. "Hey, can I have it if you decide to amputate?"

"Abstinence Goodacre!" The girl's name burst out of several of her sisters' mouths at the same time.

But Charity, to her utter mortification, let loose a laugh that would have put The Wicked Witch of the West to shame. And the harder she tried to curtail it, the more hysterical she sounded. Aghast, with her hands clamped tightly over her traitorous mouth, she turned to dash inside, but when she saw Binks, she staggered to a halt.

He'd fallen back into his chair in hysterics; he was laughing so hard that tears were squeezing from the corners of his eyes.

Frank, too, began to chuckle, and then no one bothered trying to hold back.

Abby, unabashedly irreverent as ever, pushed off the swing and made her way to the door. "And... my work here is done," she quipped in a raised voice before heading inside. The door swung open again, and she said, "Thanks for the fantastic meal, Charity. Awesome as always."

To Frank, she offered one last parting shot. "Think about it, Frank. I know a good taxidermist." Then the door closed behind her.

TWENTY-SIX

FRANK COULDN'T REMEMBER THE last time he'd laughed like that, and he certainly couldn't recall Binks ever letting loose that way, not in all the years he'd known him. Charity had apologized profusely for starting it, but he'd assured her repeatedly that not only was he reasonably sure it was Binks who'd laughed first, but that their laughter had indeed, been good medicine for everyone, especially him. Because something had happened there on the Goodacre porch. Abby's seemingly callous request had broken something loose inside Frank's chest, and it was as though he could suddenly breathe easier.

Add to that the words Cord had spoken: *We're your family. We're your team.* Wasn't that precisely what Frank had come here for? In search of a team of his own? And here they were, not just available, but offering. They wanted to walk through this with him.

If anyone deserved his amputated foot, it was Abby. He'd have to ask what the hospital would do with his foot when they took it off; if nothing else, Dr. Broderick would get a kick out of the story.

If he amputated.

But then, he realized that's what had changed.

When he amputated.

Somewhere inside him, a little ember of acceptance had started to glow, and as much as he wanted to fight it, as much as he argued that there was still time, still a chance, that ember would not go out.

As he lay in bed that night, the cold pack strapped around his ankle with an elastic bandage, and for the first time, Frank spent some time freely imagining life without his mangled foot. Life without this never-ending pain. Life without pain pills and cold packs, without worrying about infection and tissue rejection. Without braces strapped to his leg, or crutches clamped around his forearms, or rubbing raw spots under his arms or calluses on his palms from the crutches. He contemplated what it would feel like to wear a prosthesis, knowing at first it would be some ugly plastic molded foot with a fixed ankle and fused toes.

Then again, wasn't that pretty much what he had now? His foot was a whole lot uglier than any prosthesis he'd ever seen, and his three smallest toes were already fused.

Eventually, as things healed, he'd progress to something more realistic, perhaps something high tech with an animatronics foot. Or better yet, all mechanical and geared-out. He pictured himself pulling on a protective compression sock over the stump that would remain below his knee, of sliding the cup of an artificial limb in place, the dead weight of it hanging at the bottom of his leg. He thought about being able to put weight on his leg without having to clench his jaw to keep from crying out. He imagined walking without limping. He closed his eyes and envisioned himself in one of those running blade prosthetics, jogging around the track at the base, or maybe even here at the ranch. Perhaps he could talk Cord into laying a track down around the perimeter of one of the arenas so he could practice walking, jogging, and even running again.

He lay in the dark listening to the familiar sounds of a working ranch—horses nickering softly in one of the nearby barns, cattle lowing in the far pastures, guard dogs barking every hour on the hour like clockwork to remind any curious predators they were on the prowl. There was something otherworldly about it all, and yet this place embodied everything that was natural and down to earth as anything Frank could imagine.

When they'd first broached the subject of amputation months ago, his doctor had explained the process slowly and carefully, leaving out no details of the procedure, the recovery, the rehabilitation, and all the ups and downs that went with learning to live with an amputated limb. At the time, it had been far too overwhelming for Frank to do any more than listen and try to absorb. Now, it was as though he'd experienced some paradigm shift in the three weeks he'd been back. Now, knowing that he was surrounded by friends and family who saw beneath the scars to the man he was, who wouldn't think any less of him if there was one foot less of him. Now, knowing that just on the other side of the finger of woods that separated Whispering Hills Ranch from Seven Virtues Ranch slept a woman who might make staying in Plumwood Hollow worth considering....

He couldn't go there, not yet. Not until he decided what he was going to do. Or rather, when he was going to do it.

Because the more he thought about his destroyed limb, the more appealing things were beginning to look without it.

At present, though, Frank had a commitment to fulfill. He had fewer than two weeks to master being back in the saddle, and to get comfortable with the job of rotating the cattle every day, by himself if need be so that Faith could get off her horse and give birth to a healthy baby in the fall. As soon as she was ready to take over again, he'd head on back to Fort Campbell, have that consultation with Dr. Broderick, and they'd get the ball rolling to get rid of this dead weight once and for all.

Monday morning, Frank arose early and headed downstairs, following his nose to the kitchen where he found Charity already at work, the coffee maker gurgling invitingly. "Good morning," he said from the doorway, momentarily wondering if he had the right to be so pleased to find her there.

"Hey, Frank," she replied, sending a warm smile his way. "I was thinking about making some French toast. I have this delicious potato bread I made this weekend, and I've never made French toast with it before. Want to be my guinea pig? See if it works?" She sounded a little nervous, but he was pretty sure she was almost as glad to see him as he was to see her.

"I'll be your guinea pig any time," he volunteered, skirting the worktable to sit on the far side where he'd be out of her way, but where he'd be able to watch her move comfortably around the kitchen. "I'll try anything you whip up."

"Coffee?" she asked without looking at him. She pulled two mugs from the cupboard, filled them, then leaned across the table to hand him one.

"Thank you. Smells amazing." He brought the brew to his nose and inhaled slowly, filling his senses with the dark roast flavor.

Charity took a careful sip of her own cup, then set it aside and began cracking eggs into a Pyrex bowl. With a long-handled whisk, she whipped the eggs into a frothy liquid, her arm moving too fast for his eyes to follow. Without measuring anything, she poured in some half-and-half, vanilla, a good-sized scoop of cinnamon, followed by several passes with a little grinder. "It's nutmeg," she said, holding up the clear contraption with its little crank arm so he could see the pecan-sized seed inside. "It's so much better ground fresh—here. Smell this." She sprinkled a little in the palm of her hand and held it out toward him. "Rub it between your thumb and finger. Doesn't that smell like Christmas?"

Frank did as she instructed, bringing a pinch of the ground nutmeg to his nose. "Wow," he murmured, appreciating the intense aroma.

"See that color? Isn't it gorgeous? My horse's mane is that color; guess what her name is." She beamed at him as though it was the cleverest thing in the world, and he couldn't help but chuckle.

"I'm going to take a wild guess and go with Nutmeg," he said.

"Ding, ding, ding, ding!" She pretended she was beating a gong or a triangle. "You win a piece of French toast, Sir!"

"So, is nutmeg actually a nut?" he asked. It wasn't so much that he wanted to know, only that he really didn't want her to stop talking to him.

"No, no," she said, carrying the bowl of egg batter to the stove top where a large griddle was already heating up on it. "It's a seed. Just like coconut," she added, pulling a huge jar of coconut oil from the cupboard. She scooped out a generous spoonful of the pure white butter, then dropped it onto the hot griddle before spreading it around with a spatula. "Best oil to cook with, hands down," she said, tapping the side of the jar. "That's a seed that's gotten a bad rap over the years; I'm so glad people are finally promoting the benefits of it. There's nothing like the hint of coconut flavor in a batch of roasted vegetables, or in a pot of steamed rice, and you don't get the carcinogens that you do from cooking with other oils."

"I see," said Frank, attempting to hide his grin behind his mug.

Charity glanced up from the slice of bread she was dipping into the batter. She smiled apologetically when she saw his face. "I'm sorry for the food politics lecture," she said, ducking her head self-consciously. "I just love this stuff; it's my life, you know?"

"Coconut oil or politics? Or nutmeg?" he teased.

"Cooking, silly."

"That's First Sergeant Silly Boy to you," he shot back.

Charity guffawed heartily and shook her head. "No, no, no. That does not have the same ring to it. I refuse to call you that."

"Thank God," Frank said, sighing dramatically and wiping his forehead with great relief. "As soon as it was out, I knew it was wrong in every way."

Charity turned and leaned back against the counter, close enough to monitor the bread on the griddle. "Yum, that smells good," she murmured, more to herself than to him, but he nodded in agreement. "Hungry?" she asked. "I'm cooking for Binks, too, since I had to come early today."

So, she wasn't here just to cook him breakfast. A man could hope, right? "I am," Frank confirmed. "Binks has been working me hard, and my appetite shows it." He propped his leg up on the rung of a stool beside him. "So other than whipping up a meal for us guys, why are you here so early?"

Charity waved at two enormous roaster ovens on opposite sides of the kitchen. "I'm slow-cooking chicken ahead of time, so I can throw it on the grill right before lunch and crisp it up quick. It needs about three and a half hours in the roasters." She walked over and lifted the lid on one, releasing an aromatic cloud of steam into the room. "Can you smell that? I make this special rub with smoked paprika, turmeric, minced garlic, a little cayenne pepper, sea salt and pepper, and some of Prudence's honey."

He loved listening to her talk about food and cooking. She was so passionate about even the simplest things, and when she got on a roll, her features grew more and more animated, her eyes lit up, and she practically glowed. "I'm kinda drooling over here just hearing you describe it, but yeah, it smells amazing. You amaze me."

She smiled appreciatively at his compliment and hurried back to the skillet to flip her French toast. It was browned perfectly. Of course. "Do you see the golden-orange color?" she asked, waving her spatula over the top of the griddle. "Know what that's from?"

Frank shook his head, grinning at her enthusiasm.

"Duck eggs. Free range ducks. Their yolks are such an intense yellow this time of year from all the protein they eat. It turns anything you use them in this beautiful, almost pumpkin color. Isn't it cool?" She scooped up two slices and placed them on a plate she'd been warming in the oven. "You ready for these now or do you want to wait for your partner in crime?" She held the dish out.

"I'm fine to wait. Gives me more time to sit and visit with you."

Charity nodded, then slid the plate back into the oven. Keeping her eyes on her task, she dipped a few more slices of bread in the egg batter—it was, indeed, a brilliant color—and he listened to the sizzle when she carefully placed each one on the griddle. Finally, she turned around again, took a sip of her coffee, and said, "Frank, I want to ask you a pretty personal question. Is that okay?"

In the large peaceful kitchen, the combination of heavenly fragrances wafting around them, Frank felt an intimacy that rarely existed in any of the places he'd lived over the past fifteen years, and it stirred a sweet memory from his childhood. He had no clue how old he'd been, but one morning, he'd awakened before dawn, and had come down downstairs to raid the pantry. His parents were already there, and although they never noticed him, he'd stood just outside the doorway in the darkened dining room and watched them for a few moments. His father, a big, burly man, stood behind his mother, arms around her waist, his hands spread flat and low over her belly. At first, Frank thought his father was kissing her neck, but he soon realized he was whispering something to her, words that made her duck her head and smile. Then she turned in his arms and reached up to cup his face in both hands, stood on tiptoe, and kissed him. It started out soft and quick, a light brushing of lips against lips, but when she started to pull away, his father didn't release her. Instead, he started walking backward toward Frank's hiding place. "Let's try again," Judge said in a low murmur, keeping his wife held against him, pulling her along with him. Frank had scurried upstairs as fast as he could, knowing he'd witnessed something private, but not sure exactly what. He'd seen his parents kiss a thousand times, but there was something in the way they held onto each other that felt different to him.

Now, in hindsight, he knew. He faintly recalled talk of another child long ago, but by the time he was eight or ten, no one brought it up, and when he asked, the answer was always the same. "You are everything we could ever want in a child, Frankie." Maybe that was why they'd insisted on having Cord come to stay with them every summer. Maybe that was why his mother had made such an effort to watch out for the Goodacre girls—she often came and went from their place throughout the week, and Frank had never been able to figure out why. Who'd want to hang out with a bunch of girls?

"I'm sorry," Charity said, dropping her gaze to her feet. "I shouldn't be prying."

"No, no!" Frank held up a hand to stop her apology. "It's definitely okay. I just got lost in a memory there for a minute. In this kitchen from a thousand years ago. My parents."

"Oh." She lifted her eyes again. "Was it a good memory?"

"It was. I happened upon them early one morning in this room," he said. "Sitting here talking with you like this? It's a good way to start a day, Charity. Thank you."

"Oh," she said again. Then she smiled shyly. "It is nice."

There it was again, that aching vulnerability in her eyes. If it hadn't been for the table between them, Frank would have taken the spatula from her hand and pulled her, ever so gently, into his arms. And maybe, just maybe, she would have reached up to cup his face, stood on tiptoe, and brushed her lips against his.

Frank's stomach gurgled, and he chuckled a little self-consciously. "That old man better hurry or I'll eat his share. I'm famished, and all this talk of food isn't helping. So, what was it you were going to ask me?"

TWENTY-SEVEN

For a moment, Charity couldn't remember. The way he'd looked at her just then, his eyes roaming slowly over her face and stopping at her mouth, the same way it happened in movies right before the guy kissed the girl. She'd had to clamp her teeth together to keep from nervously licking her lips; she didn't want to send him the wrong message and make it look like she actually wanted that...

Except that something inside her actually did want that.

The more she'd ruminated over Pastor Treadwell's message, the more she questioned her quiet determination that her marriage to Theo was forever. Her love for him, absolutely; she couldn't imagine no longer loving the man she'd married. But as she opened her eyes in the still quiet of that predawn morning, her first thought was that it wasn't gratitude that kept her bound to that beautiful, beautiful man, but complacency and false security and... well, fear.

There is no fear in love, but perfect love casts out fear. For fear has to do with punishment, and whoever fears has not been perfected in love.

She'd read those verses in her Bible that morning, lying in her big, empty bed, her back curled against Theo's pillow. The words, so simple and straightforward, had pierced her to the core, and she'd wept softly into her own pillow. "I don't want to be afraid, Theo," she'd whispered, talking more to God than to the memory of her husband. "I don't want to forget my husband, God," she whimpered. "I don't want to move on and leave him behind. But I don't think I'm supposed to stay here any longer in this in-between place."

Do you love me?

"Yes, Jesus. I love you." And before that little voice in her head could complete the conversation Jesus had shared with his disciple Peter in the New Testament, she smiled sadly and said, "I know, I know. Feed your lambs. Take care of your sheep." She brushed away her tears and turned onto her back to gaze up at the ceiling. It wasn't so dark anymore, and she could make out the feminine chandelier light fixture she'd purchased with her own money back in high school. It was made up of pale pink glass pendants with ropes of iridescent pearls strung between the lights. Theo had laughed when she'd asked if she could hang it over their bed, but when he saw that she was serious, his expression had gone from humorous to appalled to carefully neutral in under a second. Charity had left it behind, but the first night back in this room, she'd fallen asleep with the pale crystal light casting a warm glow over her.

"Are you okay?" Frank asked, bringing her back to the moment.

She nodded, flipped the bread on the griddle, then crossed her arms and leaned against the counter to face him. "How long do you think you'll be here? In Plumwood Hollow?"

The bemused look on his face told her that wasn't the question he was expecting. It wasn't exactly the question she'd started out asking, either, but it was something she decided she needed to know first.

He frowned, took a sip of coffee, and then shrugged one shoulder. "I'm not sure, Charity." He spoke with such solemnity that she felt a little guilty for asking. "A lot will depend on what I end up doing with this leg of mine."

Charity didn't say anything, but she nodded encouragingly.

"I'd like to stay long enough to relieve Faith until she's ready to take her job back. Of course, that's contingent on how quickly I can get this leg to bend to my will." He tapped his knee with a long finger.

"And if it doesn't? Bend?" she asked.

He shot her a subdued look. "I can't think like that right now," he finally said.

"Why not? You're a First Sergeant, Frank. Isn't that your job? Study all the angles, consider all the options, play out all the possible scenarios?" She was challenging him, yes, but she didn't like the look on his face. Was that denial? "Shouldn't you, of all people, be thinking about the future?"

His eyebrows rose, and he cocked his head at her. "I think your toast is burning."

Sure enough, the four pieces on the griddle were starting to smoke. She quickly flipped them, thankful to see that only the edges were beginning to blacken, then waved away the scent of charcoal until it dissipated among the other smells in the kitchen. "Thanks." She wasn't going to ask him again, but she wondered if that had been his way of telling her he wasn't going to answer her after all.

"Listen, Charity," he began, not waiting for her to turn around. "I didn't say I haven't thought about it. I said I can't think that way right now."

She glanced at him over her shoulder, then focused again on the last two pieces of bread she was dipping in her batter. "Why not?"

"Because people are counting on me. That's another part of a First Sergeant's job; to be there when I say I will. To make good on my promises." He pushed to his feet, and a wave of disappointment washed over Charity. He was going to leave. She'd upset him, and he was going to walk away.

"Doesn't seem like a First Sergeant quality to me," she muttered, keeping her back to him.

"I'm not sure I follow," Frank said, making his way around the table. From the corner of her eye, she could see him leaning heavily against it as he moved.

"You're just going to walk out because you don't like my questions? Not cool, Frank. In fact, it's pretty childish." She dropped the last two pieces of battered bread none too gently onto the griddle, then spun around to face him. Except he wasn't leaving. He was refilling his coffee and topping hers off; she'd all but forgotten about it, having set it down near the sink earlier.

"Here," he said, holding it out to her with both hands. He was only a few feet away, but the length of the counter between them suddenly felt like an insurmountable distance. "I thought you could use a warming up."

"Sorry," she muttered, barely able to meet his eyes.

He dismissed her apology with a smile, then edged a little closer to her. "Peace offering."

When she reached for the mug, he didn't let go immediately. "What?" she asked, feeling ashamed and rattled and a little breathless at the same time. He was too close.

"There are some other things that will determine the length of my stay here, Charity." He bent forward a little in an attempt to get her to look at him. When she didn't, he moved closer. If she weren't already leaning against the counter, she'd have backed away. "My doctors, for one. I have to go back every two weeks for them to decide whether or not I'm treating my leg right."

"Oh. Well, that's good. I'm glad you're being monitored by someone who knows what they're doing." He took a hobbling step closer, but to her relief, he let go of the mug. She lifted the coffee to her lips, praying it wasn't too hot.

"And there's also Hidalgo. He's doing great, but he's always spooked a little easier than most. He might do fine in the arena, but who knows what he'll do once we're out in the pasture. He used to get a kick out of trying to throw me, but I can't risk that kind of behavior with this leg. A fall could be bad." He was so close, that he didn't have to speak in more than a low rumble.

She thought she could feel the vibrations of his voice across her skin and barely held a shiver in check. "Right. Right," she murmured, wishing Binks would make an appearance.

Frank leaned closer.

"What—what are you—?"

He reached around her, picked up her spatula, and flipped the two pieces of bread on the griddle. His arm brushed against her shoulder.

"Oh," she said again. "Thank you."

"There's one more thing," Frank said, setting the tool down, then reaching for her cup of coffee. He took it from her and set it on the counter beside the spatula.

"Um..." It was little more than a whisper.

Frank didn't step back. Instead, he planted his hands on the edge of the counter on either side of her, then dipped his head so he could see her face. "Charity?"

"Hm?" She did lick her lips now.

"Will you look at me? Please?" Every word came out as a caress, making her skin tingle and her pulse race.

"Okay," she said, but it was several seconds before she worked up the courage to do so. What she saw in his eyes both terrified and thrilled her, and she held her breath as he studied her.

"You," he finally said. "A lot depends on you."

"Oh."

"Yeah. Oh." He grinned down at her. "Think you could do me a favor?"

"Um, sure." It was a shaky whisper now.

"Turn that griddle off, then put your arms around me, so I don't fall over when I kiss you."

A breathy giggle escaped, but she murmured, "Yes sir, First Sergeant Soldier Boy."

The moment her arms were around his waist, he brought one hand up to cup her face, still clutching the counter with his other one for balance. Then he lifted her chin before lowering his mouth to hers.

Not Theo, not by a long shot.

This was Frank. And it was good.

"Ahem." From a long way off, the sound of a man's throat clearing broke through Charity's euphoria. Frank lifted his head slowly, as though he, too, were in a bit of a fog.

"Oh, hey there, man," he said, the rough texture of his voice sending another shiver through Charity. He stayed right where he was, though, Charity trapped between him and the counter. "I think breakfast is ready."

Binks chuckled and shook his head. "Your mama always said you couldn't eat until you kissed the cook. It's good to see you remember your upbringing, boy." To Charity, he said, "Smells mighty fine in here, Ms. Charity. Like French toast and roasted chicken."

"Wow, you're good," Charity said with an embarrassed giggle. She knew her cheeks had to be the color of Faith's favorite Pink Lady apples, and she rested her forehead against Frank's chest for a moment before carefully easing her arms from around his waist. "Don't fall," she whispered to Frank.

"I think I could leap the highest mountain right now," he answered gruffly. "We'll finish this conversation later."

"Is that what you kids are calling it these days?" Binks asked, coming around the table to check out what was on the griddle. "Conversation?"

"Nothing wrong with your hearing, old man," Frank laughed, hobbling a few steps back to give Charity room.

Her lips felt tender, almost bruised, but the kiss had been so gentle and sweet, an intimate exploration of the way their mouths moved together. Without thinking, she reached up to touch her bottom lip, then caught Frank's knowing smile from the corner of her eye. If she wasn't blushing before, she was now.

It had been a long time since she'd been kissed like that. Years. And as awkward and out of practice as she'd felt, her body had recognized the act immediately, and she'd found herself melting against Frank, clinging to his strength, hoping he had a good grip on the counter, because if he did topple over, she'd go down with him. Every nerve ending in her body seemed to spark and hum at random, and when she pulled the hot plate heaped high with French toast from the oven, she was trembling so bad she was afraid she'd drop it.

"Go ahead and dish up, you two. The syrup is already warm but be careful. The jar is hot." She didn't use the microwave, not for real maple syrup. She warmed it by placing it in a saucepan of hot water on the stove top, instead. Not only did it stay hot longer, but it didn't change the flavor of the syrup, either. "There's butter in that covered dish on the counter over there, Binks; can you grab it?" Busying herself around the kitchen always helped soothe her nerves, and as she dug out the peanut butter and the shaker jar of powdered sugar from the pantry, then the bowl of fruit salad from the fridge, she began to find her rhythm again.

"You going to join us, Ms. Charity?" Binks asked as he pulled out a stool and lowered himself onto it. "Looks like there's enough here to feed all three of us twice over."

"I made extra so you two could have some tomorrow morning, too," she explained. "But yes, this morning, I'm starving, so I'm joining you." She quickly filled a plate and settled onto one of the remaining stools. "Which of you boys wants to say the blessing?" Without thinking, she reached out for both their hands, then giggled when Frank and Binks looked askance at each other before linking hands between them. "Actually," she said. "I'll say the blessing. I have a lot to be thankful for."

Her prayer was short and sweet, and rather than listing all the things she was grateful for; she merely thanked God for his provision and his plan. "Dig in," she commanded as soon as she lifted her head.

TWENTY-EIGHT

He hadn't planned to kiss her. Not yet, anyway. He'd planned to wait until the end of the month at least, until after he'd spent a few more mornings in the saddle. A few more coffee breaks with Charity. A few more evenings missing her. Not until after he returned from his next checkup with Dr. Broderick. He wanted to be able to give her some of the answers she was after.

But something in the way she'd looked at him, in the way she'd smiled and got all jittery as he approached....

Well, there'd been nothing to do but kiss her.

And she'd kissed him back. His heart still hadn't settled back into its normal rhythm, and he was okay with that.

They'd shared some significant looks over lunch, but then he'd missed catching her before she left for the day. Frank was okay with that, too. He had the feeling that like Hidalgo, Charity might spook a little easier than some, and if he moved too quickly, she'd retreat. Although he would never tell her so to her face, she reminded him a little of when he'd first got the Paint. The horse had been rescued with several others from an illegal breeder, and although the animal was clearly of exceptional lineage, it had a healthy fear of humans, especially men. Hidalgo shied away from him again and again, to the point that Frank had almost given up on him. Then one day, discouraged and ready to throw in the hat, Frank dropped to the ground to sit with his back against a fencepost, and dropped his chin to his chest, eyes closed. About five minutes later, a shadow fell over him, but he didn't lift his head. Instead, he opened his eyes and watched as Hidalgo pawed the ground, took a step closer, pawed some more, stepped closer, nickered softly, then stepped close enough to nibble at Frank's hair.

Frank didn't move.

Hidalgo nudged him in the cheek with his nose.

Frank didn't move.

Hidalgo nudged harder.

Frank turned on his rear-end, so his back was to the horse.

Hidalgo pawed the ground and rested his head on his shoulder. The animal remained close as Frank reached up to stroke the long nose and murmured ugly words in a gentle, soothing voice—he was still pretty ticked at the animal, after all.

It had been the start of a delicate dance they'd mastered over the years, and now, Frank felt like he was learning those steps all over again, but this time with the lovely Charity Banner, instead.

Tuesday morning, Charity arrived later than she'd intended; she'd been helping her father with his gardening because his back was bothering him, and she'd lost track of time. By the time she rushed into the kitchen, she was on a tear, barely even acknowledging him as he ducked through.

Frank made a point to let her know how delicious the meal was—right in front of Skid Maddox—and how much he appreciated all her hard work. Skid had chimed in, equally appreciative, then offered to carry Frank's plate back to the table for him. If it had been any other guy, Frank would have been certain the gesture was intended as a sucker punch to his pride, but Skid seemed to have become one of those genuinely gregarious guys who didn't take anything too personally. They sat together most lunches these days, regaling the others with old high school football glory days, or dredging up memories of those summers with half the teenage population of Plumwood Hollow working with the cattle at Whispering Hills in the mornings, then swimming in the lake in the afternoons. "Skinny dipping down at Mr. Truman's lake; remember that?" Someone always brought up Saturday nights at Teddy Truman's lake, until talk turned to the number of girls who were there—or rather, weren't there. Because as risqué as it sounded, there were rarely any female body parts being flaunted. Jenny Stuben didn't really count, not because she didn't participate, but because she never missed an opportunity to—literally—jump into the thick of things. She liked to say she was just one of the guys, but no guy ever looked like Jenny Stuben, that was for sure.

By the time he made it back to the house, Charity was putting the last of the dishes away. She looked a little roughed up. "You all right?" Frank asked. "I mean, you look beautiful," he amended when he saw her shoulders droop. "You always do."

"Thank you, Frank." She rolled her eyes, but a small smile told him he'd said the right thing. "I'm worried about Abby, that's all. She's been kinda withdrawn and moody, and I can't tell if she's still being a turbulent teen or if she's having trouble dealing with this whole growing up thing. Daddy and I talked for quite a while this morning, and he's worried, too."

"I don't know how your father is still alive. I can't imagine trying to survive seven daughters; and not because of the turbulent teens," he said with a chuckle. "I just mean I'd probably spend more time in jail than out since I know personally what goes through a teenage boy's mind."

Charity guffawed and sank onto one of the stools. "I just wish she'd talk to me. To any of us. She used to share more with Faith, maybe just because Faith was kinda like her mom after ours died, and then she was a mom for real once she had Jasmine, of course." She sighed and shook her head. "Sorry. None of this is any of your problem. I'm just dragging around a little today. I'm glad you liked the casserole, though. It was kinda thrown together last minute."

"Anything with ham and potatoes works for me," Frank said, pulling out a stool to sit across from her. "And the condition of your heart is my problem, Charity. Or at least, I'd like it to be." He leaned forward and slid his hand across the table toward her. She placed hers in his, and he covered it with his other one, her smooth, delicate skin warm against his work-roughened palms. "I'm amazed at you, Mrs. Banner." The name rolled off his tongue, the title not bothering him at all. She was a married woman; there was no getting around that. And as much as he didn't want her thinking about Mr. Banner—Theo—while sitting across the table from him, Frank knew that if he were going to break through some of her carefully-constructed walls, he'd have to convince her that he understood that Theo was a part of her, one that he accepted. "Every one of your waking moments seems to be taken up caring for other people. For your father, your sisters." He winked. "For Studmore Mad Maddox—"

"Oh, my gosh!" she exclaimed, tugging at her hand. He refused to release her. "You *were* eavesdropping that day. How long were you standing outside the kitchen door?"

"Long enough to hear you tell your sister how much you enjoyed seeing me half-naked."

"I—" She pulled harder. "Did not—let go!" He laughed and tugged back. "Say that!" she finished, but she was blushing furiously, and the slightly guilty look in her eyes made him want to tease her more, but he didn't.

"Okay, fine. You didn't say it. But I'm pretty sure you enjoyed it anyway."

"What was it I called you the other day? Egotistical, I believe it was." But she wasn't pulling away anymore.

"And here I was trying to pay you a compliment. Because I'm serious about all this. You look out for everyone, don't you? Your family. Binks. This ranch and its high-falutin' guests."

Charity laughed. "Be nice. The Bastions were lovely people."

"No, they weren't." He shook his head slowly, holding her gaze with his. "At best, they were nice. They were also self-absorbed and self-important and completely unaware of how much of a burden they were," he said, his thumb moving in slow circles over the back of her hand. "And you? You took it all in stride like the pro you are. I, on the other hand, avoided them like the plague because I'm a big chicken."

"Hardly," she shot back. "You're braver than anyone I know."

"You think so?" he asked, wondering why she'd think that.

"I know so. I know what you do for a living, Frank." Her expression grew serious. "And I can see how difficult it is for you to be here, facing what you're facing, knowing your men are still out there fighting without you. It takes a very courageous man to get up in the morning with all that resting on your shoulders."

"Thank you." He meant it. He didn't feel brave very often these days, but somehow, when she said it, he wanted to believe it about himself. "Coming from you, Mrs. Banner, that means more to me than you'll ever know."

"Why do you call me that?" she asked, just above a whisper. He didn't have to ask her to clarify.

"It's who you are," he said, hoping she'd understand his motives. "Does it bother you?"

"I—I don't know." She shrugged one shoulder. "Up until you started saying it, no."

He frowned. "I'm sorry. I don't mean to offend you." That was not the response he'd hoped for.

"It doesn't offend me, Frank. It bothers me for a different reason." She lifted her eyes to his, and hers were bright with unshed tears. "I want to tell you something, and I'm afraid to, because I don't know if you'll like what I have to say." She inhaled deeply, and the next words came out on an exhale. "But I'm going to anyway, okay?"

Frank swallowed hard, suddenly worried, but he did his best to keep his composure. "Okay. I'm ready." He squeezed her hand again to encourage them both.

"On Sunday, Pastor Treadwell talked about gratitude in the good and the hard times. He also talked about how easy it is to get comfortable when things are good, how easy it is to hang out there even when God has other plans for us that might be challenging. That's when it stops being gratitude, you know?" She paused, but he knew exactly what she was talking about. He'd paid close attention to the message, too.

"That's when it becomes fear. I know. Fear of the unknown. Fear that God won't come through for us. I know." He nodded.

"Right. Frank," she began, then cleared her throat politely and tried again. "Frank, I've been living in this—this bubble, I guess, ever since Theo—my husband—died. Faith told me Cord filled you in on the details, so unless you want to hear my version of it, I'll leave it at that, okay?"

"I've been there, Charity." He wasn't about to call her Mrs. Banner now. "I get it."

"I know you do." She sighed and chewed on her lip a moment before continuing. "I started out grateful; I did. Grieving, of course, but grateful for the wonderful man God gave me. Grateful that he loved me so much. Grateful for every moment of the time we got to share, even though it wasn't nearly enough. Grateful that my husband got to do what he loved: fight for his country. He was a soldier, through and through. Like you," she added.

Frank nodded. "I've heard nothing but good things about Theo," he said, honoring the man by calling him by his name.

Charity sent him a sad, sweet smile. "But over the years, it's changed. It shifted without me even realizing it. Somewhere along the line, I stopped living in the moment, in today, and I've gone backward. I've spent the last year, maybe longer, living in the past, too afraid to let Theo go and face the future without him. I've been so busy being grateful for what I had in the past that I'm missing out on what I have in the present."

Frank nodded again, but this time, he said nothing. Her words may have been about her, but he felt each one of them like a scalpel to an infected wound, cutting and releasing, opening and expelling, until he was left raw and bleeding, but cleaned out.

"I think that's why I'm so focused on everyone else. I want everyone around me to be happy, satisfied, and whole. I'm kinda living today vicariously through everyone else so that I can stay in the safe little cocoon of my past. Does that make sense?"

"Yes." He didn't trust himself to say more.

"Frank, I really like you. You did scare me nearly to death that first morning when you rose up out of the dark like some phantom freak." She smiled tenderly and shrugged again. "But then you threw yourself on top of me to protect me from enemy fire—"

Frank grunted in self-loathing, but she kept talking. "And you saved me. See? I survived. I'm whole and intact." Her gentle smile became a mischievous grin. "Then you took your shirt off and let me use it to blow my nose, and all I could think of was how gallant you were. And yes, how lovely you looked half-naked."

He frowned playfully and cocked his head at her. "Lovely? Doesn't sound very manly. And besides, there's all this messed up flesh," he said, gesturing to his whole left side. "You haven't seen the worst of it, yet."

"Oh, but lovely is manly, Frank. In the best sense of the word. You call someone lovely when he or she elicits love by moral and ideal value. Look it up."

"Wow." What exactly was she saying? He found he was half holding his breath.

"Your scars mean more to me than you can possibly imagine," she said, her voice growing tight for a moment. "To me, they are tangible, beautiful, exquisite proof that you—that you survived." The last word was only a whisper, but she swallowed the lump in her throat and pressed on. "And I'm grateful for every single one of them, even the ones I haven't seen. Especially the ones I haven't seen. Maybe even the ones you haven't seen, Frank." She pulled his hand toward her so that he had to lean forward over the table. She held his gaze with her own. "My sister told me about your leg. About the problems you've had and the decision you have to make. Don't risk your life for your foot, Frank. Don't hold on to your past and miss out on today because you don't know what tomorrow will bring."

"Charity." Once again at a loss for words, he shook his head in disbelief at how her words lined up with what Binks had said to him several weeks ago. How they resonated with what he was feeling about himself, his leg, and about her.

But she wasn't finished. "I don't want to miss out on you today because I'm living in the past without you, or because I'm afraid of what might happen with you tomorrow," she said, the statement coming out in a rush. "I feel like a different person when I'm around you, Frank. I certainly don't feel like Mrs. Banner when I'm with you, even if that's who I am. I feel like...well, I can't quite label it yet. Besides, I'm sure it's way too early to call it anything, anyway. At least I'm sure that's what all the shrinks in the world would tell me." She giggled nervously and closed her eyes briefly. When she opened them again, she looked directly into his. "I don't want to miss out on you. And I really, really hope you don't want to miss out on me."

If Frank could have launched himself across the table at that moment, he would have. If he could have shoved it out from between them, he would have. If he could have quoted her the most eloquent love poem in the world, he would have. Instead, he simply said, "I'm not afraid to call it as

I see it, Charity. I'm falling in love with you, and I think you're falling in love with me, too."

A hushed silence settled around them, the only sound the gentle hum of the refrigerator accompanied by the ticking of his mother's beautiful Bulova clock.

"Okay," she finally whispered. Then she carefully pulled her hand free of his and stood. He didn't try to stop her. "I need to go. I want to try to catch Abby before she heads off to work. Just to hug her and tell her I love her. Not sure what else I can do at this point."

"Sometimes that's all a person needs," Frank said, pushing to his feet, too, and sliding his forearms into the brackets on the crutches. He was getting much better with the things, and he had to admit they allowed him a little more freedom and mobility, especially with The Beast since he could put partial weight on his foot in the big brace. "I'll walk you out."

He held the door for her, then followed her out of the air-conditioning onto the porch, the tropical-esque humidity draping its sticky web around them. The afternoon air was alive with the buzzing kazoos of insects, a dog barking in response to someone's call, and the offbeat sounds of construction going on somewhere at the ranch beyond their line of sight.

Charity stopped him at the top of the steps. "I'm good from here," she said, waving a hand at her little truck parked a few yards away. "Thank you," she added.

He waited, not sure exactly what she was thanking him for, but then she turned toward him and slid her arms around his waist. Rising on tiptoe, she pressed a delicate, sweet kiss to his mouth. When she stepped back, her lips curved up into that shy smile again, and he thought she was the most beautiful woman in the world.

"It's kinda nice having you unable to fight me off," she murmured playfully, gesturing at his crutches. "I can kiss you any time I want, and there's not a whole lot you can do about it." Then she turned and headed down the steps, a little spring in her step. With one last parting smile over her shoulder, she climbed into her truck, started the engine, and took off down the drive.

"I put that spring in her step," Frank said aloud. "That was me." He reached up to touch his lips. He really liked the way her mouth felt against his. They'd have to do that again. Soon.

Because that's what people did when they were in love with each other.

TWENTY-NINE

ABBY DIDN'T COME HOME before work, but several minutes after ten that night, she schlepped into the kitchen and tossed her floppy hobo bag onto the table. "Had to work a double shift at Ripley's today. I'm starving." She glanced at Charity who was preparing the coffee maker for the morning pot. "Did you by any chance save me any dinner?"

Charity finished her task, then opened her arms to her little sister. "Come here and give me a hug, Abs."

"Why?" Abby asked, but she crossed the room anyway and let Charity wrap her arms around her.

"Because if you want food, you have to kiss the cook," she explained. "Or hug the cook, since she's your sister."

"Fine, but only because I'll die if I don't eat, and I guess I'd rather hug you than die," Abby said, resting her head on top of her sister's. "Man, you are so small. When did you start shrinking?"

"Ha ha." Charity was accustomed to being teased about her petite frame, but Abby was now taller than Faith. "You're still growing like a weed, Abs, aren't you? And you're too skinny." She stepped back and cupped the beautiful girl's face. "Forget I said that. You're perfect the way you are, and I love you."

Abby's eyebrows disappeared under her thick bangs. "Wow. Getting all sentimental on me." She stepped back and patted the top of Charity's head. "You're so cute and little," she quipped.

Charity chuckled and pointed at the table. "Sit. I'll dish you up some chicken chowder. It was really good tonight."

"Your chowder is always good, little lady." Abby dropped heavily into a chair and dragged her purse toward her. "So, is everyone in bed already?"

"Yeah." Charity glanced at the clock on the wall. "Prudence may still be awake, actually. She was still reading in the living room when I came in here."

"Cool. Can you keep a secret?" Abby slid her hand inside her purse but left it there. "I don't care if Pru hears, but I don't want it to get back to Daddy. At least not yet." She tried to smile, but it came off as more of a grimace. "Guess what I've been doing over the last month."

Charity stilled where she stood at the counter, the container of leftover chowder in her hands. Was it really going to be that easy? She angled a glance over her shoulder at the girl, keeping her expression neutral. "Studying taxidermy?" she asked, trying not to snicker.

"No. Come here." Abby lowered her voice and eyed the doorway that led to the hall. "You're sure Daddy's asleep? You know how he sometimes creeps around at night."

Charity chuckled. "He doesn't creep around, Abs. His hip bugs him sometimes, and he has to walk it off." She poured a large serving of chowder into a small saucepan on the stove top and turned the burner on low. From the breadbox, she pulled a bag of soft rolls she'd made the night before, then put two on a plate and handed it to Abby. The butter was still on the table from dinner earlier.

"I know that," Abby rolled her eyes. "But it makes us sound weirder when I tell people he wanders the house aimlessly, pacing back and forth in silent fury, looking for his next victim."

"Abstinence! You tell people that?" Charity gaped at her sister, then turned to stir the soup.

"Of course not, Miss Gullible," Abby snorted. "Enough about creeping daddies. I want to show you something. Come here," she ordered again.

Charity put the lid on the pan and wiped her fingers on the edge of a towel tucked into the waistband of her jeans.

"I want to see," Prudence said, gliding into the room on her fuzzy slippers. She wore a yellow and blue Kimono-style robe hanging open over a pair of Daddy's old flannel pajama bottoms and a Gangsta Tweety Bird t-shirt circa 1990's hip-hop wear. The cute yellow bird wore a bandanna tied around its head, white high-top sneakers, sunglasses, and a backward baseball cap. In graffiti font, the words, "Bad to the Bone" were splashed across the black background behind the bird. It was the extreme opposite representation of everything Prudence stood for, but for some reason, it was her favorite nightshirt, and if anyone ever commented on it, Prudence simply said, "I'm being ironic."

"Shh," Abby said, holding a finger to her lips. Her other hand was still buried inside her bag. "Was Daddy's door closed?"

"Yep." Prudence reached for one of the rolls Charity had put out, sliced it, then spread butter evenly over the open faces of it, making sure to cover every corner. She sat in a chair close by, then began to break off small pieces of the bread and stick them in her mouth. "These are so good, Charity-Pie."

Abby slid the plate with its remaining roll a little closer to her, but she couldn't be distracted beyond that. "I've been recording," she said in a loud whisper. "Check this out." She slowly withdrew her hand from inside her bag and slid a CD in a jewel case across the table toward them. "I've recorded an EP. It's only five songs, and it's kind of more of a demo album, I guess, but I think it's pretty good, so we're loading it up on some of the different online music stores."

Prudence leaped out of her chair and circled the table to throw her arms around their little sister. "Oh my gosh, Abs! You crazy girl. Why didn't you tell us? I want to hear it right now."

"Wait!" Charity held up a hand, then hurried back to the stove top to grab the pan of soup. She emptied the contents into a big ceramic bowl, carried it to the table, and set it in front of Abby. "It's hot; be careful. Congratulations, little sister. I'm so proud of you." She dropped into the seat on Abby's other side. "Now tell me why this is a secret."

Abby sighed and slumped against the chair back. "Don't laugh."

"Of course, we won't," Prudence murmured, resting her hand on Abby's forearm. "Is this what you've been up to whenever you disappear for hours at a time?"

Abby nodded, then sat forward and buttered the other roll before taking a big bite. At least she didn't chew with her mouth open, Charity thought.

"Okay. So, do you remember how Daddy used to say he loved us so much at the age we were that he just didn't know if he'd feel the same about us after our birthdays?"

Charity chuckled. "I do. He stopped saying that when you wrote about it on one of your school papers in second grade. You were seven," she began.

"Yep. And I was really, really scared he wouldn't love me once I turned eight. I actually prayed that I wouldn't have my birthday that year."

"Poor little Abby-Dabby-Doo," Prudence murmured sympathetically. She had a knack for coming up with silly names.

"So, I know he stopped saying that, right? And he promised me he was just teasing me, and he assured me he would love me just as much, and probably a whole lot more the older I got." She picked up the spoon Charity had set on the table beside the bowl and dipped it into the soup. "This smells amazing," she said, then blew on the spoonful and gingerly took a bite. "This tastes amazing, too."

Charity smiled, but she said nothing. She'd learned over the years with so many girls in the family that the surest way to get someone to talk was to leave a long silence that needed filling. Prudence must have caught on because she settled into her own chair and continued to pick away at her roll.

"I know it in here." Abby tapped her temple, then pressed her palm to her chest. "But there's still this little girl in me that's afraid, you guys. I'm afraid to grow up, I guess. I'm afraid to move on."

"Oh, Abby." Charity reached over to cup her little sister's cheek. A single tear landed on the back of her hand, and it was all Charity could do to keep her dismay in check. Abby rarely cried. In fact, Charity could hardly remember the last time. "Oh sweetie, don't cry," she murmured. Then she shook her head. "I take that back, too. Go ahead and cry. And I say that because Sunday night, I had a good cry, and I think it might be over the same kind of thing. So cry. It helped me, that's for sure."

She glanced over at Prudence who had no such reservations. Sympathetic tears streamed from the girl's already luminous eyes.

Abby sniffled and took the paper napkin Charity handed her. "It's just that I think if I stay here in the hollow—" Her words broke off as though her throat suddenly constricted. "I think I might go crazy," she whispered. "I know you all love it here, the whole small town vibe thing, but I can hardly breathe here, you guys." Her face crumpled, and she dropped her chin to her chest. "But I don't know if I can leave, either. I don't know how to just go. I'm afraid I'll die if I stay—in here," she said, patting her chest. "I'm also afraid I'll die if I leave—leave—" She sniffed loudly and let out a shuddering breath. "If I leave all of you. How can I leave Da—Daddy? I know he won't stop loving me," she continued, without waiting for either of them to respond. "But what if, you guys? What if, by some fluke or bad juju or evil spell or curse—what if he does actually stop loving me, even just the tiniest bit?" The last question came out a small, pitiful whimper.

"That would be impossible, child, because that would mean my love for you was conditional." Jed stood in the doorway, his arms crossed loosely over his chest.

"Daddy!" Abby gasped and sat straight in her seat, knocking her spoon to the floor. Charity bent to pick it up, wiping the splatter of soup off the floor with a napkin.

"Come here, Abstinence Joy Goodacre." Jed stepped into the room and beckoned for his youngest daughter. She practically launched herself out of her chair and into his arms.

"I'm sorry, Daddy," she sobbed against his chest.

"Hush, child. Hush, now." Jed stroked Abby's back in big circles, continually switching directions—clockwise, then counterclockwise, then back again.

Charity pressed her lips together to keep from smiling. When Abby was a baby, when Mama was so sick that she barely had the energy to feed Abby, Daddy would take the baby and rub her back in that exact same way. He swore he could get her to burp every time that way, and as far as Charity could remember, he'd been one hundred percent successful. She wouldn't be able to hold in a laugh if Abby couldn't hold in a belch, and now was not the time to crack up.

"Do you remember what Reverend Treadwell preached on Sunday morning?" Jed asked, still holding Abby close.

"Yeah, gratitude. I've been feeling guilty ever since." Abby covered her face with her hands and added, "I need another napkin, or I'm going to get snot all over your shirt." Prudence lurched forward with a stack of them; Daddy, bless his heart, didn't even make a face.

"I don't think the good pastor intended for you to feel guilty, Abby. You know what I got out of that message?" Jed leaned back a little while Abby blew her nose.

"What?" she asked, the word almost unintelligible behind her napkin.

"Remember how he talked about becoming complacent, thinking we're being grateful, but really we're playing it safe?"

"Sorta," Abby said with a nod. "Honestly, I was so busy feeling guilty for not being grateful enough, that I kinda stop listening halfway through."

Jed laughed, then pointed at the table. "Go sit and eat your soup. Prudence, do you think you could brew us up some comfort tea? I'd love some coffee, but I don't need any caffeine at this time of night. I think something to soothe our spirits is in order."

Prudence beamed, her whole face lighting up. She loved it when their father asked her to concoct something special for him. But he'd been the satisfied recipient of enough of her home remedies to know that his sixth daughter had a way with plants. Besides, he had a way with plants, too, and although they grew their botanicals for different reasons, the end result was the same—to promote a natural, healthy lifestyle—so he, of all people, appreciated Prudence's gift.

The twins made an appearance just then, coming in off the evening shift at Schooners. They joined them for tea and some vanilla scones drizzled with maple glaze that Charity had whipped up an hour ago. "Stress baking," she explained.

"No one's complaining," Abby said, nabbing the first one off the plate Charity set in the middle of the table.

While Prudence brewed tea, Abby explained to the twins about her EP, and about what she was feeling. They nodded sympathetically, having experienced some of the same stuff throughout their lives. "We always worry how the other twin is going to feel if we do something without each other," Justice told her.

"Yep. Like Justice is really worried that I'll feel abandoned if she gets serious with Brandon, but I've told her over and over that I won't. I want her to be happy because I love her, and if Brandon Stillwater makes her happy, even though I seriously don't get it, then she needs to go for it."

"Courage," Justice began, giving her sister a narrow-eyed glare.

"Well, you do," Courage retorted. Turning back to Abby, she said, "She does. She needs to stop being afraid she'll upset me. Sure, I'll miss having her all to myself, but she needs to believe me when I say that I'm happy for her." Without looking at Justice, she added, "Because I am happy for you. Because I love you."

"And perfect love casts out fear," Charity interjected as she pulled her own chair close to the table.

"Exactly," Jed said, reaching over to pat Charity's forearm. "And that's exactly what I want you to hear tonight, Abby, child. I love you. I love each one of my daughters to a fault. I am reminded every day of how grateful I am to have each one of you in my life. But keeping you all to myself isn't love or gratitude. It's fear. I admit right out that I'm afraid to lose you. I'm afraid to trust someone else to take care of you or to love you as much as I do, whether that's a husband, a boyfriend, or even yourself. But that's not perfect love, is it? Perfect love is allowing you to stretch your wings, my little songbird." He tugged on one of Abby's glorious red curls. "It's about having the confidence that even if you fly far away from home, you'll always wing your back to us when you can."

"Oh, Daddy," Abby murmured, her voice high and a little squeaky, sounding the way it used to when she was a tiny toddler. "I wasn't planning on running away or anything. I just didn't know how to tell you."

The room went silent.

"Tell me what, child?" Jed asked, his big, calloused hand covering hers.

"I—I've been invited to go to Nashville with Remington Sounder. He—his band played in Bowling Green a couple of months ago, and he and his girlfriend came out to The Smokehouse Grill because someone told him about a girl he should hear; me. I still don't know who it was, but I checked up on him. He does this; he takes young musicians like me under his wing and helps get them established in the music world." She angled a look at Justice whose expression was speculative if not outright suspicious. "Don't look at me like that, Justy. He has a serious girlfriend. He's helped both guys and girls get started. You ever heard of Toby Quinlan? Remington found him playing in a little pub somewhere in Louisiana. He also helped Lily McGrath get picked up by her label. It's not a guarantee, but he thinks I have what it takes."

"You do," Charity said without hesitation. "You are one of the most gifted musicians I've ever heard."

"Thank you, Charity." Abby stared down into her cup of tea for a few moments, then lifted her gaze to her father. "He told me to put together an EP and send it to him when it was finished. He wouldn't promote me unless I had something I could give to people in the industry, you know? Something with my name and contact information." Her fingers were busy crumbling the remains of her scone into dust on her plate. "But guess what." Her eyes sparkled, and a shy smile hovered around her words. "He says it's so good, that he wants to have his producer clean it up so I can sell the songs as singles online, or as an EP. I'll only have to re-record one of the five songs."

"Do you have a contract?" Justice asked. "I'd like to see it before you sign anything."

"Of course, I do. And sure. I haven't signed anything yet. I was going to show Daddy first before I did anything." Abby started to rise, but Justice stopped her.

"Quick question. Is he selling your stuff on his website or his social media?"

"No." Abby shook her head. "He'll promote it there, but he doesn't want to take any cuts or royalties for himself."

"Will you be covering your own expenses, or will he?" Jed asked. It was the first thing he'd said since she mentioned Remington.

"I will. I'll have to pay for my own place, my own meals, and my own transportation in Nashville. But he'll get me into all the right places, and he says I'll make more than enough from gigging to be able to cover living out there. It's pretty expensive. I looked."

Prudence refilled Abby's mug, then slid the teapot toward Charity so she could top off Daddy's cup, too.

"Say something, Daddy," Abby pleaded.

"Tomorrow morning, I want to see that contract. You around to go over it with me, Justice?"

"I am. I don't have to be anywhere until eleven."

"I can go get it now," Abby offered.

Jed put his hand on her shoulder. "Tomorrow morning will be soon enough. Your sister and I will go over the contract, and then we'll go from there, okay?"

"Okay."

Charity could tell her little sister had hoped for something more. She nudged Abby's foot under the table in a show of camaraderie.

"It sounds like a great opportunity," Prudence piped in. "I hope Remington—that's such a debonair name!—is all that he says he is. You deserve it."

"Thank you, Pru," Abby whispered.

"It does sound like a great opportunity," Jed agreed. "So great, I can't help but wonder what the catch is. Where the loophole lies. Doesn't mean there is one—there are still good men out there, child—but it does make me want to pull back the layers and see what's at the core of this man."

"I understand, Daddy. I really do."

Jed nodded slowly, then patted her hand. "I need to ponder on this a bit," he said. "But Abby, consider you have my blessing unless we uncover a good reason for you not to go." He rose, nudging his chair back carefully, then picked up his plate and mug to take to the sink.

"I'll get that, Daddy," Charity offered, taking the dishes from him.

"Thank you," he murmured, then hugged each girl in turn and headed out of the room.

"Well, I think that went well," Prudence said brightly.

"Honestly, so do I," Courage said. "Sounds like you might be heading for Nashville, Little Songbird."

"Now let's hear it!" Prudence said, bouncing a little in her seat.

THIRTY

CHARITY BROUGHT APPLE CINNAMON muffins with her to Whispering Hills Thursday morning around 9:30, but instead of heading straight for the kitchen, she made her way to the barn to see if she could catch Frank on his horse. She ducked into the cool interior and headed down the length of the wide corridor until she reached the other end that opened into the large indoor arena.

There he was. "My goodness, he's delicious," Charity murmured to herself.

"The horse or the man?" It was Faith standing off to the side out of the line of sight of those in the arena.

Charity moved to stand next to her, careful not to be seen, as well. She hadn't come as a distraction. "Both," she said, openly acknowledging her feelings. "I really like him, Faith. The man, I mean. I'm sure the horse is nice, too, but it's the man I'm falling for."

Faith nodded, but only said, "I thought as much."

"You think he'll be ready?" Charity asked, frowning a little at what she was seeing. Frank looked like he was barely staying in the saddle just trotting around the arena. "Aren't you getting kinda close to the cutoff?"

"I am," Faith confirmed. "My midwife wants me off now, but she said I could take another week."

"Faithy," Charity turned to her sister, deeply concerned. "This isn't going to work, is it?"

"I don't know how it can."

"You need to tell him. You need to tell him today. Don't do this to either one of you. All three of you, if you include the baby." Charity reached over and placed a flat hand on the cantaloupe bulge where her sister's baby rested. "What are you going to do? I mean, do you have someone else in mind who can step in?"

"I've been racking my brain, but I'm coming up empty, at least for names of people I can trust. I'll probably have to start working with the quads. I hate to do it, but the cows will get used to it eventually." Faith rested her hands over Charity's. "She's moving. Can you feel her?"

"She?"

"Still don't know for sure. We're going to wait to find out. Be surprised. But I don't think Cord will be getting a son out of this womb." Faith pushed on Charity's hand. "There. Feel it?"

"I felt her!" She giggled and bounced up and down on her heels, not lifting her hand from Faith's stomach. "Hello, princess!" she cooed. "Give me a high five." To Faith, she said, "Have you talked to Hope? Maybe she knows someone."

"I asked her ages ago, but I haven't recently. We all have been going along like Frank's got this, but..."

"But he doesn't," Charity finished for her sister, patting her stomach one more time before stepping back.

"He doesn't," she echoed. "Hey, are those your muffins I'm smelling?" Faith pointed at the brown paper bag in Charity's hand.

"They are."

"Can I have one? I'm starving." Faith held out both hands cupped together. "Please."

Charity crossed her arms, the brown bag trapped loosely against her side. "Are you going to tell him today?"

"I don't know."

"Then, no." Charity turned as though to walk away.

"Come on, Chare," Faith groaned.

"Are you going to tell him?" she asked again, this time holding the bag a few inches out of Faith's reach and waving it back and forth tauntingly.

"Tell who what?" It was Frank. He'd circled around, dismounted with Binks' help, and was now hobbling toward them. "I thought I heard voices over here."

"Did we distract you?" Charity asked, hoping her question about distracting him would actually distract him from the question he'd asked.

"No." He shook his head and smiled, but Charity could see the effort it took to act this casual. His eyes were ringed with pain, his jaw bulging from clenching it so hard. Frank was in seriously suffering and was doing his best not to show it. "I didn't hear you until I came over to dismount."

Binks walked by leading Hidalgo, both the man and the horse's heads were down, almost as though in mutual despair. Binks knew the scoop; she could see it in the droop of his shoulders, in the furrowed lines on his brow.

"Let's head back to the house and get some ice on that ankle," Charity said, waving her muffin bag at Faith. "Tell your husband I'm putting fresh coffee on. If he wants a muffin, he can come get it in the kitchen."

"But I want a muffin. I don't care about him," Faith whined.

"Yes, you do. And besides, if I give you one now, you'll gobble it down and completely forget that you're supposed to come back to the house with your husband." She winked at Frank. "Kinda like you forgot to tell me about Frank's trip out to Fort Campbell last week. And his two very important doctor appointments."

"I did not forge—" Faith broke off mid-sentence, her eyes growing wide. She covered her mouth with her hand, but they could still make out the words, "Oh, cow patties. I forgot to tell you, Charity. I mean, I didn't forget that he was gone or why, at least, right?" Faith held one hand out. "That has to count for something. Half a muffin?"

"See you back at the house," Charity called after her, leading the way ahead of Frank. They passed Binks outside Hidalgo's stall; he was grooming the horse and talking in low unintelligible sounds to it. "Muffins and coffee back at the house," she told him, then continued past him, not waiting for Frank to stop to chat.

"What's going on?" Frank asked, a quizzical look on his face. It was obvious he knew something was amiss.

"First things, first, Frank." She turned to look at him right before they stepped out into the sunlight. "You don't look so good, Soldier Boy. We need to get you off that leg. You think you can make it?"

"Yes, of course. This is nothing."

"This is nothing?" Charity looked aghast at him. "This is not nothing, Frank. You look gray around the gills, and your eyes are practically sunken in from pain. This is not nothing," she said again. "Come on."

Frank grimaced and followed her out into the sunlight. A moment later, she heard him retching behind her. Nothing came up, but he dry-heaved so violently, he collapsed onto all fours, his braced leg sticking awkwardly out behind him.

She didn't panic, but she wanted to. Was it always like this after his lessons? No wonder he wasn't progressing very quickly. She ducked back inside the barn, calling out to Binks to come help.

Between the two of them, they got Frank inside the house and resting comfortably on the big easy chair and footstool in the front room. With him downstairs, she could watch over him a little easier. "Did you take one of your pills before your practice?" she asked.

He nodded. "Can't have another one for two more hours. I just need ice. I need to rest." Charity brought him a bag of ice and a towel, and gently propped the bag on the bad ankle. He wore a sock over his foot, but from what she could see of the appendage, the whole thing was a mess.

She handed him a glass of ginger ale with extra pieces of fresh ginger in it. "This should help settle your stomach a little. Try to rest, okay?" she said, leaning down to kiss him on the temple. He didn't feel feverish, but he was clammy and trembling slightly. "I'm going to go put coffee on, and then I'll be back to check on you."

In the kitchen, she and Binks spoke in low voices. "Sometimes it's better; sometimes it's worse. Today certainly isn't the worst it's been. Ms. Charity." He shook his head. "That boy won't give up, but he should. That leg is going to kill him, either in body or in spirit, and I don't like being part and parcel to that. There certainly ain't no way he'll be ready to round up cows next week."

"I know," she murmured back to him. "I had Faith go fetch Cord. They're going to talk to him. Maybe not right now if he's too miserable, but he can't get on that horse again." Her throat tightened at the memory of the pinched look of pain on Frank's face. "Not like this. Nobody wants this."

"I'll stay," Binks said, squaring his shoulders and setting his jaw. "The boy will need us to gather round him. He's going to be angry because he's going to see it as his own failure. We all need to be here."

Charity nodded. "I agree. I wasn't going to ask you but thank you."

Just then, Faith arrived with Cord in tow. "Coffee for him, muffins for me," she said, making a beeline for the table and one of the stools. Charity had already put the baked goods on a platter. "Whoa. What's wrong?"

"Did you tell Cord?" Charity asked her sister. "About talking to Frank?"

"She did." Cord poured himself a cup of coffee and went to join his wife at the worktable.

"Good. Because things just escalated." Charity explained what had happened and was mollified by Cord's immediate, but level-headed decision.

"He's done. He can stay here and pout as long as he needs to, but I'm taking him to see his doctor as soon as he's able to make the drive. If he wants us to help him, then he needs to give us the full scoop. I have a feeling we're missing some information. Either that or the doctor is."

"But honey," Faith began. "What if it's more than just a day? I'm already supposed to be getting off my horse by the end of this week. What are we going to do?"

"I'll go with him," Charity interjected. "I can take him. I know my way around Fort Campbell pretty well, remember?" She turned to Binks. "Do you know of anyone who might want a part-time job moving cows around every day?" she asked him, not really expecting an answer.

"I can move the chickens and collect eggs right up to the last minute," Faith stated. "It would just be moving cows."

"Actually, I think I do," the old man said, his head bobbing up and down. "My buddy Joel has a boy taking afternoon and evening classes at the community college a couple times a week. He's looking for some part time work in the mornings, and he's got a good hand on a horse and a good head on his shoulders. Let me make a couple of phone calls, and I'll get back to you before the day is out."

Charity couldn't help wondering if Binks had been looking for someone to replace Frank all along.

"Well, I'm glad we asked you, Binks. Thank you," Cord said, clapping the older man gently on the shoulder. "I'm going to go talk to Frank now."

"I'm coming with you," Binks said.

"Me, too," Charity chimed in, and was echoed by her sister.

"Let's go," Cord commanded, leading the charge through the swinging door and into the living room where Frank sat still as stone, his face a terrible shade of gray.

"I heard enough," he said before they'd even reached him. "Those doors are hollow, so unless you're talking in really quiet voices, everything you say can be heard out here." His voice was drained of all emotion. "I don't need anyone to drive me to Fort Campbell. I've done the trip many times, and I can do it again. I need a day or two, then I'll get out of your hair."

"Whoa." Cord cut him off before he could say anything else. "We don't want you out of our hair."

"We want you in our hair, but healthy." Faith frowned. "That didn't come out right, but you know what I mean."

"Son, you can't keep pushing yourself like this," Binks said, moving to sit on the edge of the footstool. "I can't just stand by and continue to let you do this to yourself. It's been over three weeks, and we're not anywhere near ready to work. You know that, don't you." It wasn't a question.

"Frank?" Charity sank down to her haunches on the floor beside his chair. "I'd like to go with you if you'll let me. I can't make you take me, but I want to be there for you. With you." She laid her hand on his forearm, half afraid he'd pull away. "No matter what happens. I want to go through it with you. I want to stay with you in the hospital. I want to take care of you at the base while you're recovering. You shouldn't be alone with all this, Frank."

He scoffed at her, the sound hurting her chest almost as much as his words did. "You can't. This is government we're talking about. You can't make decisions for me or live on base with me stay with me in the hospital; you're not family."

The silence in the room was heavy with emotion, then Cord cleared his throat. "I'm family. I'll go."

"I heard the whole conversation, Cord," Frank said, a hint of anger lacing his voice. "You can't leave the ranch right now. Or your wife. And now because of my self-indulgence, I've left you high and dry with a position that needs filling next week. I'm sorry. I shouldn't have come at all." He shook his head slowly, bitterly. "I don't know what I was thinking."

"Frank," Charity began, but he closed his eyes when she said his name, a subtle gesture that told her he was shutting her out.

"You could marry him," Faith said softly, turning to rest a hand on Charity's shoulder. "Then you'd be family."

Charity froze, the idea terrifying, yet, oh, so simple. Of course.

"I bet if you talk to Reverend Treadwell, explain the situation and all, he'd do it. Or you could go to Muldoon, and the Justice of the Peace can do it for you."

"I am not going to marry her just so she can stay with me at the hospital," Frank growled, opening his eyes again, but only to glare at his braced leg.

Charity, still crouching beside him, tipped her head to look at his face. "But that wouldn't be why you married me, would it?" she said softly. "You'd marry me because you love me." She reached up to touch his jaw. "Remember, Frank? You told me you loved me."

"Yeah, but that was before—" he broke off and waved a hand at his foot.

"So, it was conditional love?" she asked, not intentionally goading him, but why couldn't he see how perfect this was? Then again, maybe he did see, but he didn't want to be burdened with her once his leg healed.

"Of course not. I do love you, Charity," he growled.

Cord chuckled, then tried to pass it off as a throat clear.

"Good. Because I love you, too. So, let's get married. Tonight. Tomorrow if you need another day to recuperate. Then when is your next appointment? Monday?" That would be exactly two weeks since the last one.

"Yes, but what about your job?" He was waffling. "And I don't even have a home of my own to offer you. I sleep in barracks and temporary Army housing. I bum off my one remaining family member for room and board, and then I don't even fulfill my end of the deal."

"Cord, do you think your men can figure out how to make their own sandwiches until you can find a replacement for me? A temporary one, mind you, because my husband and I will be coming back home to this place, at least until he can pony up the dough to buy me my own home."

Cord chuckled. "Ponying up the dough shouldn't be a problem; I can assure you. I know what I paid for this ranch, and it all went into your husband's pocket."

"I am not her husband," Frank declared. "I have not agreed to marry her."

"Wow, seriously?" Faith stepped up and flicked Frank in the side of the head.

"Ow! What was that for?"

"For being a stubborn jackass, that's what. And I mean that in the nicest form of the word. A stubborn mule. Here you have this gorgeous, capable, intelligent—although, I'm beginning to think that's debatable if she's fallen for a guy like you—sweet, loving, caring, fun—"

"I think he gets it, Faith," Charity muttered.

Faith picked up where she'd left off. "Caring, fun woman who says she loves you, who is all but begging you on her knees to marry her, and you're lying there, all beat up, and moaning over your sad life, and absolutely good for nothing, and you're trying to decide whether or not you should give it a go? Don't you see something wrong with this picture?"

That's when Binks started laughing.

Cord was already chuckling softly to himself, but when the two women got going, there was no turning back.

It took a while, but finally, the laughter reached Frank's cold, dark corner of the world. Charity saw the smile first. She rose and gingerly climbed into his lap, careful not to jar his leg. Then she wrapped her arms around his neck and kissed him.

When she came up for air, she saw he had tears in his eyes. "What is it?" she asked softly. The room around them was strangely quiet; then she realized they were alone. She could hear the others murmuring in the kitchen, though; Frank was right. That door was not soundproof. "Why are you crying, Frank?"

"I'm not crying," he said, swiping at his eyes with the heels of his palms. "I'm leaking."

"That's gross." Charity made a face. "Please just admit you're crying. It's much manlier."

He tucked a strand of her blonde hair back behind an ear, and asked, "Why do you love me, Charity? I'm such a mess. Inside and outside."

She shrugged. "Maybe that's why. Maybe it's because you're the kind of man I can pour myself into and you'll never be full of me. I'm the kind of girl who needs to be needed, Frankie. Maybe I see you as a man who needs me."

"What if there comes a day when—when I don't—" He didn't finish the sentence, so she did.

"When you don't need me?" She sighed and pressed a kiss to his temple. "I don't know. But I'm not afraid of that. I won't let the unknown tomorrow determine what I do today. Who knows? You may get so good with this new leg that you end up going back to Afghanistan. At one time, that would have scared me even more than you no longer needing me. It's still scary, but I'm not going to lose you now because I'm afraid I might lose you later."

"I do love you, Charity Goodacre Banner."

"Hey!" Faith pushed open the swinging door and stuck her head through. "You two made this a piece of cake to remember. Charity, you're going to go from Charity Goodacre Banner to Charity Goodacre Flanner! Nice!" She nodded approvingly, and then ducked back into the kitchen.

A moment later, she popped her head out again. This time she was laughing so hard she could barely speak. "Charity Goodacre Banner Flanner!"

Charity burst out laughing, the sound echoing around the large room until she buried her face in Frank's neck. He wrapped his arms around her and held on tightly. They had some rough seas ahead of them, and this was the only way they'd get through—together.

EPILOGUE

F RANK STARED AT THE bundle sound asleep on his lap. The miniature features looked a little squished and very fragile to him, and he wondered if the baby was feeling claustrophobic wrapped so snugly in a soft blanket. The longer he stared, the more entranced he became. The infant's tiny fingernails—one little fist was curled under the boy's cheek—the shell-shaped ears that were almost see-through. The pudgy little roll under his chin, the furrowed brow with no eyebrows. He could see why parents said they instantly loved their babies.

Less than an hour ago, Cord, carrying his newborn son, Elijah Dalton Overman, had ushered a beaming Faith into the ranch house living room where Frank and Binks waited. The two men were the only members of the household who hadn't made it to the hospital to moon over the baby the night before. Charity came in behind the couple with Jasmine in tow, talking a mile a minute about how awesome it was to be a big sister and how she was going to be the best babysitter in the whole world. "I might even try changing a poopy diaper."

Dalton and Carmelita Overman were right on their heels, having driven over from Louisville that morning. Carmelita hadn't seen Frank—her sister's only child—since right after his surgery, and she was anxious to get an update on his progress, to see for herself that he was whole in spirit, if not in body.

While Cord got Faith settled into one of the big, over-stuffed armchairs in the large ranch house living room, Charity brought Eli to Frank, and with careful, awkward movements, he took the tiny little boy and cradled him up near his chest first. Eli squirmed and wiggled, his little fist flailing, emitting a few squeaks and grunts with all the effort, until Charity bent over the chair and re-wrapped the blanket that had come loose. Within moments, the baby settled into a peaceful sleep, allowing Frank all the time in the world to examine the newest little human who would call Whispering Hills Ranch home.

Beyond the fuzzy little head, Frank could see the place on the footstool where his foot should have been. Instead, he had a neatly wrapped stump below his knee, and what remained of his leg rested on a pile of pillows; he kept it elevated whenever he wasn't hobbling around on his crutches. He was back to the armpit bruisers, but they were temporary, he knew. He'd already been fitted for his first prosthesis—sure enough, an ugly plastic molded foot with a fixed ankle and fused toes that didn't even come close to matching his skin tone. He'd be getting it at his next appointment in a week and beginning the stages of learning to walk all over again. Eventually, he'd graduate to better quality prosthetics—he wondered what his closet would look like by the fourth or fifth one; a whole selection of various feet or foot-like impediments and a myriad of right foot shoes. Except that eventually, he'd even get to wear shoes on the fake foot, so he had to remind Charity not to throw away any of his left shoes.

They'd taken up residence in the big ranch house, at least for now. Charity continued to cook for Cord's work crews and ranch staff, and Frank focused on getting his feet under him again. He was almost as anxious to try getting back on Hidalgo as Faith was to get back on her horse, Watson. He had a feeling he might just beat her to it; he was progressing far more quickly than he could have imagined since the amputation. Every day, he felt stronger and more confident about all that he *hadn't* lost, and he no longer awoke each morning dreading the agony of trying to maneuver throughout the day. His pain was all but gone now. The surgical site had healed quickly, and although he still suffered from some severe phantom limb pain every once in a while, it was nothing compared to the constant searing fire he used to endure.

Being married had changed his life, but being married to Charity Goodacre Banner Flanner had brought him the greatest joy he'd ever known. She gave him new reasons to get up and face each and every day.

Some of those reasons were whipped up in the kitchen. For a while, she'd served him in bed, but before long, she'd started making him come downstairs to eat. "You didn't marry me to be your maid, remember? You married me to be your chef. You want my food; you have to come and get it. And don't forget to kiss the cook first." Besides, it forced him to get up and get moving. What better lure than a pretty wife with a plate of fried chicken and lemon bars?

Some of those reasons were her sense of humor, her laughter, and her unfiltered comments. She was never malicious, so watching her stick her foot in her mouth was like watching a real live RomCom. He could take or leave romantic comedy movies, but seeing one play out in real life was fascinating and entertaining. The fact that Charity could laugh at herself made their life together... well, like something out of the movies.

And some of those reasons were simply Charity's joy in living, in helping, in feeding, in nurturing, and caring for others around her. She made him see beyond himself every day. She made him see himself more clearly, too.

Their tomorrow was uncertain in many ways, but they weren't afraid, because their today was overflowing with the kind of perfect love that casts out fear.

The Goodacre twins are an award-winning rodeo trick riding team.
They call themselves *The Twisted Sisters.*
Falling is for amateurs... especially falling in love.

The Heart of Courage: Seven Virtues Ranch Romance Book 4.

No WOMAN SHOULD HAVE *to choose between the man she loves and the sister she can't live without.*

Being a twin has always been the best part about being Justice's sister. But Courage is starting to wonder if it's the one thing standing in the way of them figuring out who they really are. Their trick riding show has become far more popular than they'd ever imagined, and Courage must decide whether or not she still wants to be the other half of The Twisted Sisters.

Loving someone should be simple, uncomplicated. It should fill the empty places and not leave you wanting.

Courage used to believe that, but she's finding out the hard way that sometimes love is fraught with sacrifice and yearning, and it can burn its own brand of pain on even the bravest of hearts.

When the twins are tested by their greatest fear, will the bond they share bend and stretch, or will it break?

Pick up **The Heart of Courage: Seven Virtues Ranch Romance Book 4** or keep reading for an excerpt.

~ ~ ~

Did you jump into the middle of the series?
Start at the beginning with **Book 1: Gotta Have Faith**.

Can a small-town cowgirl and a big-time city boy risk a second chance at happily ever after?

Faith Goodacre has overcome major obstacles to save her family and bring Seven Virtues Ranch back from the brink of disaster.

So, when her high school sweetheart shows up hoping to win back her heart - oh, and he's bought the ranch next door - her carefully ordered world she's worked so hard to build threatens to implode.

Cordell Overman is back, and he's ready to face his past and make things right. But he's got a whole town to convince that this time around, he's here to stay.

Get to know the whole family in **Gotta Have FAITH**: Book 1 of the Seven Virtues Ranch Romance Series

~ ~ ~

Keep reading for your sneak peek from
The Heart of COURAGE: Seven Virtues Ranch Romance Book 4

A Note from Becky

Dear Reader,

Charity and Frank both still have a long journey of healing ahead of them, but isn't it wonderful that they now have each other to lean on as they travel that road together?

I like to say that I write HOPE-fully ever after stories. Because life is predictably unpredictable, and even though love conquers all, it's HOPE that gets us on our feet each day, right?

I write heartfelt and wholesome Contemporary Romance, Women's Fiction, and even some Romantic Suspense. If you're looking for fiction with relatable characters and redemptive storylines, then I hope you'll check out my other books and series, too. Come visit me online at **BeckyDoughty.com** and subscribe to my mailing list to be notified of book and audiobook news and updates, plus other subscriber-exclusive content. My favorite way of communicating with readers like you is by email, so drop me a line and introduce yourself!

I look forward to meeting you,
Becky Doughty

~ ~ ~

Keep reading for your sneak peek from
The Heart of COURAGE

An Excerpt: The Heart of Courage

Chapter 1
~ ~ ~

"Burn one, walk it through the garden, and pin a rose on it," Courage called to Carl. He jutted his chin in acknowledgment without taking his eyes off the row of tomatoes he was slicing paper thin on the cutting board in front of him. Courage marveled at how adept the guy was with his knives—he had his own set that no one, not even Oz Schooner, the restaurant owner, was allowed to touch. She was even more impressed that every one of Carl's fingertips was still intact.

"Eighty-six the frog sticks; the gentleman will take a chance instead," she added, clipping the order to the ticket wheel and giving the carousel a quick spin. Phineas Thacker always ordered the same thing: a burger with lettuce, tomato, and onion, and instead of fries, Carl's famous hash browns.

Courage slid a caddy of condiments close to the man, and he looked up expectantly, his deep-set eyes almost disappearing beneath the bristling thicket of his brows. "Mississippi mud, hemorrhage, and Mike and Ike," she said, tapping the mustard, ketchup, and salt and pepper shakers with her pen. "Anything else for you, sir?"

Phineas shook his head and winked at her. "I think you got it all, Miss Courage. You know I only order Carl's hash browns just to hear you call me a gentleman, but you keep that to yourself, you hear? Wouldn't want to hurt his feelings. He's a fine chef, that he is."

Courage motioned like she was zipping her lips, then placed a kiss on her fingertips and blew it in his direction. "You're the real deal, you know, Mr. Thacker. They don't make 'em like you anymore."

Like most of Schooners' customers, Phineas appreciated the diner lingo almost as much as the delicious food—although no one ever admitted so in Carl's hearing—especially when Courage and Justice worked the same shift. When the twins got going with their rapid-fire restaurant jargon, they were as entertaining as any dinner show. On a good night, they could even eek a smile out of Carl. Folks came back time and again, often playing "Stump the Soup Jockeys," a game Oz encouraged with gusto. If anyone could come up with a request one of his wait staff couldn't translate into or out of diner lingo, they won a free slice of his famous corrugated roof.

Lemon meringue pie for those who weren't in the know.

Courage topped off Phineas' coffee, then turned to the man beside him. "And what about you, Mr. Lynxwilder?" Joe had such a cool last name, and she used it whenever she had the chance. "Need a draw?" She held up the carafe.

Joe nudged his own near-empty mug toward her. "How's the meatloaf tonight?"

"Best batch yet," she said, refilling his coffee with a flourish, not spilling a drop.

He narrowed his eyes at her. "You say that every time."

"Because it gets better every time you make it, right, Carl?" Courage shot over her shoulder at the big man working the grill.

Carl jutted his chin out again, and then saluted Joe with his spatula.

Joe slapped a hand lightly on the bar, as though finally having made up his mind. "I'll have the meatloaf and a side of biscuits and gravy."

"The usual, then," Courage said. She'd already scribbled the order on her pad; Joe came in every Wednesday night specifically for the meatloaf special. "No steamed vegetables, and you want the baked potato to go, right?" She already knew the answer to that question, too. Joe was pretty picky about his vegetables, but then he had every right to be. No one in a thousand-mile radius grew produce like Joe did at his organic farm. And not even Carl could take offense at the farmer's aversion to the standard diner vegetable mix that came with all the blue-plate specials at Schooners: broccoli, cauliflower, squash, and crinkle-cut carrots. "I'll throw in some bacon bits and shredded cheese on the side. You got butter and sour cream at home?"

Joe nodded. "I've got cheese, too, but the bacon would be much appreciated."

The baked potato was for Joe's mother, Sarah Lynxwilder. It was Bingo Night at the senior center, and according to Joe, his mom always came home from the event hungry enough to eat something, but not enough to cook anything. "So, she just mills around the kitchen like a teenager, grumbling because I never have any junk food in the house." The potato, with all the fixings, was the perfect compromise.

"Butcher's revenge, hold the confetti, and put legs on the Murphy. Heart attack on a rack in the alley," Courage called out as she ripped the top page off her pad and clipped it up next to Phineas' order.

Joe chuckled appreciatively and lifted his steaming mug to his lips. Courage could feel his eyes follow her as she tucked her pen and pad back into the pocket of her apron and returned the carafe to the hotplate. A quick glance back at him told her he was still watching as she cleared the dishes—and the pile of coins—off the end of the counter left by a customer who'd paid in change for his meal.

She wasn't bothered by his perusal; Joe was a people-watcher by nature, a studier of living things. It was part of his genetic makeup as a farmer, she supposed. On the contrary, she couldn't help being a little flattered by his attention. He was one of her favorite customers, always generous with his appreciation of the food and service, a good tipper, and a neat diner, to boot. She looked forward to seeing his face at her station, and to catching his gaze from across the busy restaurant. He'd nod or send her a half-smile in acknowledgment, and she'd eventually make her way back to his place at the counter where she'd refill his coffee or serve him pie with a smile of her own. She only had sisters, but she imagined it was a bit like having a big brother looking out for her.

Joe Lynxwilder was one of those oak tree kind of guys. The kind who withstood the push and pull of life, deeply rooted and able to weather any storm.

An old soul, if ever she knew one. Truth be told, she couldn't tell how old he was by looking at him. There were deep lines at the outer corners of his eyes; laugh lines, perhaps, but more likely the result of the long hours he spent outdoors working his farm. Although he never showed up at Schooners looking like he'd driven his tractor straight from the fields, Joe wore working man clothes—Carhaart and Levis, flannels and work boots—even to church on Sunday. His hands, though clean, were broad and rough, and often stained with the evidence of a man who worked the soil for a living.

Daddy thought the world of Joe, and she had no doubt he'd be thrilled to hand off any one of his daughters to the man. But Courage had never considered Joe as husband material. Maybe for one of her older sisters, but not for her or Justice, and certainly not for Prudence or Abby, the youngest of the Goodacre girls.

Not until a few months ago.

Then last November, her twin had developed a crush on the man practically overnight. Joe and his mother joined the Goodacre family for their big Thanksgiving dinner, and apparently, at some point during that meal, Justice sat up and took notice of the man as something other than a farmer who traded gardening tips with their father.

Coincidentally, it was the first Thanksgiving in years that Justice's on- and off-again boyfriend, Brandon Stillwater, was *not* in attendance at the Goodacre table.

"He's so beautiful. Those eyes. His arms. That smile," Justice would sigh, leaning against the industrial fridge in Schooners' kitchen as though her legs might give out on her at the mere thought of the unsuspecting farmer who sat at the counter, enjoying one of Carl's blue plate specials.

"He's old enough to be your daddy," Tanya Maddox once teased, although Tanya had been known to openly ogle Joe, herself. And Tanya was a year younger than the twins.

"He can be my daddy any day," Justice shot back with a wicked grin that made Tanya nearly snort Mountain Dew out her nose.

Courage rarely stuck around for their girlish mooning, not sure how to feel about Justice's dramatic shift in affections.

It wasn't that she disagreed with her sister's assessment of the guy. To the contrary, it was Justice's crush that made Courage suddenly notice Joe, too. And not as her father's peer, but as a man.

And as one of the few eligible bachelors in the small town of Plumwood Hollow.

For the first time in all the years she'd known him, she found herself insatiably curious about why he'd never married. From what she could recall, he hadn't even been involved in any serious relationships. At least none she was aware of.

Which didn't make sense to her. Joe was the kind of man a woman should want to spend her life with. Strong, steady, yet somehow gentle and personable, too. A pillar in the community, a good neighbor to all, a man who worked hard for his living and had the success to show for it. Courage didn't consider him beautiful as Justice was wont to declare, but there was something mesmerizing about the way he moved, about the way he carried himself. He had the sure, intentional stride and the easy smile of a man with purpose, but his was the quiet kind of confidence that made everyone feel at ease around him.

It was a combination that had Courage thinking things about one of her favorite customers that made her blush every time he sat down at her station.

Not that she was interested in him for herself. It was because she now saw him through her sister's besotted eyes, and that made it impossible to *un*-see him as a potential love interest.

For Justice, of course.

No, she wouldn't call him beautiful.

But still.

He did have nice arms.

And there really was something about his eyes that made you not want to look away... For her sister's sake, she always did.

Yet she couldn't quite imagine Oak Tree Joe and her twin sister together romantically. Justice was a bit of a wild child. A rodeo diva, a drama queen. She lived large and loud and had strong opinions she wasn't afraid to wield.

"I'm going to marry that man and have his babies." Justice whispered to Courage in church one Sunday in February, her eyes practically boring a hole in the back of Joe's head from where they sat three rows behind him.

Just like that.

Because what Justice wanted, Justice got. And although they'd never had a thing for the same guy in all their twenty-four years, Courage knew she stood no chance against her sister when it came to men.

At first, Courage had assumed her sister's interest in the farmer had something to do with yet another fallout between her and Brandon. Usually, Justice unloaded all the sordid details of her Brandon troubles on Courage, then within a few days, sometimes weeks if it was really bad, things would blow over and everything would be back to normal. Brandon and Justice sitting in a tree, K-I-S-S-I-N-G once again. This time, however, Justice insisted there was no specific problem between her and Brandon, only that the relationship had run its course, and it was time for them both to move on.

Unfortunately, Brandon Stillwater hadn't gotten the memo that things were really over between them. For a while, he showed up at Schooners during every one of Justice's shifts, but finally grew weary—or heartsick—over her refusal to give him any more attention than she did her other customers. He still came to Sunday dinner at the ranch every once in a while—he was a longtime family friend, after all. And now that he worked at Whispering Hills next door and lived in one of the onsite cowboy cabins, he was often invited to tag along with Faith and Cord and their kids, or with Charity and her husband Frank, who'd taken over the big ranch house where Frank had grown up.

More often than not, Brandon just showed up at Seven Virtues Ranch to hunt Justice down, hoping she was home and willing to talk. She almost always came up with a reason to be busy, but even when she didn't, their conversations were painfully stilted and uncomfortable.

Courage dreaded the upcoming rodeo season. A bull rider, bareback rider, and calf roper, Brandon was a bit of a local legend, and he was in as much demand as The Twisted Sisters were. It would be hard to avoid the guy all summer long, what with the three of them riding the same circuit for several months.

Usually when Brandon made his unannounced appearances at the ranch, Courage managed to duck out quietly and head next door to Whispering Hills. Sometimes she'd visit with Faith and Charity and the little ones, but lately, she'd been spending most of her time at the new Whispering Hills Quarter Horse breeding and training program. Courage's interest wasn't entirely due to the beautiful horses—although her love of all things equine was a good excuse to make herself available to help out whenever the opportunity arose.

It had more to do with Terrell Jackson, the man who'd moved to Whispering Hills with the horses from a ranch outside Louisville. He'd worked for the previous owners as overseer of the program for almost a decade, and when Cord and Faith purchased the Quarter Horse business, they'd offered Terrell the same position for a significant increase in pay if he'd relocate. Terrell hadn't hesitated to accept, and now he, too, called Plumwood Hollow home.

Now there's a beautiful man, Courage thought as she watched Terrell push open the restaurant door and make his way to the counter, greeting a few of the other customers en route.

"Hey, there, Miss Courage. Aren't you a sight for sore eyes at the end of a long day." Her name spoken in Terrell's slow drawl made her think of hot maple syrup poured over a stack of Carl's pancakes. He nodded at the two men a few seats down. "Joe. Phineas. Evening." Then he turned back to Courage and asked, "Got something tasty for a hungry man this evening?"

Chapter 2

~ ~ ~

The guy's question probably wasn't intended to be laced with innuendo, but Joe didn't know Terrell Jackson well enough to be sure. He did, however, notice the blush that colored Courage Goodacre's cheeks in response. He noticed the way she smoothed the sides of her dark green apron over her hips, and how her fingers fidgeted with the pen in her pocket. He also noticed the smile that lifted the corners of her pretty mouth, and the way her eyes lit up as the man took a seat at the counter a few stools away.

"Hey there yourself, Terrell," Courage said, her voice lifting in a teasing tone. "I'm not sure if that's a compliment, seeing as how you've been looking at horses all day." She poured a glass of iced tea, added two slices of lemon, and set it in front of Terrell, evidently confident that she already knew what he wanted.

"Oh, it was a compliment all right," Terrell assured her, taking a long swig of the cold drink. "You're as pretty as a picture in that yellow top. Makes me happy just looking at you."

Joe bit back the growl building at the back of his throat. Although every word the man said about Courage was true—she truly was pretty as a picture and Joe wouldn't mind looking at her at the end of every one of his days, sore eyes or no—it didn't change the fact that Terrell Jackson was a sweet talker, and sweet talkers usually expected a little sugar in return.

The way Courage smiled at the horseman had Joe wondering if there might already be something brewing between the two of them, and that just about made his blood run cold.

"Well, thank you kindly, then," Courage said, her chin lifting slightly, a pleased expression on her face. "And if you're hungry, you've come to the right place. It's meatloaf night. Mile-high apple pie, too."

"I could probably eat one of everything on the menu, but let's start with the meatloaf, then go from there." Terrell took another drink of tea, then cocked his head and leaned forward to ask, "Got any of those melt-in-your-mouth biscuits?" The way he lowered his voice made the question come out sounding like a proposition.

Joe couldn't tell if his jaw ached from clenching it so hard or from the high levels of syrup in the guy's tone.

"For you? Of course." The color in Courage's cheeks flared again—so she'd heard it, too—and Joe had to look away. "Would you like gravy with them?"

If the man actually requested a side of biscuits and gravy, Joe was cancelling his own order and calling it a night. Then, realizing how childish that sounded, he turned in his seat so that he was practically facing Phineas.

Best just to shut out the conversation altogether and focus on something else. Otherwise, he'd end up with indigestion and wouldn't be able to fully appreciate Carl's meatloaf, and that would be a right injustice. He had to agree with Courage; it did, indeed, seem to get better every time Joe had it.

"Is Mary still up north?" he asked the old man sitting stoically beside him.

"Yep," Phineas said, tapping one gnarled finger against the side of his coffee cup. "Her sister's got that chronic heart failure, and her ticker's been acting up something fierce lately. I get the notion they're puttin' up some good memories for when things get bad. Those two are as thick as thieves on a moonless night." His bristly brows drew together, and he shook his head slowly. Joe could plainly see the old man was troubled by the situation.

"I'll say a prayer for them both, then. Eloise, right?" Mary's sister had visited the Thackers many times in years past, and Joe remembered her as a bright-eyed, round woman whose smile matched Mary's, right down to the deep dimples in both cheeks.

"Have you heard from your wife since Monday, Mr. Thacker?" Courage moved closer to them, drawing Joe's attention back to her. For a brief, selfish moment, he hoped she'd abandoned her conversation with Terrell, but the guy had turned toward them, too, resting a forearm on the counter, clearly set on listening in. Joe shifted on his own stool again, his ingrained good manners making it impossible to keep his back to the man.

"Oh yes. We talk every night," Phineas stated, his gravelly voice growing tender as he spoke about his wife, and Joe couldn't deny the jolt of yearning he felt at the simple words. His parents had been the same way, and he'd fallen asleep many a night to the sound of their low murmurs coming from the room across the hall. After his father passed away a few years ago, his mother continued to have those conversations with her husband at night.

"I'm not going crazy, Joey, so don't you worry," his mother said to him one morning when he'd tentatively asked how she was doing. They were sharing a cup of coffee at the kitchen table, watching the sun rise over his verdant fields. He thought she'd been crying in the middle of the night, but when he pressed his ear to her door, she'd been murmuring, laughing softly, the same way she had when her husband was alive. "I just miss your father so much, and talking to him in our bed? Well, I already know how he'd respond to just about anything I have to say, so in a way, it's like he's with me, there in the dark, more so than anywhere else."

It was the kind of relationship Joe craved for himself, having had it modeled to him his whole life, but he'd struggled to find a woman he could love the way his father had loved his mother. Or a woman who might find enough in Joe to love him the way his mother loved his father. "Dad won the jackpot when he got you," he'd told her, not expecting her to read the ache behind his words. He should have known better.

"Keep praying, son. Keep asking the good Lord for his favor in your life," she charged him, patting his forearm. "I would have despaired unless I had believed that I would see the goodness of the Lord in the land of the living," she quoted from one of her favorite chapters in Psalms. "Wait for the Lord. Be strong and let your heart take courage. Wait for the Lord."

Then with a twinkle in her eyes, she continued. "Know what I think? I'm thinking he already has the right woman picked out for you, but he's just taking his sweet time making sure you're the right man for her." His mother lifted her mug toward him. "And he's doing a fine job of it, too, Joey. Your dad and I are so proud of you." She winked and added, "He told me so last night."

Then, during the Thanksgiving feast he and his mother had shared with the folks at Seven Virtues Ranch last year, Joe had looked across the table into Courage Goodacre's eyes, and there he'd seen something he'd never noticed before. He couldn't put a name on it—he didn't have the words like Terrell Jackson did—but what he saw stopped his heart in its tracks. *Let your heart take courage.* And for a moment, all of time seemed to stop with it.

"That Courage Goodacre," his mother said after they got back to the farm and were busy putting away the leftovers that they'd been sent home with. "She loves dirt almost as much as you do, son." When he'd kept quiet, still a little in shock over the revelation in his own heart, his mother went on. "Know what I think?" She always started something profound with that question, and Joe had learned to pay attention to whatever came next. "She's the one. She may not know it yet, but I think you already do."

Indeed, he did, and now, a good six months later, he was still waiting for her to figure it out.

Joe was a patient man—what farmer worth his weight in compost wasn't?—and the last thing he wanted to do was jump the gun with Courage and possibly scare her off. He was at least a decade older than she was—she called him Mr. Lynxwilder, for the love of Mike—and although on paper he had all the right things to offer a woman, he wanted her to desire his heart first and foremost. He'd wait a year, ten, if need be, if only to be sure she wanted him as much as he wanted her.

Or so he'd planned.

That was before Terrell Jackson swept in on his fancy steed, flashing that piano key smile all over town, and snagging the attention of most of the single—and some of the married—women in Plumwood Hollow. Including Courage's.

Now Joe wondered if he'd made the biggest mistake of his life by not stepping forward to offer Courage his heart the moment he knew it was hers.

Because if he was reading things right, and he was pretty good at reading people, watching Courage around Terrell Jackson was a little like watching a moth flit around a flame.

"How's Mary holding up?" Courage asked, placing a hand briefly on Phineas' forearm in a comforting gesture. "This all must be so hard for them both. Justice and I, we aren't just twins. We're connected at the soul, you know? I can't imagine how either one of us would survive if...." She let her sentence trail off, the unspoken words ringing loud and clear in the air around her.

Phineas nodded his head slowly. "She's a trooper, my Mary. Both those girls are. She sheds a tear or two on the phone with me, but she's grateful for every moment she gets with Eloise."

"Let her know they're in our thoughts, will you?" Courage said in a thready voice, a suspicious glisten in her eyes. "And so are you, Mr. Thacker. I'm sure you and Mary miss each other something awful."

Phineas nodded, but before he could say anything, Carl set two plates on the steel service station, announcing in his robust rumble, "Order up!"

Courage jumped, emitted a little startled squeak, then smiled sheepishly, patting a hand over her chest. But the mood immediately lightened, and when she turned away to load the dishes on a serving tray, Joe could tell she was squaring her shoulders against the wave of emotions that had washed over them all.

"I'll be back to check on you boys in a few minutes," she said, her eyes darting between all three of them, and Joe frowned at the inclusion of Terrell in her promise.

Adding insult to injury, as she rounded the end of the counter and headed toward a booth at the far side of the restaurant, Terrell made a low, appreciative noise in the back of his throat as he watched her go.

Joe's eyes narrowed as he cocked his head in the other guy's direction. "Come again?" he asked, the words rolling out casual as apple pie, but even Terrell wouldn't miss the challenge in them.

"Whatever she had on that tray sure smelled good, didn't it?" Terrell replied, not skipping a beat. "Carl," he called out to the cook, effectively shutting Joe down. "If you weren't so ugly and hairy, I'd ask you to marry me."

Carl didn't even lift his chin to acknowledge the backhanded compliment.

~ ~ ~

Read the rest of Courage's story today!
The Heart of COURAGE
A Seven Virtues Ranch Romance Book 4